LADY IN RED

A film of scarlet chiffon draped from the jeweled tiara sparkling between her upright ears and fell like a regal train to her feet. A twist of the scarlet circled her body covering most of her silken, smoke-gray fur.

She was voluptuous, seductive—and deadly.

And Zref knew her. The Enemy.

Pulsing waves of yearning battered at Zref, calling him into the Crown scintillating about her: "You can't escape this time, Mazemaster. Come, tell me what you've done with it! I won't be put off again!"

Berkley books by Jacqueline Lichtenberg

The First Lifewave Series

MOLT BROTHER
CITY OF A MILLION LEGENDS

A MILLION LEGENDS

JACQUELINE LICHTENBERG

BERKLEY BOOKS, NEW YORK

CITY OF A MILLION LEGENDS

A Berkley Book/published by arrangement with
the author

PRINTING HISTORY
Berkley edition/February 1985

ISBN: 0-425-07513-3

A BERKLEY BOOK ® TM 757,375
The name "BERKLEY" and the stylized "B" with design
are trademarks belonging to Berkley Publishing Corporation.

PRINTED IN THE UNITED STATES OF AMERICA

CITY OF A MILLION LEGENDS

JACQUELINE LICHTENBERG

BERKLEY BOOKS, NEW YORK

CITY OF A MILLION LEGENDS

A Berkley Book/published by arrangement with
the author

PRINTING HISTORY
Berkley edition/February 1985

ISBN: 0-425-07513-3

PRINTED IN THE UNITED STATES OF AMERICA

Acknowledgments

I'd like to thank the people who have, wittingly or not, contributed to my development of the peculiar theory of karma and reincarnation which I use as a background for the Book of the First Lifewave: Judy Thomases, who reawakened my interest in the occult in the early seventies; Marion Zimmer Bradley, who clued me in to some excellent occult writers; Sybil Leek, who has the gift of clarity; Grant Lewi, Noel Tyl, Robert Hand, Mark Schulman and Donald Yott, whose writings on astrology have proved most valuable; legions of occultists who discuss such things as the theory that the twentieth century is seeing the reincarnation of many of those involved in the fall of Atlantis; and the hoards of sf/f fans who have allowed me to read Tarot for them or who have argued my hypotheses with me.

The theory of the workings of karma used in the Lifewave novels are my own derivations, and not to be confused with the theories being tested by working esotericists, nor with Reality. The Lifewave novels are not textbooks, but works of fantasy, using the serious theories of esotericists with as much literary license as hard-sf writers use the modern theories of physics.

One of the esoteric laws which Jean Lorrah has pointed out that I play fast and loose with here is the Magic Circle of twelve or thirteen. Jean has argued to get me to add two more to Zref's aklal, and I've refused because of a technical theory I'm using underneath the background of these books.

That theory is not at all relevant to the drama of this story, so it is unmentioned. I don't even plan to get into it in the sequel to *City of a Million Legends*, currently titled *The Last Persuaders*, although that book does have a schooling sequence at Mautri where that theory is taught.

But I would dearly love to hear from anyone who feels this book has been spoiled by the omission of discussion of the theoretical underpinnings of the background. I'd like to know what you feel should be included so I may cover it in future novels. Jean Lorrah and I always love to hear honest criticism from our readers because that is how we become better writers. Honest praise is also helpful—without it, we might well omit your favorite thing from the next novel!

Write us at the post office box below. Enclose a legal size, Self-Addressed-Stamped-Envelope (SASE), and we'll send information on current and future Lifewave and Sime/Gen novels and fanzines.

Ambrov Zeor
Lifewave Department
P.O.B. 290
Monsey, New York 10952

Table of Contents

Inscription Found Outside the Ancient Ruins of the Maze

TO ALL WHO COME AFTER——BEWARE: DANGER: WARNING. SEE WHAT WE HAVE HAD TO DO TO THE GLORY THAT WAS OURS. WE HAVE DE-STROYED IT.——OBLITERATED UTTERLY. THE CAUSE WAS——. HEED THIS TALE.

IN THE HEIGHT OF OUR——THERE CAME ONE WHO——ALL THE——POWER. HE CALLED HIM-SELF OSSMINID AND WALKED THE MAZE RIGHT HERE AHEAD OF WHERE YOU STAND NOW. HE EMERGED SUCCESSFUL, ACQUIRING THE POWER TO PERSUADE ANY LIVING CREATURE TO HIS WILL.

BUT THIS WAS NOT ENOUGH FOR HIM. HE—— THE CROWNS AS WELL. USING HIS POWER, HE BENT THE CROWN COUNCIL TO HIS WILL AND WAS GIVEN THE CROWN——AS WELL. HE IT WAS WHO SET OUT TO PROVE THERE WAS NO REAL NEED TO— —CROWN AND MAZEMASTER.

FOR A TIME, THE GLORY OF OUR——IN-CREASED. OSSMINID RULED AS MAZEMASTER AND LEFT THE CROWNS TO THE CROWN COUNCIL. BUT AS HE RULED, HE CHANGED.

——HE SOUGHT TO CHOOSE CANDIDATES TO WALK THE MAZE. FEW OF HIS CHOICES SUC-CEEDED. FEWER AND FEWER PERSUADERS EMERGED TO DO THE WORK OF OUR——.

ONE DAY HE WRAPPED HIMSELF AS MAZEMAS-TER AND WALKED INTO THE EMPEROR'S CROWN, AS WAS HIS RIGHT. HE HAD NO PERSUADER TO SEND TO THE WARRING PLANET, AND SO HE SENT HIS OWN THOUGHTS THROUGH THE EMPEROR'S CROWN.

THIS WAS NOT JUST A MESSAGE FROM THE EM-
PEROR OF CROWNS. THIS WAS A FORCE FELT OVER
THE WHOLE PLANET. NONE COULD RESIST. THE
POPULATION WAS——.

WE SOUGHT TO REPLACE OSSMINID. HE WOULD
NOT LOOSE THE——HE HAD GATHERED. THERE
WAS KILLIN. HE WOULD NOT YIELD. ON THE DAY
HE ENTERED THE CROWN FOR A SECOND TIME,
HE——TO DESTROY US.

TO STOP HIM, WE DESTROYED OURSELVES,
KNOWING THAT WITHOUT CROWN AND MAZE,
OUR——WOULD DISINTEGRATE.

WARNING. WARNING. WARNING.

THE MAZEHEART THAT——US THE POWER TO
PERSUADE COULD NOT BE DESTROYED. WE HAVE
REMOVED IT AND CONCEALED IT.

WARNING. WARNING. WARNING.

THE——OF HOW THE MAZEHEART——DIES
WITH US. KNOW ONLY THAT WE DARED NOT——
INTO A——FROM WHICH NOTHING EMERGES. ALL
OUR——WOULD NOT LET US PREDICT WHAT
WOULD HAPPEN.

IF THE MAZEHEART IS FOUND————DE-
STROY ITSELF.

THE LAST PERSUADER

CHAPTER ONE

Mating

Zref Ortenau MorZdersh'n lay supine on the fine white sand at the edge of the spawning pond contentedly watching the surging waters where the two kren mated. Zref was nude in the steamy air, though outside the pond room he'd have worn several layers of clothing to protect his human skin against the mountain chill.

Suddenly, all his contentedness vanished in a flush of protective alertness such as he had not felt since his first bhirhir, his molt brother Sudeen, had died.

He sat up, gathering his legs under him, scrutinizing the two kren in the pond, Arshel and Khelin.

"What's the matter?" asked Ley, Khelin's bhirhir.

Zref shrugged, peering about the room, half expecting to see ghosts lurking in the steamy air.

Ley brushed his hair back from his face and whispered, one human to another, "Come on! You know Khelin's never attacked any female, let alone Arshel! Relax."

Zref shivered, realizing he'd broken out in a cold sweat. He searched for a logical cause for his alarm. Arshel was not yet truly Zref's bhirhir; they couldn't pledge until the mating finished. But he already felt as protective as he'd ever felt with Sudeen. And now it seemed a *presence* invaded this most private room threatening Arshel—his brothers Khelin and Ley—himself.

The heart-pounding surge of alarm was abating, the presence gone. "I trust Khelin, too," he whispered to Ley.

But Zref remained sitting, inspecting the room.

The kren had salted the pond water and warmed the air simulating Arshel's native tropical island, so she could suffer the rigors of egg-laying in comfort. But the rest of the room was typical of all freshwater spawning ponds. The water filled half the floor. The other half, almost all the way to the door

1

leading to the rest of the immense MorZdersh'n family home, was a gently sloping sand hill. To Zref's right hulked the free-standing arch, the "door to the room without walls" of kren philosophy. To one side, pegs jutted from the wall, holding street clothing. On a table set beneath the clothing, Zref and Ley kept toiletries.

Focusing on Ley, Zref noted that his fellow human's tan was fading, and he seemed to have gained some weight during the long mating, though he still had a muscular build.

Ley flipped his long, sand-colored hair back and whispered, "They're going to want us in there soon."

"Maybe not," answered Zref. He focused on the kren pair in the water. Iridescent scales flashed in the artificial light, but it was easy to pick out Arshel's darker saltwater-spawn coloring. Two earless heads surfaced and the sound of kren voices reached them over the lap-rush-lap of the water. Soon, Arshel would be laying her egg.

An uprush of curiosity swept aside the soft murmuring of the water as deep inside Zref's mind the comnet Interface signaled a message had dropped into his private file, that part of the Interface Guild's comlink set aside for Zref to use as his own memory. Years ago, his brain had been surgically altered to give him access to the webwork of connected computer banks located in all the far-flung centers of the Hundred Planets civilization, so that now opening the Interface was natural and peculiarly satisfying.

The Urgent Flag on the message had caused the high-intensity curiosity. Mating or no, he had to read that message. *There's someone waiting to see you in the reception room of your house. Youta.*

Youta, an Interface of the Jernal species, had been on Camiat long enough to know not to interrupt a kren mating. Zref opened and dropped a return message into Youta's private file. *"The person will have to wait. Zref."*

"This is a Hundred Planets security matter, and a Guild Policy matter. Rodeen will not break her word and order you off Camiat while you are still obligated to Arshel, but we all believe you both should go. Youta."

No! But Zref didn't drop that reply, and before he could frame something diplomatic, Ley was shaking him.

"Zref, pay attention. You can't open now!"

"I'm sorry, did they call us?" Zref searched the churning waters while lowering his blood pressure to control his curiosity, determined not to be seduced into opening when Arshel needed him.

Ley, restraining Zref with one hand, warned, "Not yet, but it can't be long now; Khelin is frantic." Ley pulled his hand back, glancing sideways at Zref. "Is something wrong? You've never opened when your attention should be on them."

Zref arranged his face into a grateful smile. Ley was treating him as if he were actually Arshel's bhirhir. "The Guild is dropping me messages demanding my attention." He hadn't intended to say that, but Zref had served the Hundred Planets as an Interface long enough not to be surprised at what came out of his mouth in answer to a direct question.

"During a mating?! You shouldn't let them do that!"

Zref was relieved that Ley hadn't phrased his advice, *Why do you* . . . which would have compelled him to answer. As it was, he felt nothing.

Ley frowned. "Khelin hasn't raised a drop of venom in almost five days. He must be in agony, but he's so involved he can't even feel it. I never thought kren *could* behave like this . . . as if he wants the mating to go on forever!"

Zref averted his gaze and opened briefly, then said, "According to the literature, the three years they've gone, with this being their fifth consecutive egg, already is a record. And no such mating has occurred between a pair that had mated with each other previously."

Ley looked at Zref in chagrin. "My brother the Interface. I'll never get used to it." He shook his head, then wondered, "Could it have something to do with Khelin's priesthood?" He gestured at Zref not to answer.

The Mautri disciplines both Arshel and Khelin had mastered seemed to have gentled their mating habits while intensifying their concentration on the process. Zref squelched the bubbling question of why this was, and why he, knowing Ley was human and not at all likely to be inflamed by Khelin's condition and attack Arshel himself, still felt a growing sense of threat. He decided the entire threat to Arshel came from the messages still dropping insistently into his private file—threatening to interrupt them.

Ley scrambled to his feet. "Look."

Khelin poked his head up above the rim of the pond, his skull outlined by the soaked down fluff that normally haloed his head. His hide gleamed, cascades of rainbows adorning his earless skull. He raised one hand, webbing spread, to beckon. "She's ready."

Shoulder to shoulder, Zref and Ley walked down the sloping sand and into the water, until they stood waist deep, facing one another with the kren couple between them.

If they had been kren, the situation would have them squaring off as potential combatants, venom flowing into their venom sacks, fangs lowered to strike position. Since they both happened to be human, they had worked out a symbolic gesture which helped to put the kren subliminally at ease. Making fists, they touched knuckles across the two kren who were floating nearly submerged, hyperventilating in preparation for the long submergence.

Arshel floated on her back. The bulge of her abdomen which contained the egg broke the surface, rippling as the powerful muscles drove the egg into her fully extended ovipositor. She reached for Zref's hand and squeezed, her eyes closed as she concentrated on the Mautri disciplines to relax her sphincters and pass even such a large egg as this easily. He returned her squeeze reassuringly.

Khelin urgently motioned Ley aside. Then, in one swoop, he flipped Arshel over, submerging them both as he thrust his male organ deep, both pushing the egg down its channel and lubricating it with his sperm.

Zref saw Ley's lips moving in a silent count as the kren disappeared beneath the surface. "I'm timing them," Zref said.

Ley smiled. "Just don't get lost in the comnet."

"If I do, my watchdog function will alert me at four minutes. If we have to bring them up, we will, but I don't think that's what they wanted us here for." Over the last five matings, Zref had built these routine monitoring functions into his private file so that they would operate even around a sheaf of unread messages.

The movements below the surface churned Zref off balance, dragging him into neck-high water. Ley followed, swimming. "That was awfully strong," said Ley. "I'm worried." He hyperventilated, and Zref followed suit.

"That's three minu...
They submerged. Khe... "Let's go down."
around Arshel's abdomen, e.c ... bbed hands were spread
the ovipositor as he gripped h... he egg to descend into
was relaxed into a sublime ecstasy hind. Arshel's face

The two humans watched critical... s into rapture. Ley
puffed, "They're both getting enough ...en surfaced. Ley
skins. They can stay down three or four m... through their
Zref sculled to keep his balance in the ... more."
"Arshel's color was good: I think she can ma... ing water.
not sure about Khelin. He's doing all the work."

"Ah, but he's having the time of his life! Did yo... see the
expression on his face? I think he'd strike at *me* if I tried to
make him stop now!"

They breathed together, and Zref said, "That's five minutes." Together they jackknifed straight to the bottom, but by
the time they got there, the egg was a pearlescent blob against
the pale grains of sand. Khelin was happily scooping sand up
around it, beckoning Ley over to help him.

Arshel turned to Zref and, in self-conscious imitation of the
human gesture of acceptance, embraced him.

The flexible, kren scales were familiar. The venom sack at
her throat was still flaccid, empty from the long mating. Her
ovipositor had already tucked itself away and the pleated skin
of her abdomen was coming back into place. Her firm muscles
were pliant, not tense. Her overflowing vitality filled Zref with
inexplicable joy, so rare for an Interface.

Khelin's exuberant egg burying had kicked up so much sand
Zref couldn't see. He signaled, and together they surfaced,
Zref panting while Arshel floated, breathing easily.

Moments later, Khelin and Ley surfaced, laughing. The
image evoked precious memories of Sudeen finishing a mating.

Khelin swept Arshel aside. "At last, Arshel! That was the
final time for us!"

Her wide, dark eyes bloomed with a new joy. "Truly?"

"Yes, my magnificent mothering-lady, I'll never have to do
that again." There was a deep, abiding affection in his voice
that Zref had never heard from Sudeen. Khelin moved Arshel
toward Zref, catching Zref's eye. "So now at last you can
immunize Zref to your venom, and Zref can offer you im-

munization to MorZdersh'n in pr ...nes, and Zref knew
you truly MorZdersh'n!" ... pledge to allow the
Bhirhir, not mating, bour...nced Arshel's webbed hand
Khelin appreciated their...ef's shoulder. "I apologize for
mating. Nevertheless, ...don't even understand my own feel-
in Zref's, his own ... y to make amends. I owe you so much,
my disgraceful be... ...ings now; I can...
Zref."

Had Zr...manded it even during the mating, Khelin, as
brother ...Sudeen and thus Zref's nearest relative in Mor-
Zdersh'n, would have had to provide venom for Zref to immunize Arshel in the sealing of their bhirhir. Thus immunized,
Arshel would be infertile to all MorZdersh'n, and her odor
couldn't trigger Khelin's mating. Zref put his own hand on
Khelin's shoulder. "Brothers don't owe each other." Glancing
to Arshel, he added, "Nor do bhirhirn."

"Tomorrow, then—we can go to Hengrave to pledge," said
Arshel, glowing.

Zref strangled back a surge of curiosity, remembering all
the unread messages bursting his private file. Sighing, he trudged
up out of the pond followed by Ley and the two kren. They
all watched him as they toweled off and dressed. But he didn't
want to spoil this moment by mentioning the summons to leave
Camiat—but not for Hengrave.

Khelin brought Zref his shoes. Khelin's head fluff was already dry, though the two humans were using hot air blowers
on themselves. As Zref turned his blower off, Khelin searched
Zref's face with the look Zref had once labeled his "blue priest's
gaze," a look that meant Khelin was using his peculiar psychic
gift for probing motivations. "Zref, I remember you with Sudeen. You feel for Arshel as you did for Sudeen. Despite being
an Interface, you *feel.*"

Zref felt no impulse to answer. Ley said, "He may be the
most peculiar Interface in existence, but he's still an Interface
and won't answer you unless you ask." Zref was the only
Interface made using a combination of modern techniques and
recovered First Lifewave knowledge. As a result, he had access
both to the comnet and to his own unconscious, making him
the only Interface who could feel anything other than the Primary Emotions.

"It's not that I won't answer. It's that I—can't."

"Then answer this," said the kren. "The Guild has granted you permission to exist as both Interface and person. Why can't you grant yourself the same permission? Why did you walk away from Arshel just now—knowing how it would hurt her? I can't be party to establishing a bhirhir where such callousness is practiced."

"No!" Zref turned to Arshel. "You didn't think I—Arshel, if you're ready, we *will* pledge bhirhir tomorrow. The Guild can take their offworld job and—"

"Offworld job?" asked Arshel instantly, and Zref had to tell them then about the message drop.

"In *our* reception room?" asked Khelin. "Now?"

Without volition, Zref dropped to Youta. *"Is that person still waiting for me at MorZdersh'n? Zref."*

"Yes, with less patience every moment. Why haven't you been answering your mail? I was about to drop to Jimdiebold to say you'd had a relapse and couldn't open at all! Youta."

In a fit of temper such as he'd not had since before becoming an Interface, Zref dumped all the "mail" in his private file back into Youta's private file, then he closed.

"Yes, the visitor is still waiting." Free of the question, Zref added, "I must see him, Arshel. I'll turn him down, though. Even Rodeen concedes that's my right."

Khelin's gaze seared Zref with the intensity characteristic of his talent. Ley moved to Khelin's side, an alert bhirhir. Suddenly, the three of them formed a solid front founded on a deep mutuality which excluded Arshel.

"Something threatens," pronounced Khelin. It wasn't the usual Khelin utterance. Hardly recovered from mating, the Mautri blue priest was raising venom.

Zref put one arm around Arshel's shoulders, almost in position to express venom—an intimacy bhirhirn practiced only in total privacy. But she didn't shrink away. "The *four* of us," said Zref, "will stand before any threat." With his other arm, he embraced Ley.

The exclusivity of their three-way bond held fast for a moment, and then a coldness invaded the room. As if in response, something changed in Khelin. He shyly touched Arshel. The three of them became four, and the coldness vanished so quickly Zref reeled in an odd, euphoric vertigo.

He looked down from a glittering tower upon a city served by wide boulevards, dotted with parks and lakes.

Health, serenity and enthusiasm rose from the city like a heat shimmer. He lived here among the gold and platinum roofs, the balmy breezes and open shopping arcades where most goods were free. All citizens shared the capacity to experience penetrating beauty.

Because of a single moment of faulty judgement, he had destroyed this city. Neither he nor anyone else would be reborn here again.

And in the pond room, he knew that the end of his exile was at hand, if he could bear the cost.

The reception room was artificially lit, its windows buried entirely under midwinter snow. After the tropical heat of the spawning pond, it felt cold. But the room was done in the warm, welcoming elegance of MorZdersh'n.

Before entering, Zref paused to flip his Interface Medallion out of his breast pocket. He was wearing his oldest Guild uniform, with kren-style house shoes, and his hair was wild from too many immersions. But he fixed his most forbidding expression on his face, and marched into the room as if it were his private office, Arshel at his shoulder as bhirhir, Khelin and Ley flanking the two of them.

The man, a human, was pacing restlessly before the large polished stone table in the center of the room. There were a number of small conversation pits throughout the large room which was divided by rows of columns into private areas. But Zref chose to keep the atmosphere businesslike. He strode to the table and seated himself at one end.

"I am Master Interface Zref."

The human shoved his knee-length coat back behind his hips, and braced his fists on his hipbones. He wore a fur brimmed hat tilted onto the back of his head, and knee-high black boots. He was the image of high-powered Business.

"I have been waiting a good while to see you, Master Interface."

"You will be billed only from this moment," said Zref.

"Are you going to introduce me to your friends?"

"I had not planned to," said Zref.

Amusement chased exasperation across the man's face until he gave a courtly bow in the latest fashion and amended, "Will you please introduce me to your friends?"

Zref did so, and the man repeated, "Arshel Holtethor Lakely. I'd been told I would not be allowed to meet you."

Arshel began to answer, but Zref held up his hand. "State your business, sir." He glanced aside and queried the comnet for the man's identity.

"I've come to invite you—both you and your bhirhir Arshel—to come on a Schoolcruise Pilgrimage Tour to the spiritual shrines of the galaxy. Your duties would be exceptionally light. You would be free to enjoy yourselves."

"I go where the Guild assigns me."

"And the lady?" he asked, looking to Arshel.

Arshel held her silence, but she obviously disliked this man. Zref received the answer to his query, and said, "Mr. Onsham, we're not interested in taking any tour sponsored by Lantern Enterprises. It isn't the spiritual shrines of the galaxy that interest Lantern: it's the remains of the civilization of the First Lifewave. Such remains no longer interest us. I believe that completes our business."

"I believe that it does not," countered Onsham. "I'd hoped to keep this friendly, but now I must ask you to check with your Guild Dispatcher, Master Interface Rodeen. She avers that the Guild has ceased its vendetta against Lantern Enterprises, and therefore the remains of the First Lifewave *are* of interest to Interfaces."

Zref lowered his blood pressure to control a sudden, overwhelming curiosity. Liking this man less and less, he opened with a deliberate rudeness, looking directly into Onsham's eyes. *"Checking as per instructions of a Mr. Onsham. Zref."* That was twice in less than an hour he'd acted on a kind of angry impulse Interfaces never had. It was as if his obligations to the Guild were threatening something precious he almost had with Arshel.

"Check Guild File #9777. And, Zref, I expect you'll do this for us. Ostensibly, we support education. Rodeen."

Rising and pacing around the table, Zref called up the file. A query dropped into his private file from his physician, the human Interface Jim Diebold, asking about the status of the mating. Zref answered, and Diebold came back immediately.

"Listen, Zref, I'm privy to #9777, so if you can't get back here to Hengrave to take immunization, at least do it at the Camiat Guild hospital, not in that house. There's no telling what that venom will do to your brain chemistry. I'd come if I could. Jimdiebold."

Zref acknowledged, then opened the high security file.

It was a datafile on the search for the City of a Million Legends that had ended when he and Arshel met. He skimmed the part that he knew. Ever since the first two nonhuman species had contacted each other and begun the first interstellar alliance of the Second Lifewave, they had found a common motif buried in their legends, a city rumored to exist in some inaccessible spot or some far gone time. Fabulous fantasies came true there; people lived together without strife, every peasant lived in luxury, disease was unknown, knowledge beyond all dreams allowed them to manipulate the fabric of the cosmos—magic.

Every planet had legends of travelers straying into the City for a time and returning wealthy beyond imagining, or suddenly talented or youthful. One legend even told of a traveler who came back from the City of a Million Legends to find dead relatives returned to life.

Recently, archeologists had uncovered scattered traces of the First Lifewave civilization—the first occupation of the galaxy—and suddenly it was believed that the City of legend had been the capital of that ancient civilization.

Ancient inscriptions were found indicating that in the heart of a maze at the center of the City was an Object. Gazing upon this Object conferred the ability to persuade anyone to do anything. Such "Persuaders" had been an arm of the government of the First Lifewave. Experts averred that the Maze-heart Object might still exist, and the race was on.

Zref and Arshel had been swept up in that headlong search, until three years ago, because of Arshel's ability as an arch-eovisualizer—able to read the history of an artifact by touching it—they had been the ones to find the actual maze in the City of a Million Legends. But all they found was an inscription saying the Object had been removed and hidden by the last of the Persuaders.

Zref had thought that chapter of his life closed. But new data had been added to the Guild's file. In recent months, a new archeological expedition funded by the Hundred Planets government, had disappeared. Suddenly, books were being published purporting to instruct individuals in how to search for the Mazeheart Object; swarms of ill-equipped explorers were camping out on inhospitable planets and having to be rescued. An Interface's report indicated a probability that organized criminals were still determined to find this legendary treasure—before the forces of law and order did.

The final entry was an official HP document on their new expedition to search for the Mazeheart Object, warning that the existence of the expedition must not leak into the hands even of the member HP governments lest the panic begin anew, with each special interest group scrambling to get the Object before anyone else so it wouldn't be used against themselves.

Within yet another internal security barrier, which melted as he addressed it, Zref found the last entry. Guild research showed that the HP statisticians had discovered the Guild's unwritten policy against archeological research, and so in order to get an Interface, this Official HP expedition to find the Mazeheart Object was disguised as the Lantern Schoolcruise Pilgrimage Tour which he and Arshel were being invited to join. The ruse was expected to fool whatever criminal forces had destroyed the previous expedition, as well as the Guild.

When Zref came back to awareness of the room, he heard Khelin saying, "...once worked for Lantern Enterprises. A schoolcruise is something new for Lantern."

"Indeed. We expect the novelty to attract many students interested in the strange fact that spiritual shrines seem to outlast many civilizations. Already, dozens of acknowledged experts on such eternal shrines are among the students. We expect more will sign up when they discover an Interface will be aboard to help with their research project."

"Research project?" probed Khelin, and Zref understood that he was diverting Onsham's attention from Arshel while Zref was unable to function as her bhirhir. She stood behind him, but some odd sense told him she was raising venom.

"Each student who successfully completes an original project on the shrines we visit will receive degree credit at Camiat

University, plus the right to submit his project to Lantern. If it's selected as the basis of a Lantern novel, the author will be paid more than the price of the Cruise!"

Zref rebelled at the idea of lending himself to such use. He'd given his allegiance to the Guild only when they adopted the policy of slowing archeology to prevent First Lifewave technology from wrecking this civilization. Yet the Guild was right. With the gathered brainpower of the Hundred Planets, the curious, enthusiastic students, the Cruise might succeed. If so, he ought to be there. "Mr. Onsham, when does this cruise depart Camiat?" asked Zref.

"In three days."

"Call your superiors and have departure postponed at least three days. At that time, we will give you a definite answer— but I don't guarantee it will be yes."

"Zref!" gasped Arshel. From her tone he knew she was raising venom, feeling the threat of abandonment.

He held up one hand to silence her, and kept his gaze firmly on the human before him, more Guild Interface than bhirhir now. "The comtap is right outside that door." When Onsham had left the room, Zref was assailed with irate objections. Only Khelin kept silence.

All trace of the wild distraction of mating was gone from Khelin now, and he seemed more than a blue priest. He seemed as deep and still as any white priest as he breathed softly, "They're going to find the Object." Then as if it were torn from him, he verbalized what was buried alive in Zref's heart, "*I* can't allow them to find it!"

Only Interface's detachment kept Zref's voice from shaking. "If we don't go with them, how can we stop them?"

"Zref, no!" cried Arshel, and her voice was shaking. Her venom sack pulsed as new venom spurted from her glands. "I won't—I can't! You promised!"

The last time Arshel had become involved in the search for the Mazeheart Object, she had ended by striking and killing her bhirhir Dennis with her own venom.

"I promised to take you bhirhir," said Zref, "which I very much want to do. I promised to enroll you in the Mautri priesthood school, and stand by until you attain the white and no longer need a bhirhir—and then to dissolve our bhirhir. I'll do all those things. But neither you nor I know we'll be allowed to do them now. Tomorrow, we will go to the Guild facility here in Camiat, and complete our pledge. Then we'll go to Mautri and seek admittance for you. If you're accepted, I'll tell Onsham the answer is no."

She sighed her relief, and her venom sack relaxed. But Khelin held his grave withdrawal from them until Onsham came back with Lantern's agreement to await Zref's answer.

CHAPTER TWO
Seeking-With

"The Tour leaves tomorrow," insisted Zref, pulling himself out of the groundcar in the underground parking lot of the Mautri temple. "We have to do this now."

Khelin jumped out of the back seat to grab Zref's arm and steady him even before Arshel—who didn't feel much better than Zref did—could move. To himself, Zref admitted that the physician had been right. The inoculation with Arshel's full venom had left him too weak to be doing this now. But they'd lost too much time while he'd been delirious. He leaned against the car, breathing from the oxygen mask Khelin held over his face while Arshel and Ley also emerged. Then he pushed the mask away. "Let's go."

The elevator ride up to the plaza surrounding the Mautri temple and the kyralizth made his knees buckle. They were surrounded now by offworld tourists here for the famous sundown ceremonies of Mautri. Both Arshel and Khelin were wearing their priest's robes while he was dressed in Interface blacks. He refused to show how weak he felt.

Above, the sun cast long black shadows. They crossed the pavement and entered the Mautri school compound by walking through the tunnel-like free-standing arch, the door to the room without walls, which was decorated with high relief carvings out of history.

Off to their right, on a lower terrace, was the open air parking lot where locals and tourist buses parked, and the entrance to the underground trains. People of every species were pouring up the wide stairs, hurrying to get places around the kyralizth.

A pair of offworld humans passed them as they emerged from the arch, and the woman raked Zref with a glance, commenting to her companion, "Wonder what he's doing here?"

Khelin said, "Let's go this way," and bore left, toward the

15

high walls surrounding the temple. The towers and turrets of the temple building jutted up above the walls, hulking shadows in the rapidly gathering dusk. Khelin led them into a fenced area next to the huge, formal temple gates from which the priests would come—the area reserved for the bhirhirn of priests and those who had left the temple.

Here, the press of the crowd let up, though the curious glances continued. They found places next to the rail facing the gate, but still in clear view of the kyralizth. The huge, flat-topped, stretched-out pyramid had its long "tail" end toward them from this vantage, and Zref could almost count the steps set into the sharp edge that led to the firepit at the top. Each of the other edges of the kite-shaped edifice was also set with steps. Everyone in the crowd, which now completely surrounded the pyramid, would have a good view.

Zref caught his breath, waving aside Khelin's offer of oxygen, and noting how Ley clutched the medic's case he carried against the chance Zref might collapse. He let Arshel lean on him reassuringly stroking her hand. She, too, had suffered a bad reaction to Khelin's venom, but it hadn't been unexpected. Saltwater and freshwater kren were just not compatible. But Zref had run a perilously high fever, a condition neither Arshel nor Khelin was experienced with.

The kren were not cold-blooded, like Terran reptiles. Their body-temperature regulating system only acted to keep their temperature above a certain level, not to keep it below a given temperature. And they didn't run fevers.

"Are you sure you can stand here the whole while?" asked Arshel.

"Yes," answered Zref. "It doesn't take long." But he leaned on the fence.

"I don't know if that's such a good idea," said Ley. "It's cold out here, and you've been *sick*, Zref!"

"But I've survived. If we're going to go there's so much to do! We have to arrange for the children..."

Ley said, "I've taken care of that." He named relatives who'd volunteered to surparent while they were gone.

"We can't go," said Arshel, pleadingly. "Has everyone forgotten, there's one more hatching?"

Ley caught her eye. "I'd stay for that hatching, Arshel, at

risk of my life. But Khelin has decided to be on that cruise. He's going to molt soon. Do you think I'd let him go alone?" Ley as surparent to Khelin's children was responsible for seeing them through their childhood molts, and socializing them, but his bhirhir had to come first.

Khelin had strayed out of earshot, searching the railed compound. Skanqwin, his first-hatched son by Arshel when Arshel had been bhirhir to Dennis Lakely and Khelin's student at Mautri, was now a yellow priest at Mautri, though young for the status. Not high enough in the ranks to climb the kyralizth with the other priests, he usually watched from here. But Zref saw none of the red or orange or yellow robes of the younger priests yet.

Arshel clutched Zref's arm, staring off toward the setting sun. "They'll readmit me, Zref. I know it. But will you miss Khelin and Ley too much?"

"Interfaces don't miss people," answered Zref, wishing his words could reflect his knowledge of her emotions better. "Look, here come the reds!"

Khelin and Ley were standing a short distance away, facing the postern door that opened into the railed compound. It opened, and a flood of red robes issued forth, followed by the orange and then the yellow in decreasing numbers. At last, Khelin darted forward to greet Skanqwin, a stalwart young male with a dusky complexion, halfway between saltwater and freshwater norms. He was short for a MorZdersh'n, but the whole family was proud of his accomplishments at Mautri and held great hopes for his siblings. Inzin Tshulushiem, Skanqwin's best friend, who had won the right to the orange robe, was not with him, and Zref concluded he must have been invited to climb, a singular honor.

Ley took one of Skanqwin's arms and Khelin the other, and hauled him over to the railing where Zref and Arshel waited. But as they arrived, Ley seemed to sense a reticence on the youngster's part to be handled in public by his surfather, and he withdrew the contact. Skanqwin bowed to Zref and Arshel, as if they were strangers, and said, "Our Chief Priest sends greetings and extends welcomes." Then to Arshel and Khelin, he added, "You're both invited to climb." Arshel tensed, and Zref knew she expected this was the first sign she would be readmitted. But then she said, "My bhirhir is not wholly well. I would stay beside him."

Zref, about to protest, was interrupted by Khelin, "Tell Jylyd they have just pledged, and are still weak." He overrode the bright congratulations that leaped to Skanqwin's eyes, saying, "Ley and I will stay beside them—and later beg permission to sit in on their seeking-with. We'd be honored if he would hear us."

Zref had known they'd go to a white priest to ask for Arshel's admission, but he'd no idea the Chief Priest himself might honor them. Skanqwin bowed again. "I must hurry." He left, signaling his delight in their pledge with a cheerful glance.

When the boy had gone, Ley asked, "Do you think Jylyd really will hear us?"

"He was a red with me," answered Khelin. "We've been friends. He knows I wouldn't ask lightly."

A hush was falling over the assembly now, souvenir hawkers retiring to the parking lot as the sun touched the horizon. The city spread beneath the peak on which Mautri sat was sparkling with lights flung against black velvet, while the sky yet held light pierced only by a star or two. The world held its breath.

Slowly, the giant gates decorated with polished carvings creaked open. In the measure of time this took, Zref lived the many hundreds of times he and Sudeen had witnessed this. And it seemed his familiarity with it all went even deeper, lifetimes deeper. Familiarity made it a meaningless routine, and then turned that routine into burnished memories throbbing with enriched emotions. He blinked, and told himself it was only a data leak from the comnet setting up resonances in his mind.

The gates came to rest, and from the darkness emerged the white priests, four abreast, their ranks thin. Behind them came the purples, and then the dark blues like Khelin. The light blue was followed by the greens where Arshel could have taken her place. As the rainbow completed itself, the ranks split to encircle the kyralizth, each of the four climbing the stairs leading from one of the four points toward the flattened apex.

It was timed beautifully, the whites arriving at the top of the kyralizth just as full dark blotted out perception of the spectrum of colors now edging the kyralizth. A breathless pause, and white fire erupted among the white priests at the top. Each priest now held a torch. The leading white priest from each of the four sides dipped a torch into the fire, and turned to light the torch of the one behind him. Very quickly then points of fire rippled down each edge of the kyralizth, outlining the structure in diamonds.

Gasps of amazement whispered among the tourists while the natives of Firestrip, humans and kren alike, held a reverential silence, knowing this was the most sacred mystery of the Mautri disciplines. Its true meaning was taught only to the whites. Zref had been told that it had no inherent meaning other than what each person could extract from it, but tonight, he felt deeper stirrings from which he flinched. An Interface didn't cry.

The fire hung in the air, and then as quickly as it had been kindled, darkness swept down the lengths of the kyralizth as each priest upended his torch and extinguished it. The entire area was plunged into the profound darkness of the mountain peaks, the city lights only the merest haze below. Silence ruled, then the rustle of movement as the priests descended in darkness. As they joined ranks to reenter the gates, the parking lot lights went on, dazzling all with their crass brightness, dispelling the mood.

Skanqwin was beside them, breathless from a hard run, and then standing still without panting. "Jylyd asked me to escort you all to his chamber."

They followed the younger priests back through the postern into a narrow, dim hallway carved from the stone of the thick walls. Through an inner door, up a winding stairway where troughs had been worn in the treads by generations of feet. Deep inside the temple where outsiders were never allowed, they ascended again and turned this way and that, passing many robed priests hurrying about their evening duties. Here the stone seemed even more ancient. Niches were carved in the passageway walls, some empty, some holding abstract carvings of surpassing beauty. In places a thin carpeting decorated the floors. Elsewhere hangings curtained archways. Always, abstract designs were executed in clear, clean rainbow colors.

Once, Skanqwin started down a side passage, and Khelin reached out to stop him. "Ley and Zref can't go that way."

They took another turn then, and Zref sensed they were circling until they came to a long hallway hung with antique chandeliers that must have been worth a fortune, all lit now in bright welcome. The floor was covered, wall to wall, with a fluffy white carpet, and the walls were painted with purple textured shadows that made them nonexistent. At the end of the hall, a closed door gleamed metallic gold. Without stepping on the carpet, Skanqwin bowed again. "Jylyd expects you."

Khelin walked into the decorated hallway and turned to Skanqwin with a slight bow. "No doubt he does. Thank you."

Skanqwin hurried away, and Ley joined Khelin. "I can't help it. I'm so proud of that boy . . . !"

Khelin's face melted with affection. "With good reason. He was so nervous, I don't think he could remember which end of a bead to string—yet he only made one error, and he hardly raised prevenom at all."

As they reached the door, it swung open to reveal the white-washed and well heated room the Chief Priest Jylyd used. The windowless room was hung with faded antique tapestries. At one end, a fire filled a huge fireplace.

Jylyd, a kren almost too young to be Chief of the Mautri temple, gestured to them to be seated on the four plump cushions in a circle around him. He offered them all cups of hot soup and inquired solicitously of their health.

Once, when he was but á very small child, Zref had wanted to be admitted to the Mautri priesthood so much that he had sat in their outer courtyard day and night for nearly a week until his distraught parents had come to take him home. He'd kicked and screamed in protest, desperately sure was he that his future lay within these walls. But the kren who had been Chief Priest here then had told him his future lay elsewhere, for he had no psychic talent worth training.

He'd never been allowed to approach these private chambers until now, when he'd become an Interface, brain mutilated so that whatever slight talent he might once have possessed was forever gone. Or so it was reputed to be with Interfaces.

Jylyd and this room were familiar to all three of Zref's companions. That knowledge beat in on him until suddenly, he saw it all through their eyes, familiar.

"Zref?"

"He's going to faint!"

Khelin had the oxygen mask ready, but Zref waved it away. "No. It's just that for a moment—"

Jylyd grinned in the civilized kren manner, lips closed over fangs, but his eyes unveiled of nictitating membranes. "You *do* remember, Tschfa'amin!"

The final word was a proper name, pronounced with the resonant click of the fangs before the dental fricative. The white priest held his eyes. The world bulged in and out around Zref. He felt the word/name pry at the Interface within him as if he were reading another Interface's private file—but he wasn't.

For an instant, he sat on the pile of cushions Jylyd now occupied. The tapestries about them were bright and new, the fire as warm as ever, and his body was fanged and scaled.

And then it was gone. He slumped, panting, suppressing a whimper as an overlaid memory told him he was raising venom in simple shock/fear of a perfectly ordinary past life memory, which he shouldn't have because he was an Interface.

"Now you know, Tschfa'amin, why my predecessor could not allow your young self even into this room. Your memories here run deep. But they are comfortable ones."

Zref shook his head. "No. Not for an Interface . . ."

". . . who's hardly over a pledge immunization!" defended Arshel.

Jylyd agreed. "The stresses in this room run deep. We are all seekers, and . . . Arshel's decision affects us all."

"I've made my decision," said Arshel. "I'm ready to try for the blue whenever you're ready to let me."

Finishing off his soup, Jylyd set his cup aside and gazed at her mournfully. "If only it were that simple. But, now that I've met Zref, I'm beginning to understand." His gaze rested on Zref for a moment, then he rose and went to a tall antique wood cabinet which stood against one wall. When he returned, he had cradled in the spread fingers of both webbed hands, a large, perfectly round, green sphere covered with a snatch of white gossamer.

He set this object on a blue pillow at the center of their circle, and drew aside the sheer cloth.

Khelin looked from the object to Zref and back again several times before he whispered, "Tschfa'amin." Then he turned to

Jylyd pleading, "I never suspected! Jylyd, I never suspected!"

Jylyd seated himself answering the unspoken questions from the others. "Tschfa'amin was a white priest here, Chief Priest among us—nobody is sure how many times. The last time we knew him, he was called Tschfa'amin, and he left instructions that we must educate Arshel for him, but not admit him to the studies even if his young self asked." He raised his eyes to Khelin. "When he was Tschfa'amin, Khelin was one of his students.

"Tschfa'amin's last instruction," said Jylyd to Arshel, "was that when you sought readmission to complete your studies, you must be required to take all the vows and obligations of the Mautri, forsaking the Vlen traditions of your childhood. Are you ready to do even this now?"

"I think I did, a long time ago—when I first realized I couldn't live with Dennis."

"And do you believe that you cannot live with Zref?"

She considered him for a long time before answering, "No. Zref is the oddest bhirhir anyone ever had, but I think he will not be able to use me as Dennis did."

Zref was sad that she had not said she trusted him. But one couldn't lie to a Chief Priest when seeking admission to a degree level.

"If you have matured sufficiently to manage your bhirhir, and if you've found a bhirhir you can live with, why do you seek the blue?"

"And after that, the purple, and even the white," added Arshel boldly. "Because I discovered at great cost that I have a dangerous talent which I alone am responsible for."

Dennis had used her talent as an archeovisualizer to gain wealth, power and prestige, but Jylyd feigned not to understand. "Zref is better qualified to manage your small talent than you are."

"Perhaps, but my talent is for me to manage—or mismanage. If I am to grow, I must do this myself."

"Is there some other reason you mistrust Zref?"

"I don't mistrust Zref! Jylyd, I killed my bhirhir with hate venom! How could it be easy to take another bhirhir?"

"Look deeper, Arshel. We don't teach people to live bal-bhirhir because they dislike bhirhir. You can't learn to live balbhirhir if you aren't truly bhirhir."

To live balbhirhir was the goal of Mautri training, but only the whites lived without the assistance of a bhirhir even for molt. Most kren felt this was unnatural, but those who sought to train their psychic talents found it necessary.

Arshel was raising venom now, as a human woman might break down and cry under such pressure. She had just finished a long mating, and taken a difficult immunization. Her hormones must be in riot. Zref edged closer to her, offering the contact of one hand on her knee to steady her, while he stifled an urge to answer for her and shield her from the brunt of Jylyd's attack. He was startled at how hard it was to suppress his new bhirhir's instincts.

"Arshel, I'm not going to judge the quality of your current bhirhir. Our doors are open to you now, if you choose to enter them. But that is a decision you are going to make once you are sure you understand who Zref is, and what his business with you is."

Her gaze whipped around to rivet Zref with hot inquiry. The Guarantees which bound all Interfaces never to harm the comnet, never to waste its resources in useless queries, compelled him to say, "I doubt such information would be anywhere in the comnet." And his eyes went of their own accord to the green sphere before them.

"Yes," said Jylyd. "You recognize it."

"No," denied Zref mildly. But it felt restful.

Khelin offered, "I've only been called to it once—in this lifetime. Venerable—should I inform the aklal?" He began to rise, beckoning Ley with him, but Jylyd motioned him back to his seat.

"When I knew you would come this morning, I warned the aklal. Ley—" Jylyd considered. "Ley you may sit with us if you choose. You are part of this."

"I'd like to stay, Jylyd, Venerable."

"Please—I'm not so old as to be called Venerable yet!" As he said that, he leaned forward to place one naked finger upon the very top of the limpid green sphere. The sphere glowed red, and Jylyd took his finger away. "This was once part of the Wassly Crown. It was brought to us by Tschfa'amin in one of his previous visits, and it has been used for generations to focus the aklal on matters that concern us all."

Zref had always thought his mastery of colloquial kren languages adequate, but he had to glance aside and open quickly
to consult a dictionary for the term, aklal. He found it designated a group-mind or spirit, the collective mentality that any
group has in common. This meant little to him until Jylyd
touched the top of the sphere once more, flooding the room
with orange light.

"Tschfa'amin, if you refuse to permit it, we cannot do this
for Arshel."

He knew to answer, "I won't open again until it's finished."

"Khelin?" invited Jylyd, tapping the sphere twice more to
produce flares of yellow and bright emerald.

Khelin touched the sphere starring the interior with a blue
light. Jylyd touched it once more, and the room dimmed to
dark violet shadows. "Tschfa'amin—bring in the white priests
for us. Please."

As he automatically reached forward to touch the sphere,
Zref noted that Jylyd didn't ask, which would have compelled
the Interface to respond. His fingers touched the sphere and
the room exploded with brilliant white light. It thrilled through
every nerve and brought tears of joy to Zref's eyes as if he'd
never been an Interface.

Zref flew along stretched rainbows, whirling through time
and space. Below him, mists cleared and he saw a city—no!
The City. Clear blue sky, bright yellow sun, balmy sea breezes.
And the City. Like a flat, spoked wheel the City's streets led
him to the central hub.

And there, beside the sparkling rainbow encrusted Emper-
or's office building, lay the Emperor's Crown, a violet so bright
it seemed like dark shadows.

The Crown, as all the Crowns located on the Habitation
planets of the galaxy, appeared to be a stone circle, formed of
four concentric circles of monoliths, some of which were joined
by lintels. Within the circles, offset to one focus of an ellipse,
stood a platform flanked by uprights and lintels. Leading into
the Crown from the Emperor's Road, a long avenue bordered
by monoliths ended in a slanted stone placed outside the circle
and sighted on the line with the central platform.

Each pellucid stone seemed to be that same shade of violet

just beyond the reach of the human eye. And Zref knew they were synthetics designed by Philosophical Engineers to have specific psychic properties. When a qualified Crown Operator entered a Crown, at the calculated time, he could send and receive messages to another attuned Crown across the galaxy. This Crown, the Emperor's Crown, was the one which had access to all the others. From here, a galaxy was ruled.

The City—not yet the source of a million legends—teemed with a dazzling mixture of species, though one form of erect biped predominated. Covered with bright feathers, crested but wingless, draped in feathered cloaks to match their plumage, these people filled the streets and offices.

Within the Emperor's office building, Zref joined a formal meeting of many species. He was feathered, robed in feathers only slightly less splendid than the Emperor's own, and he was perched on a writing bench before the Emperor as were a number of other dignitaries. He was there as the Empire's Philosophical Engineer, appointed for building the Crystal Crown to house Cheeal's Golden Sphere. Now he defended his latest scheme. "My students and I can forge the Selector to reject anyone who will misuse the power of Persuasion."

Cheeal rose from her perch, her feathers new and perfectly groomed. *"Anyone* involved in governing will misuse the power of Persuasion, though I wouldn't expect a Philosophical *Engineer* to understand that!" Behind her scorn, Zref sensed real fear. And he shared it.

But his then-self also rose. "The principles of the Universe with which we've engineered this Habitation of the galaxy do indeed show us the dangers of Persuasion. But only Persuaders can save our civilization from extinction. We're far too large, too diverse and too querulous to survive without the Persuaders to be the messengers of the Crown Emperor, bringing the legendary peace and prosperity of the City to every planet. It takes a Philosophical *Engineer* to understand the necessity, the danger and the precautions which make the Persuader Corps our salvation."

"But only the Material Artist," argued Cheeal, and now Zref recognized her as his bhirhir, "can perceive the way in which power over another destroys the one who wields it. Even in the hands of a good person, the power of Persuasion will become Coercion and then Compulsion. The Emperor of Crowns is elected for life by the Crown Operators from among their own to administrate the communications flow of this civilization. The Emperor of Crowns owns the Crowns—not the people. Our civilization is too great a work of art to allow this new power to destroy it in the time of the Fortieth Emperor." She looked to the feathered figure before them.

The Fortieth Emperor wavered toward Cheeal. Desperate and outraged, Zref raised one hand and filled the room with echoes of power such as only a Master Philosophical Engineer could raise: "I call into witness the Laws of the Universe, the collective mind of all mortals, the collected minds of all immortals, that I will prove to Cheeal that the Persuader power itself does not destroy the one who wields it."

The echoes subsided. The Emperor challenged Cheeal, "Match that, Material Artist!" And when she could not, Zref had won his argument—as well as an enemy.

For a moment, reality faded in around Zref. Once the Theaten archeovisualizer, Iebe Arai Then, had told him he'd been the Mazebuilder, but he hadn't believed it when he'd read it in the Lantern novel, *Maze Builder,* nor even when Arshel had told him her version. But now he'd been there, and he knew. All his mixed feelings for Arshel made sense. She was indeed the most important person in his universe. Another scene grabbed at him: a pall of doom suffused an aerial view of the City, the Crown and rectangular Maze at the center. But new buildings had been added to the skyline, and the outskirts stretched well past the old limits. New creatures moved about their business, the City filled with statues of them.

Zref stood in a new body, an erect biped, scaled and gilled, more at home in water than air. Of a long-lived species, he was nevertheless at the end of his span, having been Mazemaster for many years. From the door of the Maze Residence building, he could see the top floors of the Palace of the Emperor who had walked the Maze to become Persuader and now aspired to be Mazemaster as well as Crown Emperor.

The identity shimmered sickeningly. With a lurch he was sitting on a cushion in Jylyd's room, looking into the globe—which was swollen to ten times its size—watching a holographic projection of the story he almost remembered.

But this time, there was no aura of impending doom, no throb of evil barely leashed, as he looked at the jewel encrusted building which housed Ossminid, Emperor of the Stars. No Philosophical Engineer himself, but only an amateur dabbler in the Wisdom Arts, Ossminid had nevertheless discovered a new way to use the Persuader's talent, and today Ossminid was to become Healer of the Galaxy.

The procession began precisely at noon, so he'd arrive at the Emperor's Crown when all the Crowns of the Empire were attuned to it. Glittering in their grandest finery, the twelve Crown Operators of the Emperor's Council preceded Ossminid. Dressed in rich but modest apparel, the twelve Maze Escorts, Zref included, followed the procession.

No! He'd never have lent his high office to such dangerous perversion.

As Ossminid stepped between the two pillars which marked the entry to Emperor's Avenue, the bright violet of the pillars radiated purple shadow. The people of the City who had gathered in stillness to watch, all cheered as Ossminid's presence activated each pair of standing stones as he passed.

"No!"

It was a kren voice crying out in the chamber of reality. Khelin.

"No!" Zref joined that objection. The scene before them was from the latest of the Lantern novels, *Healing Day.*

"No!" cried Jylyd simultaneously with Zref.

The swollen green globe throbbed once, as if fighting their collective will, and then subsided to its normal size. Arshel let out a wheezing sob, covering her eyes with the spread webbing of her fingers. On Khelin's other side, Ley suddenly crumpled forward in a dead faint.

To his credit, Khelin inspected Zref before turning to his bhirhir. But Zref was moving to Ley's side, knowing Arshel needed a moment of privacy. Jylyd reached Ley first, and spread the web between his thumb and forefinger in front of the human's nose. "He's breathing."

The white priest stretched the human out supine on the floor and then ran both spread hands over his body. His eyes closed for a moment of total concentration, and then he brightened and proclaimed, "He's unhurt. He's very strong."

A moment later, Ley came to, bewildered. Khelin helped Ley up and Jylyd poured hot brew for everyone. Zref went to Arshel who was still bent over, hugging herself. Moving slowly, mindful of her hair-trigger reflexes, he massaged the strike muscles at the back of her neck. Her venom sack was half full; embarrassing for a green.

"Whatever it was," he whispered, "it's over."

"No it's not," she said, shaking. "But I'll be all right." Her tone said, *I don't need your help*.

That stung. But Zref didn't recoil. He now knew why she didn't trust him. He had been a child blinded by his own brilliance when he'd thrown that oath at her. His current self shuddered in revulsion. No wonder it had taken him so long to accept his identity as Mazebuilder.

When they were all seated once again, Jylyd said, "Only one thing have I learned which is indisputable. You have an enemy powerful enough to reach into these very chambers, and into your own spawning pond. I shudder to think what will become of us all if you cannot vanquish this enemy." He eyed Arshel, "Or if you refuse to try. . . ."

"I had already decided to go on the Cruise," started Khelin as if to divert attention from Arshel. Ley elbowed him in the ribs. As Arshel's bhirhir, Zref should have spoken.

"The Cruise?" asked Jylyd, ignoring the bad manners.

When they'd filled him in, he said, "Yes, of course. She is behind it." Then he shook his head. "No, I must not offer advice. My vision can't be that clear."

"Venerable," said Arshel, "you gave me a decision to make. I've come to seek-with you for my answers. Help me."

No white could refuse that plea. Zref was surprised Jylyd even hesitated. Then the Chief Priest drew himself up. "We have all seen different things in the sphere, and learned different things of ourselves—until that last moment when *something* more powerful than anything I've ever touched before took over and brought us all into a warped fiction." Jylyd fixed Zref with unveiled eyes. "Your enemy; female in this lifetime; master now of a gigantic but unconstituted aklal. Her will has been manipulating your life, Zref Ortenau MorZdersh'n—as ancient and masterful as you are, she seems to have bested you. You made the Mazeheart—the Selector—and her goal is to wrest it or its secret from you. You found the City for her; you found the Maze. Now she bids you find the Mazeheart—and render it up to her."

Zref became aware of Arshel and Khelin staring at him through half-hooded eyes as if evaluating something treacherous. "No!" he said. "I'll destroy it first!"

"Remember the inscription," said Ley. "The Mazeheart Object can't be destroyed."

Zref's private file held a copy of the inscription he and Arshel had found at the entry to the Maze ruins. "The inscription says it can't be found in any ordinary way—but if it is found, it will likely destroy itself."

"But if it's used," said Arshel, "it'll destroy us as it did the First Lifewave."

"Arshel, here before the Venerable Jylyd, I swear my life is dedicated to preventing First Lifewave technology from invading and destroying our civilization."

"Your life is not your own to dedicate. It belongs to the Guild," countered Arshel.

The Guarantees rooted deep in Zref's mind made him hedge away from the secret Guild policy against archeological research. "The Guild gave me back much of my life because First Lifewave technology made me an Interface with access to a personal unconscious. The Guild backed my project to track down Balachandran and stop him. I'm alive only because you and I succeeded, and you're alive because the Guild allowed me to become the first Interface to take a bhirhir. The Guild is allowing me to decide whether to go or stay. I'll stay with you, if that's what you want, Arshel."

Jylyd added, "If you stay, Arshel, your enemy—for she is yours as she is Zref's—will have the chance to find the Object and use it before you can destroy it. If she gets it, with the power she has now, there may be no way to stop her."

Haunted, Arshel gazed at the sphere, then turned to Zref. He knew she saw him as Mazebuilder.

He pleaded, "Give me a chance to show you what I am now—not what I was then."

"I warn you—if your destiny is to find the Object, you will not use my talent to do it."

Dennis, her first bhirhir, had used her badly. "I'll take

nothing from you that is not freely offered."

"Then I'll go with you now, because Jylyd is right. I'm not free to enter Mautri again until this is finished."

Zref had never seen such unutterable grief. Her normally melodious voice was grinding, her eyes dead. He acknowledged within himself a victory—for everything in him had yearned to take up Onsham's challenge. But never had victory been so bitter. *There's no such thing as victory over one's bhirhir*. An Interface wouldn't be able to feel such pain.

CHAPTER THREE
Epitasis

"What kind of a ship's name is *Epitasis*?" asked Shui Tshu-lushiem. He hadn't been with them long enough to know it was rude to ask a direct question in the presence of an Interface you hadn't hired.

"Greek," answered Ley, who'd done graduate work in linguistics under Zref's parents. "A dead Terran language."

The six of them, Khelin, Ley, Arshel, Zref and the two kren bhirhirn, Shui and Iraem, were crowded into the forward-viewing blister of an orbiter, gazing at the outside of the void-spanner, *Epitasis*, the Cruise ship. It was the largest ship Zref had ever seen, much larger than the starhopper class which had been in use when he was young.

"Amazing," said Arshel, "that such a small ship could provide for over two thousand people."

As their pod docked, Zref listened to the computers chattering to each other and said, "We can board now."

They hefted their handluggage, the larger pieces having been sent ahead. The *Epitasis* store would have to supply many things for Shui and Iraem, who had left on four hours notice.

Shui had been bhirhir to Jylyd before Jylyd took the white. Iraem had been bhirhir to another white, and as often happened, the two abandoned bhirhirn found compatibility in one another. Jylyd had said, "I'm going to ask Shui and Iraem to go with you into this. They've made a career as discreet bodyguards to the rich—and even to Interfaces."

Jylyd had talked the Guild into hiring the pair to guard Zref, since Shui was an experienced paramedic.

Khelin and Ley had been hired by Lantern in the capacity for which they'd become famous at the Hundred Planets capital, Eiltherm. They were supposed to keep the passengers of various species from abrading each other socially.

The orbiter was full for this last trip to *Epitasis*, so Zref's

31

party waited in the crowded exit corridor patiently. Zref counted eighteen species, even a group of Ciitheen, the only other semi-aquatics like the kren.

The Ciitheen, erect bipeds who seemed humanoid enough when clothed, had noticed the four kren and had withdrawn ostentatiously, as decent Ciitheen always did because most of them were vulnerable to becoming kren-venom addicts. This cruise could try Khelin's diplomatic abilities to the limit.

Even as they neared the portal, Zref, wearing his finest new Interface Guild uniform, was not jostled by the crowd.

Arshel said, "It hardly seems you need a bodyguard." Was her bhirhir's ego injured by Jylyd's sending the pair with them, as if *she* weren't protection enough?

"I don't think Jylyd was considering our physical safety. We don't know Shui and Iraem's past lives."

She twisted to gaze up at him—the top of her head barely came to his shoulder. "I never thought of that!"

Khelin had followed Ley into the crowd, beginning their job early. Ley paused to chat with an auburn-haired human woman wearing a green shawl dripping with tassels. At the portal, four stewards—a tall Sirwini with newly sharpened blue horns; a ball of pink fluff suspended over six spindly legs, who was a Jernal; a human woman with long blond hair; and a sleek, damp Ciitheen—welcomed the passengers to *Epitasis*, emphasizing the second syllable of the name.

"Ah, Master Interface!" said the blonde. "Captain's compliments, and she requests your presence on the bridge at your earliest convenience." As she was speaking, another steward was welcoming the three kren in Camiat's trade language, and the other two greeted people behind them. The blonde handed Zref a guide beam to the bridge.

Zref saw no reason for this request, but he drew the others together at the first wide place in the corridor, and invited Arshel to go with him. She demurred, "It must be bedlam in there. I'll go see how our cabin is."

Asserting her independence, thought Zref, but he said, "I'll be there as quickly as I can."

They parted, and Zref followed the guidebeam through a series of hatchways labeled AUTHORIZED PERSONNEL ONLY and RESERVED FOR TECHNICAL AUTHORITIES, to the control room.

Zref had seen many spaceliner control rooms, but never one so spacious; it looked more like a lounge than a bridge.

Sirwini and Theatens manned the few active stations, seemingly not working. Zref spotted a single female Almurali pacing around the padded lounge chairs in the central arena. She was tall for one of the erect bipedal quasi-felinoids, and her fur was magnificently long and perfectly groomed. She was wearing the immaculate ship's white in symbolic strips anchored somehow across her cream-and-tan colored body. Captain's stars gleamed on the leather device perched atop her head between her upthrust ears.

He approached her quietly, and said, "Master Interface Zref, reporting as ordered, Captain."

She whirled to face him, almost crouching into her species' fighting stance, then recovered gracefully. "Ah, Master Interface. Welcome aboard. Have you examined our onboard controlcom yet?"

"No, Captain, but from this"—he swept his hand around the bridge—"it must be most impressive."

"This is the newest voidspanner class liner, and some of our systems are classified, so by order of the Star-Treader Lines, and by my personal order, you'll refrain from making even superficial acquaintance with our operational systems unless I so request. You're employed by Lantern Enterprises to attend to the needs of the students and faculty aboard the Schoolcruise via the Interstellar comnet, not my ship's systems. You may verify this with your Dispatcher."

Under cover of a sigh and a shifting of position, Zref opened, checked Rodeen's open file and found the new order. "My Dispatcher has indeed informed me of this new order. As per Guild Contract, I will abide by the Line's wishes."

The Captain circled Zref, casually examining the working readouts on the boards around them. Out of earshot of the crew, she said, "Between you and I, Master Interface, I feel more secure having you to call upon if this experimental design crashes. You did pronounce a personal name?"

"You may pronounce me, Zref, if you will."

"Then perhaps, now that the unpleasantness is out of the way, I may invite you and your—um—bhirhir to sit with me at the Captain's table for the first meal. It's a delightful old custom of the human species which the Star-Treader Lines is reviving. The first and the final meals of the cruise will be formal affairs, and the crew will eat with the passengers. At other times, socialization will be minimal."

Zref accepted graciously, understanding that he should regard himself as a passenger and stay away from her crew. Then she assigned him an escort back to his cabin—as if to do him honor, but he suspected it was done to keep him from exploring.

His "cabin" turned out to be a suite occupying the end of a corridor. The door opened into a high-ceilinged sitting room dotted with lounges designed for many species, a dining area and an open hearth fireplace contained in a forcefield safety net. A mezzanine rimmed the room, and from that level doors opened into adjacent rooms assigned to Khelin and Ley on one side and Shui and Iraem on the other.

Straight ahead, a door led to a bedroom containing a sandbed and a full-immersion pond. An area beyond a walk-in dressing room held sanitary facilities such as one would encounter in a luxury hotel. The room was decorated in muted skytones from many planets, and greenery from Earth, all clean and new and perfectly flawless.

As Zref came in, he heard Arshel's voice raised in fury. "I don't care what your orders are, you aren't permitted in here!"

He loped across the sitting room and through the door into the bedroom. Arshel stood before a giant Theaten woman attired immaculately in ship's uniform and evincing unruffled proprietary servitude.

"Madame, it is my duty and my pleasure to attend to the personal needs of the inhabitants of this suite. You will require service in order to uphold your position aboard—"

"One moment," said Zref, as he moved to Arshel's side. Only a slow blink of the Theaten's green eyes betrayed her surprise. Zref looked calmly up into those eyes.

She intoned, "Identify yourself! These are private quarters."

"*My* private quarters," insisted Zref. "You will identify yourself."

"Suite Steward-in-Chief Linraep, in charge of the staff of these rooms. My privilege to serve." She bowed.

"And I am Master Interfacc Zref. This is my bhirhir Arshel. We occupy these rooms at our pleasure, not at your sufferance. Is that understood?"

"Absolutely, sir." Her eyes were fixed in the distance behind Zref now, passing at least a handspan over his head.

"Perhaps you'd care to elucidate the difficulty?"

"It is my duty to have this room cleaned and to keep it in repair, as well as to provide body servants, wardrobe servants and secretarial facilities. So I must inspect the premises regularly, if discreetly in your absence. The Lady Arshel has requested that neither I nor my staff enter this room for the entire length of the voyage. I am personally responsible for this room. I cannot accept banishment."

"I understand your difficulty," said Zref before Arshel could protest again, "but our need for absolute privacy takes precendence." The Theaten surely regarded them as unworthy of these quarters.

"It would be regrettable to bother the Captain with such a minor matter," said the Theaten still at rigid attention.

"Therefore, we shall compromise," said Zref.

"I'll not have them in here!" said Arshel in a strangled whisper. Anticipating a molt, she was desperate for privacy.

Zref stepped full in front of Arshel, facing her. "They won't be—trust me." Then he turned to the Theaten. "Suite Steward, are there any kren on your staff?"

"Yes, sir."

"Would one of them be competent to take full charge of this inner chamber, without your supervision?"

"One could be trained to do so."

"And his bhirhir to take charge of the other two bedrooms?"

"This is most irregular."

"You may check my authority with the Captain."

"I will ask my supervisor to speak to the Chief Steward for permission to promote the appropriate staff to your service. Is it that a Theaten is odious to you?"

"Not at *all*, Madame Steward," replied Zref hastily. "However, kren can't tolerate even the most loyal servants in the room where the pond is located. A kren servant would detect the most sensitive moments and avoid the—dangers."

The Theaten's eyes darted to Arshel's venom sack, widened, then fixed on the far bulkhead. Zref regretted embarrassing Arshel. Her venom was already flowing too freely. "You will leave us now," ordered Zref. "Send your kren staff members to us as soon as you can arrange it."

The Theaten bowed again and intoned, "May you have a pleasant voyage, sir."

When the outer door of the suite had closed, Zref let the starch flow out of his backbone, and apologized to her.

"Why didn't you just say we'd take other, less pretentious quarters? The ship isn't full."

"Lantern seems to be intent on honoring the Guild by the deluxe treatment. Relations have been strained since Lantern sued the Guild. The Guild can't turn down Lantern's offer of courtesy. So I'm stuck with a room that comes equipped with servants trained to creep about invisibly."

She laughed, her fangs slapping against the roof of her mouth. "Do you think we can talk a kren who's been trained by that woman into leaving us alone?"

"We'll have a strategy conference over this, but first let me express you so you'll be hungry enough for dinner. We've been invited to sit at the Captain's table!"

Arshel unpacked the molded leather venom bottle Zref had given her when they'd promised to pledge bhirhir, and they settled into the deep, ultra-fine sand of her bed. She knelt, he beside her with one arm around her shoulders so his hand lay across the sensitive skin of her venom sack at the base of her throat. With his other hand, he held the venom bottle as she hooked her fangs over the padded lip.

He closed his eyes, concentrating on her breathing, the feel of her scales against his skin, the bunching of her neck muscles as the strike reflex gathered. For this to be a comfortable maneuver for the kren, the bhirhir had to trigger the strike reflex at just the right moment. Sudeen had suffered greatly to teach Zref the trick. He was gratified still to have the skill.

Cupping the distended sack in the palm of his hand to support the strained muscles, Zref set off the reflex, his other arm working hard against her repeated strikes. The last spasm came with an open-throated grunt that was half sigh. And then she went limp into the sand.

He set the bottle aside and squirmed onto his back. He had to change clothes anyway before the formal dinner. He was almost asleep when he noticed Arshel gazing at him. The tension had gone out of her, but she was still gravely reserved. "I'll bet I know what you're thinking," said Zref.

"Oh? What."

"That I'm better than Dennis at that."

Astonished she drew back, and he could almost sense her firmly discarding the old superstition that Interfaces were invasive telepaths. "I was thinking that—but also that I'd determined to stop comparing you to him. Only I can't stop."

"It's all right. I was thinking of Sudeen, and what he went through teaching me to express. But I was also enjoying it more than ever before."

"Then I wasn't imagining that," she said, sitting up.

Zref agreed and suggested, "Let's swim!"

Later, when Zref was unpacking a dress uniform, Arshel surveyed her clothes despondently. "I didn't know we'd have to live in such style—and I had no time to shop anyway. Will what I wear reflect on the Guild?"

"I suppose. But don't worry about it. Tomorrow, we'll tour the shipboard shops to get whatever you need to put our Theaten in her place."

Dressed, they visited the room Khelin and Ley shared.

They entered the room on a balcony over a living area not so spacious as their own, but gorgeously appointed in mauve and taupe with green accents, a Theaten forest. The immersion pond was disguised as a forest glade pool. Under a voluminous hanging plant, Khelin was buttoning Ley into a formal jacket that fastened down the back. Heedless of the intrusion, Ley was objecting, "But I can't take a mate now! You know you'll be molting soon!"

"I saw how attracted you were," argued Khelin, "and I can see she's your type. I'm going to speak to her tonight, and that settles it. After all, what's a bhirhir for?" He spun the human around to check the front pleats. "I've kept you tied up too long. We'll manage the molt somehow."

Before he'd become an Interface, Zref would have been embarrassed to walk in on such a private conversation, and he could feel Arshel's flush of venom as if it were his own. "I see you two have been informed of the dinner."

"A Jernal brought an engraved invitation," said Ley, "Then it wanted to stay and dress me! We had a time getting rid of it. I think we hurt its feelings."

Zref and Arshel descended, telling of their run-in with the

Suite Steward and their compromise. Khelin said, "I admit I'm relieved. Let me call Shui and tell them about it."

The kren went to a table console hidden in what looked like a canebrake, and called the others to the common sitting room. Zref, as Khelin's brother, and Arshel as immune to him, had casual pond privileges with Ley and Khelin, but Iraem and Shui were not family or mate. They, too, were intensely relieved at the compromise.

"We've traveled without luxury, but never without privacy. However, neither of us will mate or molt this trip," added Iraem. "We shall endure."

"Why did you come?" asked Arshel with real curiosity. "We've all been involved in the search for the City before—"

"We wanted to be," replied Shui. He was a little taller than Arshel, heavily built, and of the freshwater, mountain-bred stock of Firestrip. He looked young, strong, healthy and competent. "But Jylyd and Frie were studying at Mautri, so we stayed with them. It all worked out. Jylyd even got us onto this cruise, which we never could have afforded!"

Khelin laughed. "That's just like Jylyd—letting two problems solve each other! And I for one am glad you're here!" At Zref's raised eyebrow, he explained, "There's already enough greed and desperation aboard to create a vicious aklal. People can be possessed by such a force, and become a dangerous mob."

Iraem said serenely, "And we will not be possessed." He was shorter than Shui, but taller than Arshel, and shared Shui's strong look. His features were regular and handsome in the light, freshwater kren way, though as with Shui there wasn't a hint of family resemblance to MorZdersh'n. Zref made mental note to treat their venom with extreme respect.

"How high did you go?" asked Khelin cryptically.

Shui looked to Iraem as if consulting, then answered, "Light blue. But we don't claim it. We're pledged."

So, these two were priests ranked just below Khelin in the rainbow hierarchy of the kyralizth. But neither of them had any intention of pursuing the balbhirhir life.

Khelin scrutinized the pair. "I'll keep that in mind. But you should wear your medallions at least for this formal affair.

There are kren-phobes and Ciitheen aboard. It will go easier for Zref if we aren't considered dangerous."

Arshel spread one webbed hand over her breast. "I forgot mine! It's been so long since I dressed up!"

The kren departed in search of their jewelry, and Khelin hooked one elegant leg over the back of a carved mahogany perch. "I hate to ask for privilege, Zref—"

"Ask," prompted Zref, expecting a comnet query.

"We signed on so hastily, Ley and I are not sure if we initialized a salary account with Lantern. If we didn't, the Camiat taxes will be charged to the MorZdersh'n accounts, and my uncle—"

"Say no more!" Zref held up one hand and cast his eyes aside to open. When they'd first hired him to audit their accounts, the family business had filed the necessary permissions to allow Zref to audit their accounts. While he was waiting for comnet to respond, Zref felt a trickle of chatter filtering through the edges of his mind, some computer talking to the Lantern net.

". . . Zref exudes an aura of restrained power."

"Hardly surprising in a friend of Jylyd's. But it is odd in an Interface." It was Iraem's voice.

"Jylyd said he read his past. An *Interface's* past! I wish he'd explained what's so special about this human."

"That's easy. The moment I saw him, I was sure I've known him before, and I'll bet that's why Jylyd put us here."

Zref cringed away from the contact. The conversation had been compressed into a squeal and squirted at one of Lantern's dishes by the *Epitasis*'s own computer talking to Lantern. And his orders were to stay out of *Epitasis*.

There was pressure on his knees—his whole body's weight. His lungs burned, thirsting for air as he crouched gasping, his head pounding, reducing all to impressions. Khelin's voice shouting; Ley's steps pounding; a human male voice calling, "Arshel!"

The other two kren came racing from their room, skidding down the steps and falling over each other to reach Zref. Zref pulled himself up, the waves of pain receding. "It's nothing," he gasped, fending off Arshel's firm hands.

He climbed back to his feet, felt his knees begin to give

and collapsed in a deeply padded chair. Arshel sat on the arm of the chair. "Do you need oxygen?"

"No, no." And he told them of his conversation with the Captain. "I accidentally intercepted *Epitasis*'s computer, and the Guarantees threw me. It's nothing, really."

"Nothing! I thought you were dead!" said Ley.

Catching his breath, Zref rummaged in the drawer of an end table and found a pad of ship's notepaper. Tearing off one sheet, he wrote, *These rooms are sound-tapped by the ship's computer—maybe visuals as well—the information is squirted to Lantern Enterprises.*

Reading over his shoulder, they looked at each other wide-eyed. Aloud Zref said, "Here's the number of the account you opened with Lantern." And he wrote, *I don't have the number yet, but there* is *an account.*

Arshel started to say something, but Zref opened and dropped a message to Rodeen, telling her about the bugging, adding, *"Kren can't live under surveillance. I can't touch that computer to turn off the recorder. We're getting off at Sirwin unless you can do something about this. Zref."*

"Surveillance was no part of our agreement. One moment. Rodeen." She came back, *"It's taken care of. The next time the* Epitasis *checks in with a Guild astrogation beam,* Epitasis *will be instructed to black out your three pond rooms and your person. Your person only, Zref. I'm guarding the Guild's reputation, not your privacy. Rodeen."*

Zref came back to awareness to see consternation on human and kren faces. "Now let's go to dinner," he said, scribbling, *I'll tell you when it's safe to talk aloud. But even then don't mention this to anyone until we see what Star-Treader will do next.*

CHAPTER FOUR
Almural

The dining saloon was a cavernous, lozenge-shaped room with the ship's structural members disguised as towering trees from many planets. The gently blowing air was scented with living springtime, the lighting simulating the spectra of half a dozen suns. At barely half capacity, tables were scattered. Brilliant white and gold tablecloths contrasted with the riotous shapes and colors of formal attire. A Jernal with a triangle of white and gold cloth pinned to its pink fluff suggesting a ship's uniform, escorted Zref and Arshel to the Captain's table as a Sirwini led Khelin, Ley, Shui and Iraem to a table in front of the Captain's. Bending its six spindly legs in a suggestion of a bow, the Jernal indicated a long bar curved around one end of the room and said in its reedy voice, "Please help yourselves to drinks. The Captain will be along momentarily."

When it had gone, Zref asked, noting Arshel's tension, "Would you like something to drink?"

"I don't know," she answered. "It's been so long since expression, I'm afraid I'm going to disgrace myself."

Zref understood the gnawing hunger a kren experienced after a full voiding. He glanced about wishing he could check with the ship's computer, but then he found what he wanted—the doors, hidden by heavy draperies, leading to rooms for such functions as kren venom kills of their dinner.

"Come." He led the way. As expected, one door was discreetly labeled Expression Rooms, and Zref knew it would also provide pre-feeding facilities. He urged Arshel forward. "Go ahead, while I get us something to drink."

When the door closed behind her, Zref turned to the bar where Khelin was ordering drinks from the steward. Beside him stood a human woman who looked to be about Ley's height if one discounted the heaps of auburn hair piled atop her head. It was the woman of the tasseled shawl, now wearing an eve-

41

ning gown of brilliant white sequins accented with forest green satin, archaically cut to leave her shoulders bare. The full-length circle skirt emphasized her tiny waist.

As Zref approached, Khelin was saying very quietly so others along the bar wouldn't overhear, "I volunteered to fetch the drinks because I wanted to talk to you."

Recalling the conversation he'd walked in on earlier, Zref veered aside and turned to survey the room. Others were being seated at the Captain's table though the Captain herself had not arrived. Faculty and crew were spreading among the students at formally mixed tables.

When he judged Khelin had finished, he went up to the bar. Khelin turned in instant greeting, saying, "And this is Jocelyn Petrovan, the choreographer."

She smiled, lips covering her teeth politely, answering with a Firestrip accent, "Hardly *the* choreographer. I'm only well known on the Camiat University campus."

"But we've all spent our lives in Firestrip," answered Zref, "and none of us would miss one of your holiday productions! Yet I wouldn't have expected to find you here."

"Master Interface, I'm here teaching the history of religious dance, but that's just to pay my way. Actually I'm taking my Masters in archeolinguistics."

Zref pondered whether to tell her his original family name —for his mother and father had been two of the foremost archeolinguists of the Hundred Planets. And Ley had all but completed his doctorate when the Professors Ortenau were killed, and Khelin had decided to give up at Mautri to make his way in life with Ley. But then their drinks arrived, and Zref thought she'd learn of the family soon enough. "I'm looking forward to working with you," he said courteously.

As they left with the trays of drinks for their table, Zref overhead Khelin briefing Jocelyn on Zref's place in the family. *At least*, he thought, *she didn't blush and run from the room at Khelin's invitation to mate with Ley.*

When Arshel joined him, looking much more relaxed, he told her of his meeting with Jocelyn. She watched Jocelyn seating herself beside Ley. "Is Ley *blushing?*" she asked.

It was clear why Khelin had sensed the attraction between them. "It's been a long time since Ley was serious about a woman. I hope Khelin knows what he's gotten into." Before she could answer their drinks arrived and so did the Captain.

When the Almurali entered, resplendent in her dress uniform which consisted of a number of long chiffon veils that did not conceal her exquisitely groomed pelt, everyone in the room stood, coming to order behind their own chairs and falling silent. The Captain marched the length of the saloon, flanked by her First Officer and her Astrogator. Zref and Arshel hurried to their places. Having reached her chair, she didn't signal the company to sit, but said, "I'm pleased to inform you that, despite our delayed departure, we'll arrive at Almural to pick up the rest of the students on schedule, and you'll have your day at the Shrine of the Huntress."

As she seated herself, the live waiters promptly entered carrying gleaming platters heaped with intricately decorated edibles. Species had been seated with care that none would be nauseated by the odor of their neighbor's meal, yet the air circulators whined as they dealt with the aromas.

As soon as their table had been served, the Captain pronounced the name of each of her guests, then opened the dinner conversation. "Our delay in orbit has one advantage. We picked up the very newest Lantern novel, *Assassin*."

Some of the academics donned expressions of distaste. The First Officer hastened to say, "I've heard this one is more like the earlier ones—authentic."

"There hasn't been any spectacular new find recently. What could it be based on?" someone asked

"I'm not sure, but it's by Mithal Meguerian, who wrote *Skanqwin and the Emperor of Crowns* and *Maze Builder*."

Maze Builder had been written by a trio of authors Zref had met while auditing Lantern's accounts and it had been based on a past lifereading they had taken on him.

The Captain said, "Previews said it was about a Kinrea woman opposed to Ossminid's uniting of Crown and Maze. Because Ossminid, instead of the Mazemaster, was choosing the Persuader candidates, there was a drastic shortage of Persuaders. This is the story of Ossminid's first attempt to put his Crown Operators through the Maze, and this Kinrea woman assassinates the candidate. In the end, a mob storms the Maze and Ossminid massacres them." She reached for a platter. "I'll probably stay up all night reading it."

"I'm also interested in the Meguerian titles," said Zref. "I certainly wish I could read this one." The urgency for each new Lantern novel he'd felt as a youth had gone after his surgery, but he still read them. Now, after the seeking-with, he suspected there was more to it than simply acquiring the means of small-talk with non-Interfaces.

The Schoolcruise Director, a hulking, suntanned human male with light brown hair and eyes, queried Zref. "Can't an Interface read any novel in the system free of charge?"

"By no means," answered Zref. "The Guild pays the ordinary fee when we access published matter. But Preview Releases are exorbitantly expensive for the first few days, so the Guild archives won't have them until libraries do."

"Why don't you read it from the ship's computer then? They certainly wouldn't charge *you* for it!"

"Star-Treader Lines has forbidden me access to *Epitasis* systems," said Zref, more frustrated than he wanted to admit.

The Captain turned to Zref. "But certainly you can use the comtap in your quarters, as everyone else would?" She added as if the subject of money were distasteful, "There'll be no charge for that, Master Interface."

"Using a comtap is probably the last thing an Interface would think of," commented the Cruise Director.

In fact, it hadn't occurred to him, but Zref answered the Captain, "I've been forbidden access to *Epitasis,* not just by Interface, but access itself. With your permission, Captain, I'll be glad to use the comtap."

Zref couldn't interpret the expression in her eyes, but the Captain only muttered, "Permission granted," and opened a discussion of the way Lantern Enterprises had funded serious research into First Lifewave excavations from the profits on the Lantern novels. When someone mentioned that this cruise was the first such effort in several years, the First Officer added, "And Lantern stands to lose a lot of money, unless this cruise turns up something big."

Another ship's officer said, "We're not going anyplace new, so how can we find anything new?"

"That's not the way research works," argued the Cruise Director. "When we understand the sites we have, we'll understand a civilization whose artifacts have survived a turn of the galaxy. Why do you suppose the Wassly Crown and the Crystal Crown are intact while the Maze and Emperor's Crown aren't? Maybe the Mazeheart Object disintegrated millions of years ago? Most of the shrines we're visiting are near First Lifewave sites, and have lasted for phenomenal spans. Perhaps our students will discover a more recent mention of the Object than the plaque in the City."

As dessert was served, an argument erupted over whether the Object should be brought to the light of day now.

One of the professors, a Sirwini woman whose blue skin was darker than any Sirwini race Zref had ever seen before, asked, "Should Merlin have destroyed the sword in the stone before Arthur retrieved it? Certainly that sword made Arthur as potent a Persuader as any Mazemaster!"

The conversation swirled around Zref and Arshel without including them, but Zref noted Arshel listening carefully, not seeming to feel excluded. The discussion was so loud, Khelin and Ley turned to listen. Soon Jocelyn, Shui and Iraem were also paying rapt attention. At last, the Sirwini professor suggested, "Let's have the Interface arbitrate, since he can be dispassionate. Master Interface, do you want to learn that the Mazeheart Object has been destroyed?"

It was an unfortunate wording for a question to an Interface. Yet the advantage of Interfaces over comtaps was that casual phrasing could get intelligible—even intuitively accurate—results. But he couldn't give his own opinion, nor even consider the effect of his words on Arshel. "No. Your allusion to the magical sword seems appropriate, though Arthur had been trained by Merlin to use it. However, a tool, no matter how powerful, is just a tool. Tool making is the universal mark of sentience. If we are to understand people who've lived before us, we must understand their tools. Loss of the Object might be a great loss indeed—"

Abruptly, Arshel rose, shoving back her chair rudely, and sped for the exit, missing Zref's final words, "—though the misuse of the Object may have destroyed the First Lifewave." Khelin lunged after Arshel, but Ley restrained him; he was not Arshel's bhirhir. Jocelyn gazed after Arshel, but everyone else was staring at Zref. He rose, folding his napkin and facing the

Captain. "Allow me to thank you on behalf of myself and my bhirhir for the regal banquet, Captain, and to tender apologies for our precipitous departure. Rest assured I shall be available as scheduled."

Zref had to use his key to enter their suite, and he found Arshel burrowing into the sand of her bed, gasping with the uprush of venom. He closed the door, thankful for the quiet opulence. Aware of his presence, she only wormed her way deeper into the sand. "Arshel, it's bound to be difficult being bhirhir to an Interface."

She raised herself, showering sand all about. "Just tell me, then, yes or no. Are you going to destroy the Object, as you told Jylyd you would?"

Any moment, *Epitasis* would take a position fix. He temporized, stripping to his immersion wear. By the time he'd finished, the signal came. "There!" he reported. "This room— and my person elsewhere in the ship—is now free of the recorders." He felt no sense of triumph, only a vague curiosity about what Lantern's countermove would be. He repeated the last half of his sentence. "I know its dangers, Arshel, just as I'm aware of its value."

She shrank from him. "You're still the same as you were then," she said in a strangled whisper.

He knew she meant when he'd built the Maze. "I don't think so, but I can't *remember*. I'm an Interface. I must answer all questions—and truthfully. The Sirwini phrased her question very badly. If she'd asked whether I'd destroy the Object myself, I'd have said I'd destroy it at cost of my life if necessary, to keep it from being abused."

"What does abused mean? That anyone but you uses it?"

"No. That it be used to override the conscience of any individual or group."

"I wish I could believe that!" Her voice was reduced to a raw whisper now as her fangs descended to strike position in response to the increasing tension in her sack. "But I'm so afraid you're going to turn out to be just like Dennis."

One day it's going to come to a choice between Arshel and preserving the Object. The professors had shown him how much it was going to hurt to destroy it—if he could even remember how with the Interface surgery blocking his life memories. *But if we find it, the Guild will order it destroyed, and I'll have no choice.*

He fetched her venom bottle and, moving very slowly, joined her in the sand. "I swore not to try to use your powers to locate the Object. I'm not like Dennis."

She shuddered on the verge of blue-voiding, the reflexive emptying of an overfull venom sack. He coaxed, and at last she allowed him to express her. Later, he got her to read *Assassin* with him on the viewer.

About midway through the book, he regretted that, for the main character's attitude of reverence for the Object was so graphic, she raised venom. But she insisted on finishing the book with him. After, in their lights-out discussion she admitted she understood, emotionally, why such a horridly dangerous thing had also to be considered a vast treasure. But still, everything in her screamed for its destruction.

Slowly, the days settled into a routine. Zref lectured on using an Interface; most of the students and faculty had no experience. Arshel gave a seminar in archeovisualization. Khelin and Ley kept busy interceding in minor interspecies frictions, and Ley began attending courses with Jocelyn, who was always witty and cheerful. Inevitably a chance comment revealed his knowledge of archeolinguistics, and he ended up almost teaching the course. Jocelyn found out he'd been a graduate student of Zref's parents, but she didn't gossip.

The gangway bulletin boards blossomed with diagrams of their first stop, the Shrine of the Huntress. Shui and Iraem were right in the thick of it, creating humorous works of art illustrating the endless facts about the Shrine to make them easier to memorize. But while they participated in shipboard life, one of them was always with Zref.

When they arrived at Almural, Zref told Arshel, "You don't have to go down with me. We'll be gone only a few hours."

"You don't want me to go?"

Their relationship had been painfully strained since the banquet, but Zref could only answer, "An Interface cannot 'want' one way or the other. But I did promise not to ask you to use your talent at the sites we visit."

"I'm not going to let you go by yourself. Besides, I promised to show some of the students how to dowse a site."

But as they were getting dressed, she relented, "Zref, I don't mean to be so—belligerent. You're my bhirhir."

He smiled, circling her shoulders with one arm in the most intimate gesture. "And you're mine—whatever may have gone between us in past lives."

Zref went down with the first shuttle load, prepared to stay in the hot sun at the Shrine for the entire day. The site was a desert oasis where a cliff ten times the height of an Almurali split the continent. Climb the cliff, said the Legend, and the Huntress's luck would bring you to your goal.

As Zref was drinking cold juice at a refreshment stand in an open shed, he watched the students and faculty crawling all over the site. An old Almurali came up to him. "I wouldn't expect an Interface to believe in the Huntress's blessing, but I hope you will insert this into your files. It *is* true. I've seen it work many times. The Huntress, worshiped or not, guards and guides us all. Climb the cliff to her abode, and your quest, too, will be fulfilled."

Already, a number of the students were attempting that climb. Zref checked with *Epitasis* via the local traffic control computer to make sure that medical supplies had been sent down. "My species isn't particularly gifted at rock climbing without tools," demurred Zref.

The adobe houses of the small staff of devotees of the Huntress were shimmering in the heat, accentuated by the exhaust from their air conditioners. The tree-bare rock basin around them was striated with pink, black and gold obsidian gravel that could shred even the best shoes.

On the cliff above, a small shrine, nothing but a roof raised on carved columns, held a bowl hollowed from living rock and filled with water. This was the most holy spot on Almural, and Zref could understand why. The best hunters among them were the females with cubs to feed, and so their goddess was the best of the hunters, feeding all Almural.

Shui ducked into the shelter. "Zref, how long did you say we have to stay here?"

"It will take most of the afternoon for them to finish their assignments." He handed the kren a glass of the juice.

"Thank you. Some of us are going to be heat-sick."

Zref tried again to convince the kren there was no need for them to stay so close to him, but Shui wouldn't hear it. "Very well, then," said Zref. "I was about to take the cable lift up to the top. Come ride with me."

"It won't be any cooler up there," said Shui glumly.

They rode in a small gondola from a point near the devotee's house to the top of the cliff, which was just as barren and hot as the colorful basin below. There, Zref demonstrated the use of an Interface to record and index every detail of a find. It was sweaty work and busied volumes of comnet memory with redundant data, but they learned.

After that, Zref visited the actual Shrine. It was cool under the stone roof, and the large basin of water added a kindness to the air. Tourists who shared the Shrine with the Cruise jammed into the area following their guide. When the guide moved on, some of them remained in the cool, and Zref turned from gazing at himself in the water to stumble over a pink ball of fluff which was standing on three of its six legs, gesticulating at the basin and talking to someone.

The Jernal fluff was silky and limp with the heat. Briefly, Zref felt a hard, bony case covered with a hot, thin skin. Hastily, he pulled back, apologizing. The Jernal were very sensitive about body-space.

"Master Interface Zref!?" exclaimed a Theaten male.

Zref recognized the Theaten member of the writing team, "Arai! Iebe Arai Then!" He looked down at the Jernal, who was now standing on all six limbs. "Waysjoff?"

"Who else do I look like?" challenged the Jernal.

Arai, towering over the crowd as any Theaten would, was a deep reddish brown, his toothpick body now covered with the white dust of the desert. He called behind him, "Neini! Come look who I found!"

The petite human woman who appeared still had her darkly good looks. "Master Interface! It must be true! All I did was climb the cliff, and here you are!"

Shui, noticing that every eye in the place was now fixed on Zref, said, "Maybe we could hold the reunion down below?"

On the way down, Zref introduced everybody while scanning the grounds for Arshel. He found Khelin and Iraem, and then Ley and Jocelyn who were sitting on some rocks, more interested in each other than in the site. But no Arshel.

Stealing a moment, he accessed the comtap at the hospital tent, but she hadn't been admitted there. However, three climbers had fallen, one tourist to his death.

A big refreshment tent was now open. They all took drinks and settled at a corner table. Zref opened by saying, "I thought *Assassin* was the most perceptive thing you've written since *Skanqwin and the Emperor of Crowns*."

"Where did you read it?" asked Neini, as always their spokesperson. Her astonishment seemed all out of proportion until she added, "It was withdrawn before publication, and all our other books are being pulled, too."

"*Epitasis* picked it up as a preview just before we left Camiat," and Zref had to explain the Schoolcruise.

Arai cut him off. "We know—we wanted to go on it!"

"When Lantern turned us down for the Cruise," explained Waysjoff, "we came here, hoping to find out why Almurali dislike our writing." The Jernal's reedy voice was strained.

Aghast, Shui asked, "Your books have been canceled because Almurali don't like them? What kind of censorship is that?"

"Not censorship," protested Arai. "Someone high up in the Lantern hierarchy suddenly hates our work, and Lantern's committees and Boards are dominated by Almurali females."

"True," said Zref, wondering if they were anything like their Captain. "Well, have you discovered why your books aren't to Almurali tastes?"

"No," answered Neini, "but we've got some material for future novels. We met a kren—tiny little female, odd coloring. Have you noticed her?" she asked Shui.

"Arshel?" asked Zref, and at their nods, explained his relationship.

Arai regarded Zref in that unfocused way which meant he was seeing flickers of past lives. He was the writing team's archeovisualizer and had read Zref's life as Mazemaster.

Neini said, "Lantern won't touch what we've got, though. I don't know if anyone else will—word is out on us."

"Lantern will sue anyone," said Waysjoff, "who publishes any First Lifewave novel we write, on grounds that we researched it under contract to them."

"Which means we need new material—and plenty of it," said Neini with one raised brow. "This Cruise—when do you leave? Is there any room left?"

Zref checked and answered, and Neini said, "We could pay our own way. We'd be broke, but—what do you think?" The other two looked at her as if she'd gone crazy.

At that point, Khelin and Iraem came up to the table, panting. "Zref! Arshel is climbing the cliff!"

Shui was on his feet instantly. Zref ran, too. The kren from the mountain city of Firestrip could climb anything for fun, but Arshel was from a flat tropical island. When he got to the base of the cliff, she was halfway up. The brown crumbling stone face sent a constant shower of gravel down into their eyes. Zref swallowed a hard lump of fear. Arshel was panting, and he thought he could see her legs shaking.

From below, her students called instructions to her, while Neini said, "Maybe *I* convinced her the Huntress legend really works."

Ley and Jocelyn elbowed their way into the group. "Zref! Why don't you *do* something?"

"Like what?" asked Zref, feeling helpless.

"Maybe she'll make it," said Khelin. The kren's voice was strained and Zref could see venom pulsing into his sack.

Ley moved to Khelin's side. "She's got to make it."

She was three quarters of the way up now, and suddenly her feet slid out from under her leaving her hanging by her hands, a position kren were unsuited for. Zref couldn't breathe, couldn't think. Despite the hot sun, the world about him seemed to go black.

He was aware of Arai staring down at him, of Ley clinging to Khelin, of Jocelyn frowning at Ley, of Iraem and Shui at his back, of dozens of people gathered to watch this feat, and terror gripped him as imagination he wasn't supposed to have showed him a graphic picture of Arshel, smashed and broken at his feet, sharp rocks protruding up through her chest, her kren blood spattered on his shoes.

Then he pulled back from that vision as if it were hot enough to burn. "No!" he said aloud, and put his arms out to Ley and Khelin on one side, and Neini and Shui on the other, calling the nine of them together almost as it had been in the pond room before the four of them had gone down to meet Onsham. He proclaimed, visualizing. "Of course she'll make it. See her looking at herself in the Huntress's basin?"

"Yes," exclaimed Arai. "I can see it!"

Waysjoff emitted a strangled squawk then agreed.

Zref clutched his companions, straining as if he could reach up and place Arshel's foot on the ledge he could see near her. And suddenly, her foot moved onto it. She pulled herself up and reached again. In moments, she was at the edge of the cliff, rolling over it out of sight. Zref was the first to break for the gondolas, with Khelin right on his heels. The others followed. The nine of them piled into one gondola over the shrill cries of the Almurali operator, Waysjoff saying, "I don't weigh much!"

On the way up, Waysjoff seized Zref's jacket in one hot, gritty claw-hand and demanded, "What did you *do?* I *saw*—I *saw* as if with your eyes—and I believed!"

Zref answered the pink fluffball automatically, but without conviction, "Anxiety spurred your imagination."

The moment the car stopped, Zref squeezed out and raced to the edge of the cliff where one of the Almurali attendants was already giving Arshel something to drink.

"Zref!" Sloshing water over him, she clutched him around the waist. "I was so scared! Until about halfway up, I knew I could do it—and then all of a sudden, I saw myself—crushed and broken at the bottom of the cliff, and I knew I was going to fall, and then I slipped! I must have almost passed out because I thought—"

"Easy, easy," he said as the eight others clustered around. "You didn't fall. It's all right now, no need to raise venom here!" *Did she see what I saw? Or did I see what she saw?* The thought was total nonsense.

After Arshel had been given the briefest introduction to the three writers, they had to leave with their tour. Zref worked with other groups of eager students until late, then rode up in the last shuttle with the paramedics who wanted him to do something about the Almurali who wouldn't let them rig even a minimal force-net under the climbers. "Religious nuts! They think it'd bring the cliff down!"

Without warning, a shuddering jolt hit the bottom of the craft. "What's that?" cried Shui, the only one of their party who stayed down with Zref.

Zref opened to the traffic control computer, and answered instantly, "Gravitic pulse! Something exploded—a ship! A large one!" He remained half-open, reading the tracker scopes as if he had a picture window view.

A small Hundred Planets Escort ship was hurtling toward a large, black hulk that was bearing down on *Epitasis*. Washes of focused gravitic fields were ripping from the hulk into the sleek cruise ship, while the Escort fired blasts of particle smoke into the hulk's uptake fields. In moments, the amount of noise in the planet's vicinity had blanked out the non-military traffic control scopes, and the telemetry of every ship in orbit including their own shuttle.

CHAPTER FIVE
Human Mating Dance

Zref noted several other ships coming in, about to make orbit, and a sudden cacophony of Interfaces comparing the views of the different astrogation computers, all concluding that the HP ship was in hot pursuit of a pirate of some kind.

"Zref, take planetary traffic control. I've got the HP node. Bittins, take the Guild Astrogation Dome. Kribs."

The Interface on the HP ship had taken command. Zref flashed the military telemetry to the incoming ships then assigned every ship in orbit to safe slots. He found a hole in the pattern where a civilian ship had been blown out of existence, and called in a military scooper to clean up the hot debris. Canceling civilian takeoffs from the three moonbases, he gave the clear orbit data to the military ships which were now lifting from Almural. He shouted to the other shuttle passengers, "Brace!" while juggling ships' orbits, flinching as the pirate ship imploded, then exploded.

"Zref! Zref, are you all right?" Shui was unstrapped, bending over him, fangs down in sheer fright, venom pumping.

"Fine!" Zref reassured him. "Wait a minute," he said, opening to the dataflow. Then it was over. Closing, Zref coaxed Shui to sit and calm himself by the disciplines of the blues. "Fine sight you are! We weren't in any danger!"

"I thought you were dead! Your face went so lax, your eyes glazed over and the pupils dilated and stopped moving."

"I'm sorry," Zref apologized. "It was an emergency. But everything's fine now." And he told all the paramedics what had happened. "The HP Escorter got the pirate, though."

Later, in the common sitting room of the suite, Zref told of the attack while they waited for the ship to break orbit and serve supper. Arshel was contrite. "While they were firing on us, Zref, I remembered other times when I watched you die—

and lived out a lifetime of futility. We have to finish this, this time. I shouldn't have climbed that cliff! I'm sorry, Zref."

Dusty and sweat-stained from their day in the open, they were sharing a pitcher of iced juice before going to bathe. Jocelyn joined them, and Ley, pink under a layer of sunscreen oil, sprawled on the floor by her chair, massaging her feet. He asked, "I suppose such talk only confuses you, Jocelyn?"

"No," she answered. "If I'd been kren, I'd have gone to train at Mautri. I often think I—sense—things."

Ley looked at her, surprised. "You never told me that!"

"You never asked, and—I admit I'm a little jealous of you all, even though I chose dance rather than Mautri."

"Was that when you refused to take Jtsor bhirhir and went to study dance on Sirwin?" asked Ley.

She nodded, lips pressed tightly together, eyes big and liquid. "And I regret it—but only sometimes."

"Jtsor," repeated Khelin thoughtfully. He described a gangling, awkward adolescent with defective hearing and a supreme talent for the written word. "His bhirhir took him away from Mautri, and we all thought that was a tragedy."

"With me, it would have been the same," she agreed. She fixed Khelin with a candid stare. "You disapprove of me."

Ley's fingers froze on her feet, his eyes riveting Khelin. Khelin's gaze seemed unfocused, his face set in what Zref termed his blue-priest's look. Then he said, "No, Jocelyn. I just need a little time. It will be all right."

Zref made an intuitive leap, and mouthed silently, "No!"

Jocelyn scanned Iraem and Shui, as if aware they were not family. "I guess the family has a right to know."

Ley stirred. "This afternoon, I asked Jocelyn to marry me— if Khelin will consent to immunize her."

"We're willing," said Jocelyn, "to wait." She spoke to Zref as if it were important to relieve him, despite his lectures about Interfaces not needing consideration. "I know what a bhirhir is, and I'm not going to come between them."

"And you're not going to be jealous," suggested Khelin, knowing the grim statistics on marriages of a human bhirhir.

Jocelyn met Khelin's eyes in unguarded honesty. "I'm already jealous. I dislike myself for it, but that's the way humans are in mating. If I can understand how kren are about bhirhirn, can't you understand how humans are about mates?"

"But he does," protested Ley in a perfect bhirhir's response to an emotional challenge. "When Zref wanted to marry Tess, it was Khelin who explained it all to Sudeen."

Zref then had to tell the story of Tess, the only woman he'd ever wanted to marry. "But she died in the raid that killed my parents and Sudeen." He smiled at Arshel. "You don't have to worry about me. Interfaces don't mate."

Jocelyn looked self-consciously at the outsiders, Shui and Iraem, who were seated together in an immense bag chair. Shui said, "I guess we're lucky. Our lives are so simple!"

They all laughed. Bhirhirn of advancing Mautri priests faced complex problems. Suddenly, chimes warned of impending departure, though in such a highly advanced ship, they'd feel nothing. Zref couldn't resist surveying the system via traffic control computer. All was back to normal, except—"We've got company!" he said aloud. "The HP Escort ship. It's pacing us off our stern." The obvious inference was that pirates had discovered this was the official HP expedition—which even his companions didn't know—and were determined to destroy it as they had the other one.

Alarmed, Zref searched the entire comnet for tampering with Guild or HP security files, and reported, "Lantern's computer demanded the HP send the Armored Escort well before *Epitasis* reached Almural orbit."

"Did Lantern know a pirate was after us?" asked Iraem.

"No," answered Zref as he digested the data dump he'd taken. "They only knew their security had been breached." *But not by the Guild, and Guild files are still sealed.*

Was the enemy whom Jylyd had detected a member of some giant pirate organization, such as the one that had once loosed a Wild Interface into the comnet and wrought havoc with the HP economy? Zref had lost too much in that battle to relish another encounter. But before he could share these speculations, the door signal announced three guests in the foyer. Shui rolled to his feet and went to the security screen. "It's a Jernal, a Theaten man, and a human woman—the three we met at the Shrine!"

Zref came to his feet. "Let them in!"

It was indeed Waysjoff, Iebe Arai Then and Neini Mori.

Zref padded barefoot across the carpet to greet them, taking Neini's hand and then Arai's. "Come in, have a glass of chreel!" The three were still in desert gear.

Arai held the ship's official passenger folder picturing the public areas of the ship, giving directions for operating the comtaps and the species customizing features. The three marveled at the room and the beautifully carved balustrades leading to the mezzanine. "I really feel out of place," summarized Neini for them. "You're too important for us!"

Arshel went to pour drinks for the three, rummaging out one of the tall, narrow Jernal vessels with its long sipping tube. "If this impresses you," she said conversationally, "you should have seen it when I got here. There were live servants standing against the wall spaced only a few paces apart—seeming about to leap on me for trespassing!" As she served the drinks, she narrated the fight Zref had with their Theaten Suite Steward until they all laughed.

Straddling its drink, Wàysjoff enveloped the sipping tube with its pink fluff, drinking until Arshel finished her story. Then it said, "We actually came here to query Zref."

Arai, weaving himself into a half-kneeling position atop a carved blackwood rack, shuffled a page out of the ship's folder and handed a gold and white bulletin to Zref. "At request of kren passengers and crew," Zref read aloud, "the Captain has ordered the cabin safety recorders blanked."

"What are cabin safety recorders?" asked Neini.

Zref explained how he'd caught transmissions of a private conversation and then had their own cabins blanked. "But how did anyone else find out?"

"This seems to be an evening of confessions," observed Khelin. "I told our Room Steward and one or two passengers."

"We did the same," said Iraem.

"You could have told me you were starting a rumor," said Zref. Despite being an Interface, he felt betrayed. He noticed Arai was watching him again, as he had down on the planet's surface. "I doubt if anything is lost, though."

"I understood," said Shui, "why you wanted us to wait. I don't know why it seemed so—impossible."

Khelin said, "I felt it was immoral not to mention it. But now I'm not sure . . ."

Ley casually moved from Jocelyn to Khelin while Arshel returned to Zref, nervously eyeing the three. Yet none of the kren were raising venom against the intruder's odors, though they'd continued to speak as if within family walls.

Zref moved to the center of the room, the others arrayed about him. He felt *safe,* as if a subliminal vulnerability he'd felt since that moment of illogical protectiveness during Arshel's mating had finally been banished by the three joining them. "Perhaps it was wrong of me to ask you to wait. If I were kren, I doubt if I could have waited."

"No," said Arai, "it was more than that. There was another influence . . ." His gaze rested on Jocelyn.

Jocelyn's eyes unfocused. "It knows it can't get to us now." She wrapped her arms around herself and shivered.

Ley murmured something to Jocelyn while Zref caught Khelin's eye and said, "I want to tell them of the seeking-with, and what we're doing here."

Khelin said, "It was Arshel's seeking-with."

Arshel joined Zref, surveying them all. "This afternoon," she said, "I thought it was my imagination, but no—I did feel Zref's hand on my foot, placing it on that ledge—but all of you did it. We all climbed that cliff! Zref, tell them everything."

Arai said, "Now I understand why we had to come. Neini, you were right. Nine of us have been together before, scattered for millennia into our various lives, and now Zref has reassembled us—with a purpose."

"No," denied Zref. "I haven't done anything!" He told them of the seeking-with down to the last detail of Ley's faint and Jylyd's surmises. "So that's what we think we're doing here," he finished.

Arshel looked at him peculiarly. "I didn't know you were recording that session in some computer!"

He had recited it all word for word, with every movement and gesture he had observed, and some he hadn't been aware of observing. "I have no memory other than my private file, but rest assured now that there are no more Wild Interfaces, my private file is safer than your organic memories."

They discussed it then, wondering if the enemy was behind Lantern's computer surveillance attempt, the forbidding Zref access to *Epitasis,* and the cancellation of the Meguerian titles, or the pirate attacks.

At last everyone fell silent. Then, with an air of sudden understanding, Shui scrambled across the carpeting to Khelin and gingerly touched the other kren—a gesture Zref had never seen between nonfamily kren before. *"That's* why we betrayed Zref! The enemy set a compulsion!"

Khelin's eyes closed in pain as he fended off Ley's attempt to protect against the stranger's touch. "Yes! Jylyd was right. This *enemy* is enormously powerful."

Iraem came after his bhirhir, consoling, "Anything that could invade a seeking-with in full aklal must be more powerful than any of us."

Arai said, "I was trained at the Glenwarnan School on Sirwin where we learned to respect such techniques. To think someone's raising a massive aklal to manipulate and destroy!"

"That may be only the viewpoint of the Mautri," said Waysjoff. "I tried once for admission into the Mautri school at Finjs and was rejected—oddly enough, not because of what I am, but because of what I once had been."

Neini said, "This seems to be a time of total candor. Do you feel like explaining that to them?"

The Jernal settled down beside its empty glass, hiding its legs under its pink fluff in embarrassment. "It's a matter of considerable shame, but it seems you must know. Once, many lifetimes ago, I made the mistake of using skills of psychokinesis to delude people into thinking I was a great prestidigitator. I won much fame and fortune in that life as a performer. For this, the Mautri rejected me—so you see they're capable of very twisted reasoning."

"No, I don't think so," contradicted Arai. "You've been asking me for years about that rejection—you know I often fail to read lives close to my own. But now I see! In that life, you profaned the Persuader power to support a minimal ability at psychokinesis and Persuade audiences to win fame."

"And for that I was hatched, not born, and Mautri rejected me?"

Hatched! Jernal were either born or hatched depending on when the ovum was fertilized. From that biological fact, the Jernal cultures had erected elaborate myths of the superiority of the born over the hatched. For a Jernal to admit this status to any non-Jernal was rare.

Khelin said, "I doubt the connecting threads of your lives are so easily untangled. Perhaps you're needed here, in your current form, to work with us."

"You are kind," muttered the Jernal, its fluff wilting.

"And that work is?" asked Neini swirling her glass.

"I think," said Khelin, "the first and most urgent task, is to restore Zref's memory."

"Impossible," insisted Zref.

Arai argued, "I read you, surely you can read yourself."

Arshel pointed out that the only glimpse Zref had ever had of a past life was in the Wassly Globe, aided by the whole Mautri aklal, and that had not been a personal memory.

"Your mind is different now," conceded Khelin, "but no other Interface has yet been made as you were. If there *is* a way, you'll have to find it yourself."

Jocelyn asked in a small voice, "Is there some procedure for restoring past life memories?"

The four Mautri priests all spoke at once, and then Khelin finished, "There're exercises for inducing the recovery of memories, but they're nonselective, and they take years. Presumably, though, Zref who was many times a white, has possessed all of his past during those lifetimes. His current amnesia may be his attempt to protect himself from the enemy, or it could be induced by that enemy."

Neini cleared her throat and offered, "I've only theoretical knowledge in these things, but if we all were once an aklal, then if we all work at recovering past memories, perhaps Zref will be drawn along?"

"I told you she was brilliant!" said Arai beaming.

"Regardless, this is not work to be undertaken on a full sack or an empty stomach," commented Iraem.

"The ever-practical!" said Shui rising. "Let's eat!"

As Zref led Arshel into their private pond room, he saw Khelin climbing the stair while Jocelyn followed the three writers. Ley stood irresolute between them. Khelin paused, looking back at Ley silently. At last, Ley moved to the stair, but Khelin gestured urging Ley to go with his mate.

Zref made a mental note to speak to the Captain to see if

Jocelyn could be moved to the room next to Khelin's.

While they were stripping for immersion, Arshel made a little sound in the back of her throat.

"Something wrong?" asked Zref. Kren rarely suffered sunburn.

"Stiff, that's all," she said, tossing the shirt away.

"Let me see—Arshel!" said Zref grinning fully behind her back. "Your molt is starting!"

Startled, she twisted to try to get her own fingertips onto the stiffening skin. "I guess—so . . ."

"Well, then, first a good soaking, and then we'll get some venom onto that dry patch. It'll be a while until that skin is ready to come off, and I'm not going to let you get into such bad shape as you were last time."

She'd been in molt when she'd struck and killed Dennis with hate venom. When she'd run from the scene to her shipboard cabin, Zref had followed, unable to let a kren go untended in molt. Entering against her will, he'd found her skin showing criminal neglect on Dennis's part, and any sympathy he'd had for the man had fled. Because of mating with Khelin, she hadn't molted again under Zref's hands. He was determined to see her through this one without pain, for agonizing molts could sour a kren personality irretrievably.

In the water with her, he checked every scale on her hide for drying and cracking, and scrubbed her down with a molting compound to keep the old skin supple.

"Enough!" she complained at last, "or I'm going to use that smelly stuff on you!"

He laughed, and let her scrub him, but before she finished, a message dropped into his private file. *I'm informed an emergence has taken place, a male to the MorZdersh'n Ley. Youta.*

Zref whirled Arshel around. "You have another son! Or rather Ley does. I've got to tell them."

Dripping, heedless of the carpeting, he went to the comtap and punched code for Khelin and Ley's room, impatient with the slothful instrument.

It took awhile, but then Khelin answered, visuals turned off. Zref said, "I hope Ley can hear this—"

Khelin interrupted, "He's not here just now."

"Well get him! Khelin—"

"I won't disturb him now. He's with Jocelyn."

A tremor of foreboding washed through Zref, but he delivered his news in a steady tone, thinking, *I hope Jocelyn will be happy.*

"Is Arshel there?"

"Of course. And—uh—her first molt bubbling has appeared." She came up beside him wrapped in a towel.

Khelin sighed as Arshel pronounced the emergence ritual, "A future lives!" adding, "Your future lives!"

"Our future, and many futures," Khelin finished and Zref remembered the times Khelin had given Arshel's children into Ley's hands with those words. Before they left, Ley had given this one into the hands of a foster surfather, but still he knew Khelin was aching to have Ley there now.

The main saloon was aglitter when they arrived. Many of the passengers had already eaten and left, but Zref spotted the three writers just claiming a large table. Iraem said, "Let's join them." Zref agreed, turning to look at the group with him. Jocelyn was there, but not Ley and Khelin. If he hadn't been locked out of the ship's computer, he'd have flashed a message to them on their comtap.

Seeing his search, Jocelyn said, "Ley was late going to express Khelin, but they'll be along presently."

Arai, towering over the seated diners, gestured for them to come to the table. Shui gestured back and led the way, Zref trailing, telling himself not to worry about Khelin.

The missing pair joined them just as a Theaten waiter delivered a written message which crackled like real woodpulp paper when Zref unfolded it. The script was black on the white background, a spidery handwriting which Zref could decipher only by calling up a cryptography program. He read it aloud, "My compliments, Master Interface. Be pleased to report to me in my office within the hour. Captain Rrsee."

"Imperious, isn't she?" asked Ley rhetorically.

"She's Almurali, and a Captain," answered Khelin.

However courteous they tried to be, Almurali seemed to assume other species existed only for their convenience.

Khelin seated himself between Ley and Jocelyn, and seemed

his usual contented self, though Zref searched for signs of molt. Khelin, too, had had a very rough time of it at his last molt, when he and Ley had been imprisoned and deliberately kept apart. *And now Jocelyn!*

Zref ate without participating in the conversation, and departed for the Captain's office which turned out to be as sumptuous as the rest of the *Epitasis*. When Zref was shown in, she was at ease in a huge chair behind a gleaming glassite desk. At the side of the desk, standing to attention was a human male arrayed in the HP law enforcer's dress uniform. Zref made his insignia out to be that of a ship's captain. He was looking inordinately pleased with himself. And Rrsee was not.

"Ah, Master Interface, at last. I'm glad you could join us. May I present Captain Regardy of the Escorter *Minth*."

"I am honored, Captain," replied Zref.

"And I," said Regardy. "We're discussing how odd it is for a passenger carrier not to use an Interface Astrogator."

Since it wasn't a question, Zref felt no compulsion to answer. He simply waited in attentive silence.

With a gesture of disgust, Rrsee said, "Captain Regardy has convinced Star-Treader to invite you to access the *Epitasis* system directly. He argues it's unsafe to have you under such a ban—after the incident at Almural. So I hereby grant you full access to our operational systems."

Grateful acceptance washed through Zref, and he bowed low in acknowledgment. Checking Rodeen's files, he found the ban had been lifted officially, but no appointment of himself as astrogator had been logged, for which he was thankful. "This will greatly enhance my efficiency at handling student queries, Captain. The Guild thanks you." To the human, he said, "There seems no need for a ship of this class to use an Interface for astrogation."

Regardy argued. "I'm responsible for the safety of this ship now, and I'll rest easier if I know you are monitoring its internal functions."

"You anticipate sabotage?" asked Zref.

"It's more comfortable to rule it out." He shuffled his feet a bit, then met Zref's eyes forthrightly. "However, we also have our orders that in exchange for this concession on Star-Treader's part, we are to bar you from access to *Minth*'s systems—an edict which doesn't set well with me, since I respect the Guild. But I have my orders. Master Interface, you are hereby requested not to access *Minth*'s operational or internal systems, not even to read our outgoing beams."

"It would be convenient, if I could communicate with your bridge directly," countered Zref. He knew now where the recording devices which still operated within the public areas of *Epitasis* would be dumping for transmission.

"The whole prohibition seems nonsensical to me, but orders are orders. You may message our screens only via *Epitasis*'s own outgoing beams."

Moving about the room as a cover for once again checking with Rodeen, he acknowledged, "I'll comply, of course. I hope that in any emergency, I may be of service." Then to Rrsee he said, "You'll only be billed for the few seconds I spend in routine checks or in pursuing something suspicious. I bill Lantern for any student's use of your systems I make."

"That will of course be satisfactory," answered Rrsee. Zref again moved, attempting to thaw the atmosphere. "I wonder if I might ask an indulgence, Captain Rrsee?"

"Certainly. I expected you would understand that any personal use of *Epitasis* you cared to make—"

"Of course," said Zref, "but this is another matter. Could you arrange to have Jocelyn Petrovan moved to the room next to that occupied by Khelin and Ley MorZdersh'n? They're working closely together, and it would be a great convenience to them not to spend so much time traveling the corridors."

Rrsee hid a smile behind one hand, saying, "I see you are a sensitive man, Master Interface. It's good to see such in a member of the Guild. I'll attend to it immediately."

When Zref got back to the suite with the news, he found them all waiting for him in the sitting room. He related the conversation, trying to paraphrase rather than recite, so as not to seem machinelike. "So that's the enemy's counter to our acquisition of privacy despite their surveillance."

"I'm not so sure," said Shui. "I'll bet the program that's sending that spybeam to *Minth* is beyond your reach, behind a security lock they didn't give you a key to."

"Probably," agreed Khelin, "but the use of *Minth* as a relay implies the HP itself is doing the spying. If the enemy is behind

the surveillance, she isn't a pirate, unless she's another Balachandran."

They all shuddered. Balachandran had been a high HP official *and* mastermind of an attempt to take over the galaxy by
using a Wild Interface.

"If this's a countermove," said Neini, "it's only an opening
gambit. They're giving you *Epitasis*—what do they expect you
to do with it?"

"Take us to the Object," said Arshel, her eyes haunted.

But I can't, thought Zref. *I don't know where it is.* And he
suspected he never had.

CHAPTER SIX
Sirwin

Epitasis now headed toward the edge of the galaxy and its farthest stop, Earth. Zref had never been to Earth, and was looking forward to it. But well before that, they'd visit Sirwin, the blue world of blue people. He'd been there before and had found the Sirwini affable and law-abiding.

Their habit of sharpening the two small blue horns that sprouted from the fronts of their heads made the otherwise humanoid Sirwini seem formidable, and so they were valued law officers and body guards.

As they neared Sirwin, Zref was swamped with queries on the history of the Glenwarnan School on the ancient site they were to visit, so he enlisted Arai's aid as a lecturer because the Theaten had trained there as a lifereader.

Soon, the group of ten began to breakfast together in the common sitting room, and then disperse for the day's classes, lectures and office hours. Zref's new access to *Epitasis* saved him enough time so that each night, before the group gathered for supper, he could relax with Arshel, tending her now itching hide and expressing her properly.

Evenings were often spent in their sitting room coaxing past life memories to surface by discussing dreams. Neini was the most eager in this, Jocelyn and Ley often absent.

One day, just as Zref was putting away Arshel's venom bottle after giving her hide a thorough anointing, the comtap sounded a message. It was Khelin on the screen.

"If you two are free a moment, I think we should talk," he said. Ley was not on the screen with him.

Zref consulted Arshel with a glance and told Khelin. "You're both welcome to come over. Arshel's still soaking."

Khelin hesitated. It had been some time since they'd exercised pond privileges. "I'll be right over. I could use another good soaking, myself—if you don't mind."

Zref made a handspread welcoming gesture and faded the contact. He was settling luxuriously into the water, when Khelin arrived wearing only a towel, which he cast aside as he immersed beside Arshel. After a polite interval, Zref said, "I assume Ley is with Jocelyn?"

Khelin's glance went to Arshel, surprisingly shy, Zref thought. "I can't grant her pond privileges yet." With an effort, he added, "Soon, I think."

There was no other place Zref could have asked such a personal question, so he indulged his curiosity. "She hasn't been pressing you to immunize her before your molt, has she?"

One pulse of venom, and the kren had his emotions under control. He swam away, submerged his face for a moment— the skin there showed a few blotches already—and said, "I've been talking to Jocelyn, and watching them together. I like her. It sometimes frightened me how much I like her—until I began dreaming of her. And now—"

"You've recovered a memory!" exclaimed Arshel.

"I think so," said the blue priest. "In some far distant lifetime when we both wore feathers, Jocelyn and I were mates. I'm not sure—Zref, did Persuaders mate?"

The raw urgency in Khelin's question prompted Zref's unthinking response. "Of course, but only with Persuaders, for who would dare stand up to such power in intimacy?" Only after he spoke did he realize he hadn't consulted the comnet, but had answered out of private file.

"Is something wrong?" asked Arshel, grabbing his elbow.

"The comnet wouldn't know that! *I* knew it. But I've never known it." He searched the entire file of the Lantern novels, and found no such reference in fiction. He put his dripping hands over his face. "How?"

Khelin swam at Zref. "You *do* dream! You don't recall, but you do dream."

"No," denied Zref. Yet once or twice before. . . . "Except as a symptom of dire illness," he amended.

"And what was that dream?"

"Nothing—well, I dreamed I was kren—a white priest. But that was when I was so sick—before I met Arshel."

Arshel had made him relive Sudeen's death, hearing Sudeen's death cry without the distortion of shock, and that had cleared an emotional block he'd had against opening.

"Did you dream of building the Maze?" asked Khelin.

Arshel complained, "He's an Interface, Khelin. You shouldn't question him like that . . ."

"Hold your venom, Arshel," replied Khelin softly, but retreating just a bit. "We all decided the only way out for us is to trigger Zref's deep memories."

She apologized, adding, "But Khelin, I can't!"

"She's pre-molt," said Zref fiercely, "and doesn't have your control. You and I can continue this in private!" Zref climbed out of the water. "Don't fret, Arshel, his questions might even work!" He grabbed towels and tossed one to her. "And to answer your question, Khelin, I'm not sure. Somehow, I can believe—what I've seen and been told about myself. But my files contain nothing!" Having distracted Khelin so Arshel wasn't torn by conflicting instinct, he tossed Khelin a towel, too, and added, "We ought to get dressed."

Over supper, talk ebbed and flowed around the topic of the Glenwarnan School. Finally, Arai said, "I never did apply to Mautri. I doubt I'd have been accepted."

Many humans had been trained by the Mautri of Firestrip. Zref said so, and Shui added, "The primary requisite, besides a talent demanding training, is an understanding of the kren, which can be gained only by living a lifetime as kren."

"I don't think I've ever been kren," said Arai, "but I'm not sure. Our methods don't work on one's own past."

"Perhaps you've been Sirwini," suggested Shui.

"Do you do lifereadings?" asked Arai, eagerly. Neini glanced up at the towering, toothpick form, and Zref read a tender sympathy on her face.

Iraem answered for his bhirhir. "We haven't mastered that discipline yet, though we have studied ourselves."

Jocelyn said, "Perhaps Shui knew you in a previous life. It seems many of us have associated before." She glanced at Khelin but spoke to Ley, "As it seems very important to me— that Khelin *like* me, not as your mate, but for myself."

"Have any of your memories surfaced?" asked Khelin.

Zref thought, *They haven't discussed his dream!*

"No," she said. "But maybe now would be a good time to start the technique you promised us." They adjourned to the suite sitting room, Zref noting how Ley and Jocelyn walked ahead while Khelin was left trailing the group.

When they'd all been served drinks and settled into their favorite lounges, Shui said, "As senior, Khelin, you should conduct."

Ley shared a chair built for one with Jocelyn, but as Shui spoke, he cleared his throat to make a bhirhir's answer when Khelin said, "I should defer to Zref. Jylyd does."

"No," denied Zref. "I don't know your methods!"

"I wonder," said Waysjoff, its pink fluff swaying in the air, "if any such methods are truly suitable for those who have not done the hard work."

Neini folded herself cross-legged on the floor and said, "As I understand, it's not harmful to access past lives, but the greatest caution to the beginner is not to *believe* the first results of his efforts. Most of what you get right away is bound to be fantasy. When a real memory surfaces, it's apt to be a powerful emotional instant which warped your judgement anyway, and so should be discarded."

"Yes," agreed Khelin. He raked them with his eyes. The last few days, Zref had watched Khelin talking with each of them, and with various fragments of the group, preparing for this decision. "I think the best technique for us is the Reversing Method. It's difficult enough that any who aren't ready will be unable to accomplish it, which is its built-in protection. Yet, it seems we've all had this training perhaps ages ago under Zref, so it should work for us."

Iraem was the first to comment, though Shui and Arshel also joined in, then deferred to Iraem. "I expected you to start with something more tactile."

"But we aren't searching for trivia, or random flashes just to convince ourselves we've lived before. We must recover memories of the lives when we learned this skill."

"I am curious," said Zref.

Khelin leaned his elbows on his thighs and dangled his large, webbed hands between his knees, measuring Zref with a stare. "It may be too easy for you, as an Interface. And then again, it may be too easy because you spent so many lifetimes perfecting the technique." He fell silent until Zref was frantic with roused curiosity, barely able to keep from a futile opening, and then he shot a question at Zref. "What would you expect the Reversing Method to reverse?"

"Time," answered Zref, blankly, then shuddered deeply.

Khelin held Arshel at bay with a gesture. "That's the second time you've answered a question like that. That place within you where those answers come from—can you access it at will? Shut out your usual Interface memory?"

Zref reached out a soothing, restraining hand to Arshel. "I don't think so. It only happens when you ask, Khelin."

"You must try, though, when Reversing." He looked up at the rest of them, and Zref felt Arshel relax. "It's simple. At the end of the day, when composing yourself for sleep, remember vividly the most recent event—such as cleaning your teeth. Then go back into the day, one event at a time, in reverse order until you get to the morning. If you can still remain awake, then remember your dreams of the previous night, and your pre-sleeping actions and so on back to the previous morning. Let your mind scan the events of your life in reverse until you fall asleep. When you wake, record your dreams, your thoughts, whatever seems to be in your mind."

"Often," added Shui, "it takes years of diligent effort to be able to scan even a single day perfectly—and years after that until any reliable memories surface."

"It sounds so simple," said Neini.

Khelin answered, "I've read books from ancient Earth, before space travel, recommending this method."

Waysjoff settled on its six stick-like legs. "It sounds unnatural, to make the mind work backward."

"My problem with it," said Arai, "isn't the direction, but the internal, personal act of remembering. My training is toward the external, objective, universal."

"Waysjoff," whispered Khelin, "why are you frightened?"

The Jernal's fluff had fallen, and was clinging to its legs. Zref compared its attitude to a chart of Jernal body language and concluded Khelin was right. It was scared.

"I'm not . . ." it protested weakly.

Khelin came off his chair and knelt beside the Jernal, his hands spread around the pink fluff. "Tell your fear, and it will become powerless."

Ley struggled out of the deep chair he shared with Jocelyn

to kneel beside his bhirhir. "Listen to Khelin," advised Ley. "He really knows what's he talking about."

Waysjoff said, "I dream sometimes—very clearly. Suppose I dream of when I was evil—and I can't wake up?"

The kren sat back on his heels, his legs flat under him. "Remember this morning, at breakfast, when Arshel itched so much she had to go soak?"

"Yes," answered the Jernal in its small, reedy voice.

"You also remember the rest of the day?"

"Naturally."

"You can stop remembering and think about the future?"

"Yes."

"And so you can when you dream."

"Not always." Its voice trembled. "Since we came aboard this ship, I've dreamed—ugly things about people. And they don't go away when I wake up."

It had never mentioned such dreams. Zref asked, "Whom do you dream about?"

Neini had to coax the answer out of the wilted Jernal, but finally it confessed, "Jocelyn! I dream she's Almurali and would like to eat me!"

That was not irrational. The Almurali had discovered Jern and at first had thought the Jernal a game animal, eating them with relish.

Jocelyn cleared her throat. "I hate to say this, but I think I've had that dream, too. Maybe I was one of the Almurali explorers first on Jern?"

Khelin was absorbed in Waysjoff, but Neini answered. "That would be the simplistic explanation. Doesn't the dream have any emotional texture to it?"

"Well—being Almurali, there's this tremendous sense of gratification at giving myself up wholly to those more powerful than I. I can't retain it when I wake, but it's so seductive, I want to." At Ley's horrified glance, she added, "It's nothing! I only dream that when I sleep alone."

Khelin had not missed a word. Now he gestured Jocelyn to kneel beside the Jernal, who began wretchedly dissociating itself from the dream. But Khelin demanded silence in his blue priest's voice, insisting Waysjoff allow Jocelyn to clasp one of its claw hands in hers. The Jernal were supreme xenophobes, and even Neini couldn't get the Jernal to allow that contact. Khelin, resigned, spread his webbed hands between the two, his face blank, eyes veiled for a moment.

"This *is* the work of the enemy. As she struck through Ley into Mautri to plant false images, so she insinuates herself into our aklal through Jocelyn, who is now our open medium." He pulled himself to his feet bringing Ley with him. "From now on, my bhirhir, you will always sleep with Jocelyn. Waysjoff must not sleep alone either."

Joy fought with dismay in Ley's eyes, but Khelin turned and walked away. Only Zref saw the kren's anguish. He knew Khelin wanted desperately to immunize Jocelyn, but with the tides of molt ripping through him, he couldn't even take her into his pond as Ley's mate. So he'd given up the comfort of his bhirhir on the long nights ahead.

Waysjoff quickly recovered its fluffiness under Neini's ministrations, and Khelin sent them all off to attempt Reversal, saying, "We'll discuss the results over breakfast." Then he trudged up the stairs.

As the group dispersed, Zref called after Ley, "May I talk with you a moment, Ley?"

Khelin turned on the stairs. For once, Ley had been voluntarily following him rather than Jocelyn, and now Zref was pulling his bhirhir away. Zref called, "This'll only take a moment, Khelin. I have to anoint Arshel again, too."

Khelin assented and went on into their room. Zref motioned to Ley as he approached. "Watch him."

Puzzled, Ley waited until Khelin closed the door. Then he turned, cocking his head in silent question.

"It's not my place to interfere," said Zref, "but I'm the only family you have here—and I have to say something about the way you seem to be neglecting Khelin."

As he spoke, Ley's face registered shock, then indignation. "No, it's not your place to meddle! Khelin has never had reason to complain of me, and he never will!"

Reading past the instant defensiveness, Zref said, "I know Jocelyn doesn't mean to monopolize your time—"

"You keep Jocelyn out of this!" Hands on his hips, he added, "I don't owe you an account of our private affairs."

Ley, as Zref himself, was a product of the human community on the kren world. "Ley, don't you remember when Tess and Sudeen and I were in the same situation? I know how the three of you feel! And I only want to be sure you're tending Khelin because I care for him. He's ambitious to take the purple so he might not demand as much of your attention as he needs. With Jocelyn around, you might not notice."

Coldly Ley said, "Are you finished insulting me?"

Zref sighed and nodded, gesturing Ley toward his room.

Ley whipped about and stalked up the stairs, but at the top, he relented, turned and said in a kindly voice, "I'll chalk all that up to an Interface's social clumsiness. You shouldn't try so hard to hide it, Zref. I know you don't really care anymore. I forgave you for it, long ago."

Zref stood in shock as the door closed behind Ley. *So that's how he really feels!* Zref was hurt by Ley's parting shot, in a way an Interface shouldn't hurt. But it was also true, Zref admitted in the ruthless cool of the Interface's private file notation, that he didn't *care* anymore.

All he had was the memory of feeling and caring. The actual physical responses were missing. In all honesty, he couldn't chase after Ley to convince him caring was still his primary motivation. Yet, he couldn't retire into the Guild, divorcing his family as all other Interfaces did, and live fulfilled as they did. Some crack in his Interface oozed a white-hot lava of feeling and caring through to plague him. He could neither deny that, nor claim it as a virtue.

As he went in after Arshel, he realized that wherever it was inside him that the caring came from, that was where any real past life memories were rooted. If he could do Khelin's exercise while *caring*, perhaps it would work.

The next morning, Shui and Iraem were waiting as the group began to gather for breakfast, the suite stewards having delivered their standing breakfast order and left.

As Zref arrived, he saw that the dining table he'd asked for had arrived and was even set with flatware and china monogrammed in gold with the symbol of the suite. There was one chair, matching the suite decor, perfect for each of them. He smiled. "Luxury like this could be addictive!"

Iraem commented blithely, "Of course the gheeling is fattened before being tanked for the venomkill."

Shui asked, naturally matching his bhirhir's mood, "I wonder who considers us so choice a delicacy as a gheeling?"

At that point, Khelin and Jocelyn were descending the stairs, and Khelin put in, "Perhaps we're not gheeling, but popayunze to the enemy, for she must deal with our venom!"

"He's right," asserted Jocelyn, seating herself next to Khelin instead of waiting for Ley. Her eyes were sparkling this morning. "Khelin may be our most wonderful weapon."

"No," denied Khelin. "Zref is that."

Khelin seemed more energetic this morning than since the molt symptoms first appeared. Perhaps his talk with Ley had born fruit. Joining in the banter, Zref replied, "The Guild would fire me if they thought I could be a weapon!"

Mischievously, Khelin said, "Now I wonder where fired Interfaces find employment."

"You're talking about a Wild Interface!" accused Shui.

Khelin looked up from his inventory of the table's offerings, puzzled. "I'm sorry, I didn't mean it that way."

Iraem intervened, "Khelin wasn't implying Zref could become a Wild Interface! After all, he once wore the white!"

But Zref had once been perilously close to going Wild, blackmailed by Balachandran's torture of Khelin during molt, and only Arshel's striking and killing Balachandran had saved him. They exchanged haunted glances, but the awkward tension was broken by the door's opening to admit Neini, Waysjoff and Arai, showing Zref a glimpse of the two kren stewards who stood outside the door, waiting to serve.

At that point, Arshel and Ley joined them, coming from their separate doors. Khelin announced, "Well, now we're all here, we can announce our first success. Jocelyn?"

"I dreamed—like I never dreamed before in my life, and even recorded it, waking Ley in the middle of the night. That's why he's so sleepy-eyed this morning. But it seemed so important. I was a feathered woman." She looked at the three writers. "You named them Kinrea, rightly I think. I was a Persuader student, living near the Maze after having survived the walk—which I didn't dream so I don't know what the Object was like. But I remembered Khelin: Mazemaster, my teacher—and my mate." She blushed bright pink against her auburn hair. "We were both of the same species then, of course. And we loved each other—terribly."

When she fell silent, Zref put one arm around Arshel. Ley sat between Jocelyn and Khelin with head bowed as Khelin took up the narrative. "As it happened, just the other night, I had a very similar dream/memory. This morning I showed Ley and Jocelyn the record of it. The details match so closely, I believe we can consider it a verified fact that at some time, Jocelyn and I were both Persuaders, and mates."

"This doesn't tell us much about the enemy," said Shui.

"No," agreed Khelin, "but it does explain what's been troubling me about how I feel about Jocelyn." He turned to Ley and spoke as if they were in private. "I will immunize her—when you're ready." He was a Mautri Priest of the dark blue rank. He could do it, even in molt, Zref thought.

Later as Zref was sitting in his rather tiny office, juggling seven separate programs for various students, and contending with an eighth, a Jernal who was trying to catch up on course work before orbit by using the Interface, the Cruise Director presented himself at Zref's door.

"Excuse me, Sthwhish," said Zref to the Jernal while tripping the door opener.

The Director's massive body nearly filled the remaining space within the cubicle. The Jernal took its leave hastily, and while the human seated himself, Zref completed the chores for the other seven students who were working at their comtaps in their own rooms. "At your service," said Zref.

"This isn't a query. I just wanted to talk to you."

Zref waited.

"You aren't making this any easier for me."

"I'm sorry. I still don't understand what 'this' is."

"The Captain asked me to speak to you about it because you're technically faculty, even though you now have command of the onboards. She feels you don't know how to wield that power. How can an Interface cause such a problem?"

"What problem?"

"Your little group. The ten of you. You mix socially only with each other, giving orders to the crew and students as if you own and run this ship."

"I've not been aware that anyone I know has overstepped the bounds of propriety."

"That's just it—they haven't. They all obey the Quintana Code in mixed species society as if born to it. But they're giving the impression that they're your elite guard, a closed group which is the real power behind both the way this ship is run and the grades given for the courses because they control access to you. That Jocelyn Petrovan, for example, has everybody thinking she's the Cruise Director!"

"How?"

"Look, I'm not here to issue an itemized indictment, just a warning. See to it that it stops, or we'll stop it for you." With that, he rose and left.

Disturbed, Zref closed and mulled that over. It could be than an Interface had no business with a family, for the essence of the Guild Guarantees was total impartiality.

After supper that night, Zref related the conversation, and they compared notes about their activities. Zref questioned Jocelyn, but the only incident she could single out was a rumor she'd overheard a student repeat that she was sleeping with the Cruise Director. Rumors like that were inevitable in close quarters, and she'd ignored it. They dredged up other gossip then, and found it added up to a barbed indictment. The Director wasn't just on a personal vendetta. However, the only accusation that held up was that none of them spent any social time outside the group.

Ley looked at Zref. "You're not going to order us to spend more than our working hours with strangers, are you?"

"I've no authority—" said Zref, but Shui interrupted.

"We're under your orders. We work for the Guild."

Khelin added, "I'd take your orders, Zref, anytime, because you wouldn't order anything to distress a bhirhir."

The three writers consulted with a mute glance, and Neini said, "We'll take your orders, no arguments."

Jocelyn said, "If we're electing a president, or something, I nominate Zref."

"Seconded," said Ley. "And I apologize, Zref."

"Aye!" voted the others.

"You're being silly, all of you," complained Zref.

"No, we're not," said Khelin. "The group has been attacked as if—" He stopped. "Why did I say that?"

Ley said, "Sometimes you know things without evidence."

"Well, we were waiting for the next move," said Iraem.

"But the enemy—attacking with petty gossip?! Ridiculous. To accomplish what?"

Ley defended, "That remains to be seen, but Khelin's insights are accurate."

"Was it an insight, Khelin?" asked Arshel.

Khelin assented with obvious reluctance. "Which means she has agents aboard. Do any of you read auras?"

The priests all stared at him. Zref looked up the kren word he'd used and translated it for them. The kren accepted the translations after some argument. Then Khelin reiterated, "Well, anyone?" There was silence.

Jocelyn said, "I once thought I could—but . . ."

"Ah!" said Khelin. "Of course you'd have that talent! How much training have you had?"

"None," she answered.

"Then tonight, I'll try to teach you the rudiments—though it's something I can't do myself. Tomorrow, when we go down to Sirwin, you'll mingle with the staff and students, and search for our hypothetical agents of the enemy."

"We go down?" asked Zref, looking from Arshel to Khelin.

"I have a few more days at least," said Arshel. "I'd enjoy open air. It's a long way to Earth!"

"It's awfully dry around Glenwarnan," warned Arai. Then he suddenly thrust his lanky body forward. "Do you think— could they be complaining you appointed me to teach that seminar on Glenwarnan? Did you ask the Director first?"

Zref was astonished. "Of course—by dropping a note onto his deskpad. And I got an immediate affirmative."

Arshel asked, "Could the reply have been forged?"

"The origin of the reply was the Director's own deskpad. A number of people evidently have access to it."

"If he never got that query," said Neini, "or others like it—"

"Then," finished Waysjoff, "he has cause to feel shriveled."

"I can check," said Zref. "I'm still monitoring *Epitasis* systems regularly. It'll be easiest while we're making orbit and all systems are activated." Reluctantly, he added, "But that's not enough. I'm not going to order you—because Ley's right. Off-duty, your time's your own. But as an Interface, *I* must remain accessible. So I'm going to have breakfast in the saloon tomorrow with Arshel."

"That's probably a good idea," said Shui. "And the rest of us should make a conspicuous effort to mix with others, and not do or say anything authoritative."

They immersed themselves in their plans, and the next morning Zref and Arshel took the first shuttle down to Glenwarnan. Sirwin was a blue world. Not only the sky, but the soil and the vegetation were gradations of blue from light grayish to deep indigo. Even the skins of the Sirwini natives were shades of blue. With the advent of interstellar trade, the Sirwini had taken to colored clothing, but their eyes perceived only shades of blue in the offworld fabrics.

The skimmer they took from the spaceport was a clear force-field bubble, like the most luxurious tour buses. Vistas of blue-misted mountains closed in and then opened into lush, blue valleys, dotted with crumbling ruins. They were at the interior of a continent of a very old world.

The Cruise Director himself had the front seat beside the driver, as if he'd chosen to take this skimmer because Zref was on it. Twice Zref tried to start a conversation so he could ask if the Director had ever seen his memo, or the ones Jocelyn had left for him, but he ignored Zref with a passionate diligence.

At last, they came out onto a high plateau, and followed a narrow, snaking road through open woodlands and across plowed fields.

"This is the approach to Glenwarnan," read the Director from a brochure. "Note the occasional standing stone at the edge of the road. As we get closer, you'll note the stones are more numerous until they stand in matched pairs as if guarding the approach. Most of these stones are restorations.

"Sirwini legend has it that this was the actual site of the City of a Million Legends. At least, there are about a million legends native to this part of Sirwin, as you have learned. Witaker and Strumfield, seventy-five standard years ago, disproved the claim to the site's being the City, but could not discredit its claim to being First Lifewave—at least in part. And documented miracles have occurred here.

"However, some five thousand Sirwini years ago, the site was destroyed by the local residents in a religious purge. Thus the need for reconstruction, which was done by a Lantern Grant twenty-five Sirwini years ago. They used the original construction technique, so it's impossible to distinguish reconstructions without the map provided with your seat.

"The Glenwarnan School has aided the reconstruction, though experts disallow their claim to teach the psychic skills practiced by the actual builders of the site."

Over Arshel's head, Zref gazed out at the roadway which led to a huge molded earthwork, surrounding a giant standing-stone circle within which were two smaller circles, located at the foci of an ellipse. The pattern was hard to see for a small village sprawled within the giant stone circle.

"This place is dead," said Arshel, "long dead and gone."

They landed in a parking lot on the outskirts of the big circle, and the Director issued instructions: "Note where your skimmer is parked. You have until twenty-eight-fifty local time to examine the site. The first aid station will be set up here in the parking lot. The souvenir shop will open in one hour, local time. Ship's meal service will provide takealongs three hours from now. Be prompt."

Zref didn't want to stray far from Arshel, as he had on Almural, for now impending molt could make her short-tempered without the calming influence of his scent on her hormones. So at first, he just followed her along the winding road, through cobbled village streets and among houses built ages before electricity or running water.

But then, students came to consult him or to ask him to put references on their pocket screens or to have him record a specimen for their reference. It was interesting work. Some theories entertained by this group were more exotic than any Zref had heard before, and their devotees were as excited and industrious as any archeologists. *What if one of these charming lunatics actually does find the Object?*

"What's wrong?" asked Arshel. "You can't be cold. It's a lovely day."

Actually, it was much too warm for Zref. He voiced the thought that had occurred to him.

"I know what you mean. Some of these people have more impressive finds to their credit than I do."

Zref could debate that, but let it go, strolling along one of the paths, avoiding the dung of the local village cattle. The path led toward the center of the large circle where a cluster of stone buildings was fenced about with solar collectors and

NO ADMITTANCE signs. The Glenwarnan School itself.

"There's only one thing we can do," said Arshel, "to keep the enemy away from the Object: shake her off our track, and find the Object ourselves. Then destroy it."

"It does sound simple when put that way."

"You sound defeated before we've even started. I'm the one entitled to feel depressed and out of sorts, not you!"

He laughed. "Interfaces don't get depressed, remember?"

"I don't believe that. At least not about you. And I don't believe you don't dream. You had *some* kind of nightmare last night."

"It wasn't a memory, though. I was watching you—this you, Arshel—drowning."

"Was *that* all it was?"

"Why? What did I do?"

"Oh, you were just groaning and sounding frantic."

"Look—the memory of Sudeen's death is still pretty raw, and the idea of losing you is pretty frightening. Life has been very comfortable for me since you came into my life. But, Arshel, I promised I'd see you through Mautri as soon as may be, and I will. Our relationship can't be permanent."

"Khelin says the practices of the blues are designed to strengthen bhirhir. The theory is you can't give up what you've never had. The strength of the individual has to spring from that partnership. If it's hard for you now, it'll be harder then—if I can take the blue."

"I think in a lot of ways, you already have. It simply isn't acknowledged at Mautri yet."

They stopped at the outskirts of the array of solar collectors, and Arshel leaned on a truncated stone. "Oddly enough, that's what Khelin said. Did he tell you that?"

"No. We don't discuss you much anymore."

The sun was behind Zref as he faced Arshel, her eyes veiled in nictitating membranes. Zref put his elbows on the stone, which was just over waist high. She cocked her head to one side and went quiet. For the moment, no students were tagging along behind Zref, and he just stood there enjoying his bhirhir watching him. It was a sensuous experience. The countryside around them was deeply still, the silence swallowing up the babbling of the students.

Suddenly, a bell began to toll richly, reverberating across

the circle. Arshel shuddered and buried her face in her hands, delicate webbing spread thin.

"Hey?" he asked, reaching out. She squirmed away, then turned back with sudden decision.

"All right! I'll read for you." Staunchly, she stated a Mautri maxim. "A talent is to be mastered, and a Master must employ talent to a purpose." She took a deep breath and announced, "Zref, we've been here before—just like this, the two of us, at this very stone. Listening to that bell."

CHAPTER SEVEN
Glenwarnan Diorama

The tolling reverberated deep in Zref's mind, evoking an episode of déjà vu such as had not afflicted him since he'd become a functioning Interface.

Arshel spread her hands on the dull blue agate surface of the stone between them, her touch a reverence to the ages. As he gazed at the ancient stone with her, he searched for some memory. But there was only deadness in the stone.

At length, she looked up at him, eyes still shielded. "We were Sirwini, Glenwarnan students, not bitter enemies, but rivals. I strove to equal your feats, much as Dennis strove to equal his father, and I never succeeded, just as Dennis never could. You taught me never to accept only the *appearance* of being equal, as Dennis sought the appearance of success. You taught me appearance is of value only when backed by achievement in excess of appearance."

Her nictitating membranes slid aside to reveal her gemlike, fathomless gray eyes. "Watching how you get what you want, how you react when authority misunderstands you, how you worry over Khelin, and respect Arai, and manage not to step on Shui and Iraem for doing their jobs, and bully the Suite Stewards without belittling—Zref, I'm beginning to believe you actually *are* what I first thought Dennis was."

"I don't do anything difficult. Interfaces don't experience emotion as others do." But he was feeling, as no Interface should. Moments like this, with Arshel, made him certain he'd destroy the Object to keep her. *She hated Dennis for such personal greed.*

Arshel made a noncommittal gesture scanning the circle as if looking for a landmark. The village used the field as a cattle pasture. The grass was a rich blue in the bright sun, the small grazing furry animals a lighter blue with dark indigo horns. "We spent lots of time here. I watched you die young, and lived on—emptily. You were buried—there, near where Arai is standing." She added in a voice almost too soft to hear, "I don't want to go through that again."

Arai was fondling one of the small cattle they'd been warned not to go near. The timbre of the bell changed abruptly. Arai gave the animal a firm pat and ambled toward them with a loose-jointed stride across the uneven ground.

Arai called, "I was thinking to seek admittance. Would you like to join?" He gestured to the dark entryway between two sections of solar collector fence.

It was the hour appointed for the *Epitasis* kitchens to dispense the picnic lunches. All over the far-flung site, people were tromping toward the distant parking area where Zref saw a skimmer landing. "Hungry?" Zref asked Arshel.

"No," she answered. "But the three of us shouldn't go off together as a group."

"This won't take more than the time allotted for the meal," argued Arai. "They'll never miss us."

Zref was curious about the School—a precinct closed to outsiders. But he couldn't plead curiosity to Arshel—it would be the kind of manipulation Dennis had used. Her sensitivity would leave her open to painful memories in there. And she was too close to molt to leave her.

"You go ahead, Arai," said Arshel. "We really should go and mix socially with the faculty."

At that point, an elderly Sirwini wearing light blue pants and dark blue, waist length cape, horns not even filed, stepped out of the tunnel entry between solar collectors. He waved to Arai. Arai lit with recognition. "Sidenl!"

The distant Sirwini now turned to face Zref and Arshel, and beckoned. Zref consulted Arshel with a glance. Reluctantly, she assented and followed Zref.

Arai introduced them to Sidenl, saying, "I've invited them to Renew Sequence with us."

"Had you not invited them," said Sidenl, "it would have been my duty and my pleasure to do so."

The old Sirwini reminded Zref of Jylyd as he gazed through the both of them in the abstracted way Arai did when reading past lives. Zref inquired of Arshel with one raised eyebrow. With concealed reluctance, she gestured for him to decide. He told Sidenl, "We'd be honored to join you."

Sidenl added, "Our honor, for there is that within which you've forgotten. And now, you urgently need to remember."

Arai added, "Yes. I want to show you what I saw the first time I read you—on Raynat, at Lantern Headquarters."

Arai had nearly fainted at that reading—and had said only that he'd seen Zref dying in the Maze.

After a few feet of dark tunnel, they emerged into a lighted rotunda, domed by some translucent blue substance. In the center of the huge, round area, a fountain threw water up into concentric plumes. Mist spread from the water, and fractured the blue sunlight into muted rainbows. The air held a delightful moistness such as the kren treasure.

"How beautiful!" exclaimed Arshel in genuine surprise, as if she'd been expecting only horrors within.

"At night," said Arai, "lit from within, it's even more beautiful."

In boxes around the rotunda, fresh flowers grew—all in multiplexities of blues, but a splendor of aromas. One flower-box held an abandoned digging tool and a sack of plant food. All about it, the soil of other boxes had been freshly turned. Leading the way, Sidenl said, "We're meeting now within. Join us, and then I'll escort you."

Through the archway on the far side of the fountain, they entered a lofty groined corridor which seemed familiar—almost kren in its avoidance of squared corners.

Sirwini were converging on the room off the far end of the corridor. Zref and Arshel followed, each searching for the echo of familiarity indicating a memory surfacing. But Zref felt nothing like that.

All the Sirwini were dressed exactly as their host, but in various shades of blue. Zref's references insisted Sirwini saw all these shades differently.

The assembly room was a perfect cube. In the center of the floor was a solid white cube, its corners facing the middle of each side of the larger cube. It was the first object Zref had seen here that wasn't blue. Perhaps it was the only object on Sirwin that wasn't blue.

Around the edges of the room chairs waited, empty. The

entire population of the school, some two hundred Sirwini and a sprinkling of offworlders, was standing in a circle around the white cube, and not a sharpened horn on any Sirwini head.

As Zref watched, a spot of sunlight leaped into being upon the white cube, turning it the palest blue Zref had ever seen. Gradually, the light intensified. The white substance reflected the light like a photomultiplier until it penetrated the Sirwini bodies and they glowed translucently.

Zref blinked, and the room became quite ordinary again. Or—no. Not entirely ordinary. The sun had passed the point at which it could shine upon the cube, leaving the white cube in shadow again. But still, somehow, it *glowed*.

Suddenly Zref knew: Once, the standing stones outside had all been white, glowing in the sun and the focused concentration of thinking beings. Something niggled at the back of his mind, itching to be recalled.

But just then, the Sirwini broke ranks, murmuring to one another, some stopping to greet Arai warmly. Arai touched the horns of some of them, an intimate welcome. Arshel stood very still beside Zref, hardly breathing but not in distress. Zref swept the room with his most minute recording vision as if it were an archeological site. Perhaps he could recover that almost memory later.

When the room was empty save for Arshel, Arai, Sidenl and Zref, Sidenl turned to go. "It's right through—"

"Wait," whispered Arai. "They're remembering!"

The old Sirwini inspected them both closely, "You're going to tell me the cube is white."

"No," demurred Zref. "I'm going to say it's *alive*. Those out there are the same—but they're dead."

"Yes," agreed Sidenl. He turned and led them across the cube and out an archway flanked by two freestanding columns. Arshel paused, examining the array. It didn't—quite—go to make up the Mautri "door to the room without walls."

Arshel said, "The symbols are familiar, yet all wrong."

Arai and Sidenl had paused at another door at the end of a long, down sloping tunnel. Arai turned, beckoning with the relaxed mien of someone at last home among the familiar. "This I couldn't share even with Ncini and Waysjoff. You've a right to know—but—this we do not reveal."

"Because," added Sidenl, "it's very powerful—very dangerous to the unready minds. You've passed this way before, mastering these concepts, touching these roots and being sustained by them; Arshel, more than once. Arai tells me you, Arshel, have achieved the green at Mautri in Firestrip. That is a rigorous school, and a proud one."

"I hope one day to go on there," she agreed.

"And you?" asked Sidenl of Zref. But before Zref could say he was an Interface, excluded from Mautri, Sidenl answered himself. "A white. Many times. And before that—yes—yes—ah! Arai, now I understand why you can read so very far back with such clarity. I, myself, never had a lifetime then. But you—all of you—must now finish what you then started." He flung the door wide and stood aside, saying. "One at a time. I will meet you on the other side."

Dark indigo drapes blocked the door, a photonlock. *Of course, what did you expect?* Since he'd begun Khelin's bedtime exercise, he'd become more aware of such reactions, but had never dreamed of being Sirwini. He penetrated the curtains to find another layer of drapes, and through that, he found himself overlooking a maze. Before him, a huge downward slanting chamber was divided by low walls, with several openings before him. He took the centermost course. Around a sharp angle bend, he came upon a scene.

In a niche before him, a Sirwini clothed so it was impossible to say if it were man or woman, stood before a solid cube—the very palest blue, so that Zref knew it was meant to be like the one in the cubical room. On the cube, three instruments were laid out in a triangle while the Sirwini, whose horns had not been filed, held another aloft. Above the person's head, flowers grew in profusion, while behind the figure a path of the same pale tint as the cube led away across formal gardens into a sunrise.

It was breathtaking. It was more than just the startlement of coming upon the scene, unsuspecting. The scene itself was incredibly lifelike. Zref fixed it and his reactions in memory, and proceeded.

Another choice of direction, and around another bend he came upon yet another scene. Here the figure stood upon a distant mountain peak. The only light was a faint glow from the lantern the figure held. Zref studied it, equally impressed.

Beyond, yet another scene, and another. He heard the two others enter the chamber, and wanted to call to Arshel how to follow him. But she hadn't called to him, and she had a right to her own adventure. Yet he could imagine her revulsion. The maze itself represented what she fought most. Yet this one had no mazeheart. The Glenwarnan were not Persuaders.

Intent on meeting her when she came out, he turned, and turned again, studying each new scene a few extra seconds until the cumulative significance began to affect him. Within a few minutes, he had the key to the layout. There were really ten superimposed mazes, and at certain points it was possible to transfer from one to the other.

At intervals, he came upon scenes that were merely differing numbers of the same object, arranged in patterns fraught with significances he couldn't fathom. Lost in this richness, awed beyond measure, the Interface within him shut to a tiny crack into his personal file, Zref found the caring part of himself stirring. Momentarily, he'd learn how to be person or Interface at will. He dashed onward, seeking.

He found himself staring helplessly up at two small figures facing each other under the immense wings of a benign Sirwini holding gong and hammer poised over the heads of the two. Tears in his eyes, Zref ripped himself loose and proceeded to what had to be the final chamber for him.

Before he'd gone two steps into the last area, he froze in his tracks, his breath caught in his throat.

Blocking the exit so he'd have to walk through the tableau to get out, a plumed and feathered biped danced, holding crystal wands in each hand about which snakes were twined. The figure was caught in the midst of a leap high over a path that led off into blue mist. There were no wings though a feathered cloak floated gracefully about the figure.

The feathers were all shades of blue and blue-gray, but Zref couldn't fail to recognize himself, as he'd been in the green crystal sphere in Jylyd's audience chamber. That poignant sense of exile gripped him in a part of himself that no longer existed.

At length, he gasped and commanded his legs to carry him forward. He knew, now, why Arai had gone to his knees in shock when looking back into Zref's incarnations as a Kinrea.

He walked into the scene, following the path, passing so close to the feathers they brushed his face, and climbed hard into blue mists among blue mirrors until he was dizzy.

Emerging through layers of draperies, he came out into the refreshing blue daylight of the fountain chamber.

People were moving about their business. The gardener was working her way along a new row of containers. In the distance, someone was playing a flute. Sidenl waited beside Arai and Arshel, their expressions bright and hopeful as Zref went toward them, trying to hide the weakness in his knees.

By the time he reached them, the sharp emotions were fading like a dream, and he was again Master Interface. Arshel, her venom sack not visibly distended though she reeked of strong emotion, wrapped her arms about Zref and said, "I'm no longer afraid—not even of the frustrated loneliness I knew here." She looked up at him. "You didn't see what I saw, did you?"

Sidenl answered, "No two trips through life are the same. The experiences depend on the decisions one makes before and during. The lessons depend on what one is willing to hear, and see. So even an identical trip wouldn't be an identical experience."

"Yes, of course," said Arshel abstractedly. "I caught one of the partitions shifting after I passed." And then, as if something had just come clear, she asked Sidenl, "Did you mean to say before that Arai was right to take the writing job with Lantern after all?"

Sidenl answered, "I meant to say his work has proved of the most astounding significance, awakening Zref's interest in the Crown network, and the Persuader's Maze. But I still believe you'd do well to sever connections with Lantern Enterprises. The Lantern novels are not a healthy thing."

"What do you mean?" asked Zref. His growing esteem for Sidenl was suddenly challenged. He had grown up fighting his parents over those novels.

"Let me ask you," said Sidenl, "which Lantern novels did you find resonant with your own sense of life. Only the Meguerian titles? Right?"

At the direct question, Zref had automatically searched his private file which contained all his life's memories before he'd become an Interface. "Yes," he had to answer. "And they have now all been withdrawn, 'Meguerian' fired."

"What have the novels accomplished recently?" asked Sidenl, rhetorically. "The inciting of thousands to search once again for the Mazeheart Object. Just yesterday, five Sirwini were lost when their small ship was searching an asteroid belt. If they'd found the Object and gained the power to Persuade, what would that have availed?"

"Only responsibility greater than their ability," answered Arai. "We tried to show what abuse of power—"

"But Lantern won't allow it," interrupted Sidenl. "They paint only the picture of utopia regained. Someone behind Lantern wants to rule this galaxy. The Lantern novels are being used to awaken the idealistic urges of all mortal species, directing it toward acclaiming an Emperor of Stars."

"The enemy," said Arai.

"So Arshel's mentor has maned her. And she is forming an aklal out of the readers of the Lantern novels, binding them by attuning and orchestrating their emotions. Crudely done, but devastatingly effective."

Arshel said, "I must tell Khelin what you've said."

"Must, yes. But before you leave, could you indulge an old teacher, and allow me to take Zref aside for a test?" Politely, he asked Arshel rather than Zref.

Apprehensive, she nevertheless said, "Certainly, but we don't have too much time."

Zref quoted the exact span remaining in the lunch break.

"That should be ample," replied Sidenl. He took Zref back to the cubical room with the only white stone on Sirwin.

The room was dim now, but the empty air still held a charge that seemed to make every edge stand out in a too-vivid focus. "A test?" asked Zref.

"Yes, quite simple really. You've done it before. But often it's important to repeat such exercises."

Zref understood then that this was some form of initiation for the Glenwarnan. "Before we get to that, though, will you answer a question of mine?"

"If I may."

"That final figure—who is it?"

"One of the Glenwarnan Founders." He watched Zref.

Zref was somehow not surprised, though he didn't believe

it. Some well-meaning person had gotten fact and legend mixed up. "What lesson does it represent?"

"These lessons are depicted as you saw them because the mind must grasp them as a whole, and relate them to emotional states resulting from beliefs."

Zref's automatic protest, *Interfaces don't experience emotional states,* went unvoiced. Emotions resided in the unconscious, the zone of himself which Zref could access via that state of *caring* Arshel's presence catalyzed.

"Surely, there must be some verbalization of that lesson that might help me grasp it?"

Studying Zref, listening to more than his words, Sidenl stroked his unsharpened horns for a moment, and then threw his head back in Sirwini gesture of reluctant consent. "We say, Science assumes the Laws of Reality can be understood by facts, and will respond to acts. However, Wisdom assumes the Laws of Reality are as independent of facts as the Laws of Mathematics are of numbers. The fabric of the universe responds primarily to what you *are,* not what you *do.*"

"Thank you," said Zref dissatisfied.

"Here, then, is your test. In this room lies an item which belongs to you—if you can find it."

With that, Sidenl left, closing the door. The stone cube seemed gray now, not white. The chairs, carved stone, wood, and woven reeds, stood in empty ranks about the room. The tiled mosaic floor stretched away gleaming on all sides.

Zref toured the room, scanning each chair seat, and under the chairs. The most likely place to hide something would be on top of one of the freestanding columns, but Zref had no way to check there. The chairs were not cushioned; nothing hidden there. The walls were painted stone; no paneling to come loose. No alcoves or niches. No hollow statues. *Hollow?* He stared at the cube, suddenly certain it was hollow, though a reflexive search of the comnet revealed no information.

With what reverence an Interface could muster, he placed his hands on top of the still sun-warmed cube.

At once, a square section of the center of the cube, set so that its corners bisected the cube's own edges, sank into the cube's surface. It rose again, now bearing a small case.

The thing looked like an ordinary book cartridge, but when

Zref picked it up, he found one edge was transparent. It was a rectangle, as big as his hand and one finger thick. He put it to his eyes, and abruptly, he was confronting the blue-feathered effigy of himself.

He almost dropped the case, then put it back on the cube surface. He didn't need such a thing. Starting to leave, he reconsidered and picked it up again. A new scene greeted his eyes, one he hadn't come upon in the maze. Three figures in opulent surroundings, an undressed stone before the one in the middle. Above their heads floated another figure.

He rocked the device, and watched the scene change yet again. He began to understand. The holographs displayed randomly as one handled the device. Interesting, but the device wasn't interfaced so he couldn't probe it. After some consideration, he pocketed the item and left the room.

Sidenl was waiting, and as they returned to the others, he said softly, "You may not be ready yet, but I shan't speak with you again, so I must warn you. You're embarking on a task more dangerous than you know. Remember the Phailan atrocities when Ossminid used aklal to work a Soul Dispersal on the founders of the First Lifewave, which is why they haven't reincarnated among us. The power you're about to assume is awesome indeed, your enemy formidable, your danger incalculable. Yet what you've learned through the millennia should see you through—if you remember, Arshel is the key."

Once back outside in the bright sun, Zref put that visit aside, and strode toward the wave of students who were dispersing across the meadow to resume their study of the site. He had work to do.

But just as he was enfolded by the first rank of clamoring students, Ley pushed his way through the crowd, yelling, "Zref! Zref! There you are! Where have you *been?* Where's Jocelyn?"

He turned, holding up one hand to the human male who had first claimed his attention. "I don't know."

"Then she's missing!" panted Ley.

"Don't panic," said Arshel. "She's a grown woman, and has been on many planets by herself."

"Maybe one of the cattle gored her, or maybe—"

By this time, Khelin had caught up with Ley. "It's not time to imagine disaster. We've got to organize a search."

Zref checked the overhead satellite to get a visual of this

region, but had to report, "We won't be able to get an orbital view for three hours yet."

Cruise Director Plath had now spotted Zref and was bearing down on them from the parking lot. At the same time, Zref heard a reedy Jernal voice squeaking in a panic, and he turned to see a pink fluffball hurtling across the field toward them. The six spindly legs were moving so fast it seemed the fluff sped through the air unsupported. Zref had never seen a Jernal move like that before.

Plath reached them first, though. "Master Interface! And just where have you been? We need you to search for—"

At that moment, the Jernal brought itself to a stop and began to retreat in the opposite direction, calling, "Zref! Ley! Come quickly. It's Jocelyn! I've found her!"

Khelin led the pack, with Ley right behind him until Arai overtook them with his long Theaten legs. Zref pounded along in their wake, Arshel panting beside him, "That must be Waysjoff! What other Jernal would recognize Jocelyn?" Which was true. Waysjoff was the only Jernal Zref had met who seemed able to tell humans apart.

They had covered half the width of the large circle when Shui and Iraem fell in beside them. They were now trailing a phalanx of students and faculty and those who were not running with them were watching intently. It must have been a spectacle indeed, thought Zref, for the Jernal never lost its lead, soon outdistancing even the Theatens.

They followed Waysjoff into the farther small circle within the large one, almost completely restored.

Jocelyn was slumped bonelessly against the shady side of the center stone, her legs jutting out in front of her in a wide V shape, her chin resting on her chest.

When Zref arrived, Ley was kneeling, shaking her.

"She's just asleep!" said one of the Theatens, a forgivable assumption considering.

"She looks unconscious," countered Plath.

Finally, Jocelyn opened dazed, blank eyes focused somewhere beyond reality. Her face was crusted with dried tears and nasal mucus smudged with soil. Her hands wandered restlessly among the grass and rocks, and Zref saw her broken, bloodied fingernails.

She seemed to focus on them all at last, and then her eyes

widened, her face registered shock and horror beyond measure, and she twisted about, scrambling against the stone as if she could make her body melt into it.

Then she began to scream hideously.

CHAPTER EIGHT
Molt

As *Epitasis* left orbit, Zref gathered his group in the sitting room of the suite. Jocelyn had been put to bed under heavy sedation in her own room after a thorough medical examination in the ship's infirmary. Ley was with her.

Stricken by her breakdown, he'd been unable to leave her side for a moment. Khelin, after offering bhirhir's comfort, had let Zref persuade him to leave them. Now he sat in his accustomed chair, elbows on knees, hands dangling between them. Zref couldn't mistake the lackluster droop in his head fluff. His molt would not be far behind Arshel's.

The long silence made it seem as if someone had died. Zref noted *Epitasis* taking a data dump which included a preview of a new Lantern novel, *Emperor at Peace,* by Thwil, a writer who extolled the glories of the combined Empire of Stars. "Well, I know what everyone else is going to be doing this evening," said Zref, to break the gloomy silence. And at the questioning looks, he told them of the new book.

Neini made a disgusted sound, and Arai just looked like a statue carved of bronze and copper—for the sun had darkened his skin. Waysjoff continued impassively combing bits of blue grass and indigo gravel out of its pink fluff.

But Khelin raised his head. "It's a pattern!" He scratched at a spot on his arm then disciplined the hand away as his visible discomfort made Arshel squirm against Zref. "I should have seen it long ago! First you were forbidden the *Epitasis* controls, so our conclusions about the location of the Object were relayed to—well, the Enemy. Then, pirates, also seeking the Object, attacked us to stop the best chance the Enemy had of finding the Object. Then, the Enemy turned over *Epitasis* to you. And Jocelyn is the countermove to your winning *Epitasis* away from the Enemy!"

"But," objected Waysjoff, "I thought our sudden unpopularity was the countermove."

Shui said dejectedly, "The unpopularity forced us to separate, and leave Jocelyn to search for the Enemy's agent, making Jocelyn vulnerable—to something."

Shui and Iraem had already apologized, and Zref had countered that they'd been hired to protect him, not the entire group. To that, Shui had said, "And we even lost track of you!" And Iraem had added, "The Guild is paying us to protect its Interface—but Jylyd has commissioned us to Zref's mission. We can only earn our fee by accomplishing Jylyd's task, which means protecting Jocelyn, too."

Zref asked, "Why does the Enemy want to break us up?"

"The right question," said Arai. "The Interface's talent. Zref, we must tell them what Sidenl told us."

Zref relaxed into the deep cushions of the lounge he and Arshel shared, and she touched his knee as if to forestall his raising venom. "Arai," said Zref in his Interface's voice, "to guard Glenwarnan's privacy, I've had to put all of that under permanent block. There's no way I can speak of it." He was conscious of the case he'd found in the cube, now nestled in his pocket opposite where Arshel sat.

So Arai related Sidenl's perception of the Enemy.

Khelin said, absently rubbing the itchy spot on his arm, "I see. The Enemy, someone high in the control of Lantern itself, conceded to you the ship's mechanical systems while grasping control of the aklal aboard ship—using it to break up our embryonic aklal. The Enemy is afraid of us."

"That's why," added Neini, *"Emperor at Peace* arrived just now, ripped from its publication schedule weeks early. Everyone will read it tonight. What will tomorrow bring?"

One of Zref's routine sweeps of *Epitasis* systems yielded a new datum. "The Enemy may not be waiting for tomorrow. As a special bonus, because Sirwin was a disappointment to many students, we're being diverted to Raynat." Lantern Enterprises Headquarters occupied one of the moons of the giant quasi-planet, Raynat. The moon also held some long known and mostly ignored First Lifewave ruins.

"If the Enemy's anywhere," said Arshel as Zref trapped the hand she was scratching with, "She's there."

"Perhaps," agreed Khelin. "So we must constitute our own aklal formally, or *we* may become a tool of the Enemy."

"Constitute? How?" asked Neini. "I've been remembering backward but so far nothing's come of it."

Everyone else agreed the exercises had been futile.

"Only Zref knows," said Khelin, "how to constitute this aklal and use it."

"And I don't remember," Zref asserted wearily.

Scratching fretfully, Khelin stood. "In the morning, we can discuss this again. But right now, please excuse me."

The other kren exchanged glances, knowing Khelin's skin needed Ley's ministrations, and a blue could tolerate much more discomfort in molt without a bhirhir's touch than a green could. Zref also stood. "We'll eat in our room tonight. If anything new happens, I'll drop notes to your own comtaps." They adjourned, the three writers to mingle with students, Shui and Iraem to seek rumors among the crew.

"Khelin was feeling bad," said Arshel when the door closed them into the privacy of their own pond room.

"Strip," he ordered brusquely. "You're further—"

Guiltily she eased out of her shirt, showering dull scales all over. Zref said, "I was right. You shouldn't have gone down—not like that."

"I've hardly raised half a sack—"

"Oh? And what sort of drug did you take to accomplish that?" It would have been an insult to a blue. She tried to stare him down. He added, "You know I can check the medcomp to find out what you've requisitioned."

She wilted and told him.

He sighed, something deep within him quivering with unsheddable tears of compassion. "Oh, Arshel."

She stopped stripping off her grass-stained slacks. Her eyes evaluated him, and her sack pulsed with renewed venom production. "But you're not like Dennis. I shouldn't have brought it. I shouldn't have taken it without telling you."

He threw her discarded things into the laundry chute where he shed his own sweat-stained and begrimed clothing. "Did he neglect you in molt—except for that last time?"

"No. But he tended me—only because he'd been trained to take good care of tools. You're not like that."

"You know that now?"

"I discovered it on Sirwin. Oh, if I could only think!"

He took down the leather venom bottle, sloshing it to judge its contents against what she was likely to produce now, and said, "We'll save this until after a good soaking. Come on." And he urged her into the water.

Later, he ordered his dinner. She'd lost her appetite, and Zref wished he could tempt her with his own venom-kill.

The next morning, he sent instructions not to disturb him even for student queries now, but assured the Captain he'd keep his surveillance of the ship's systems as agreed. Free at last, he turned his whole attention to Arshel.

Her venom production had normalized, and her sleep was heavier than usual. When he wasn't soaking or anointing her, she meditated using her beadstring, the Mautri device called, "the key to the door to the room without walls." She insisted he could go to work, but he flatly refused. "Perhaps, during some ordinary molt, but you went through hell last time. I'm not letting you develop a molt phobia."

He passed the day reading *Emperor at Peace*. Before he'd become an Interface, he'd have thrown any such addlepated trash across the room in disgust. It would take much better writing to convince him, even for a moment, that a ruler could impose peace by decree and have every face turn toward him in adulation. But he was able to finish it and see why so many people aboard were rereading the thing.

Idling away the late afternoon while Arshel dozed, he checked the file through which mail was dispatched as they passed pickup points. Several items were flagged for Interface dispatch direct to destination, and as he handled these he was forced to note many of them were letters of praise to Thwil asking for more books like *Emperor at Peace*.

He didn't tell Arshel about all this when she woke, but later that evening, a message dropped onto their deskpad and he drew it to her attention when he saw it was about Jocelyn.

"She's better!" exclaimed Arshel. "We've won again!"

Zref wasn't so sure. The message, signed by both Khelin and Ley, had been meant only to allay their concern. Neither would want to disturb Arshel at this point.

Arshel spent a restless night. The next morning, the ship made orbit at Raynat's moon, and Zref had to concentrate to shut out the multiplex babble of the largest comnet node except for Eiltherm, the HP capital planet.

Cruise Director Plath demanded Zref's services on planet during the visit to the Crumbling Crown. Zref invoked the bhirhir's privilege clause in his contract, and refused.

After the last soaking he would give her, she settled wearily onto the sand bed, hissing fretfully as she squirmed to get comfortable. "It feels so bad, I think it feels good!" Coming to herself, she looked at him. "Am I incoherent?"

"No," said Zref. "I think I know what you mean."

"I've often wondered what it's like not to molt."

"It's probably an even trade," he replied, to keep her mind off the crescendo of itching. "Humans sweat an oily, odorous film all over the skin, and have to put up with insect stings and sunburns on dozens of planets. Nails never stop growing. Hair grows and sheds constantly. Human males have to deal with face hair, and are constantly fertile. Human females menstruate and can be impregnated several days out of *any* month. Personally, I'd rather be kren."

"Then why did you choose to be human this time?"

Troubled, he said, "I only wish I knew!"

Seeing his distress, even in the midst of her own, she stretched out her hand to him. "Oh, Zref. I'm sorry." At full extension, the webbing between her thumb and forefinger split. She gasped, realizing this was at last the molt.

While everyone was on planet, Zref worked over Arshel, helping her stretch the stiff, brittle skin until it split neatly down her back. She squirmed, rested and writhed as he eased her out of the old hide. Many times, he expressed her molt venom, laving it on the parts of the old hide adhered to the new, and dabbing it on the new, tender skin.

But because her molt had not been premature this time, the old skin had been well cured before being shed, so the new hide dried quickly, without a single scabbed wound. The new scales were tiny transparent half-moons, transforming her coloring to attract a mate. Soon, her headfluff would also be a glorious summons to the males of her species.

Zref knelt at the edge of her sand bed, watching her doze as he gathered up every fragment of her old skin. The crack deep within him from which came the *caring* now delivered up an overwhelming pride, as if he'd invented her.

Peripherally, he was aware of comnet chatter as *Epitasis* shuttles docked, returning people from the excursion. Under that, for the first time in hours, he noticed the backlog in his private file.

He'd tapped the infirmary log. Now, it told him Jocelyn had been checked and found healthy, twice. Then, healthy still, she'd been readmitted. Zref overrode privacy locks shamelessly and found she was in for kren venom treatment.

His file also held a message from Rodeen. *"We have a complaint saying you've adopted a few people as confidants and excluded the rest of our clients aboard* Epitasis. *An Interface belongs to the community of species. If you can't defuse this discontent, we must remove Shui and Iraem from the ship at Earth, and have Khelin and Ley fired as well. Arshel is yours by contract, but the others are a dispensation. I've trusted you, Zref. Do well for us. Rodeen."*

Arshel stretched luxuriously, and murmured, "I never knew molt could be like that." When she opened her eyes, the new skin puckered oddly until she rubbed her eyes. "You were right, Zref. I was afraid. But you—care—and that made all the difference. I'll never be afraid again, as long as your hands are there."

She sat up, flicking the sand out of her new, short headfluff. Glowing inside, Zref went to the disposer chute, bundling her old hide into the atomizer—as good as the traditional burning. He said the appropriate benediction in the language of Vrashin Island, her home.

She came, brushed the last residue of old scales from his hands, and clasped them, gazing into his eyes. "If I never get back to Mautri, I'll be content as your bhirhir for the rest of this life. I think this is the first time I've ever *had* a bhirhir. And all those years, I never knew it."

Zref knew she wasn't saying it just to be kind. The warmth washed away the cold prospect of giving her up as he'd promised. "I'd much prefer to keep you bhirhir, Arshel. But if you ask, I'll keep my promise—however much it hurts."

"I'll never hold you to that!" she said decisively. "We'll decide—when the time comes—as any bhirhirn would."

"But—"

"How can one make an Interface erase such a recording?"

"Simply say, 'Erase all memory of your promise to take me through Mautri.'" But as she began to speak Zref put two fingers over her mouth. "May I beg the favor of keeping my memory intact?"

Shocked, she drew back. "You mean you wouldn't even—"

"I wouldn't even know I'd forgotten something. Too many people knew of my promise. I might act inconsistently—"

"I wouldn't—! Remember then, but ignore it. Please?"

"I won't mention it again." He took her in a brief hug, infinitely touched. But then he had to deliver the news. "I think Khelin has immunized Jocelyn."

They dressed hastily, Zref transferring the flat case to his new jacket rather than hunt a place for it. It was now well into the ship's night. Only a few students, still in on-planet garb, were in the halls. Supper had just finished and the corridor lights dimmed. *Epitasis* orbited the huge sun at increasing distances, preparing to leave. Zref said, "We've broken orbit. Can't ask Lantern for medical help."

The sick bay hatch stood ajar. Inside, there was a foyer with an examining table with glaring overhead lights. The pharmacy window had a CLOSED sign flashing monotonously. In a straight-backed chair beside a heap of dirty linen, Ley slumped. Several day's growth of beard marred his usually clean appearance. He was nursing a cup of something gone cold. Similar cups littered the small table beside him.

He looked up listlessly when they came in, then leaped up, seizing Zref. "At last. Maybe you can help!" He pushed Zref toward a closed inner door, as he also greeted Arshel.

The inner room was silent, curtains drawn around one of the beds, the other two, empty. Behind the curtain, two physicians, a Jernal and a Theaten, worked over the pale sweating body of Jocelyn. The Theaten came toward Zref. "Master Interface, would you consult on this case? It's a simple kren immunization, but—here, read her history."

Zref took the notepad and opened for the details. When he closed, Ley was saying, "...don't let them do a full volume blood exchange! Please, Zref, we kept them from doing it to you..."

"She's not to be his bhirhir—" objected Zref.

Arshel said, crowding in behind them, "Khelin won't be able to accept her if she can't take the immunization."

"But what happened?" asked Zref. "She should throw off MorZdersh'n venom in a night's sleep." It had been almost a day, and her fever was still raging.

"She will," insisted Ley. "I know it."

Ley's tone made Zref leap to a new conclusion. "That was pre-molt venom!"

The two doctors looked on during this discussion as if it were in a foreign language. Checking, Zref found neither of them was expert in venom reaction; both doctors who were had mustered off at Lantern Headquarters. Another move of the Enemy? As Zref assimilated the situation, Arshel moved to the bed, reaching out tenderly to stroke Jocelyn's head. The Theaten reached across the bed to ward off Arshel's touch. Offended, Arshel said, "She's practically my sister!"

The Theaten looked totally confused, and the Jernal said, "More venom couldn't hurt her now. She's going to die." It spun as if to look at Ley. "We've told you that. Humans can't tolerate fever like this. There'll be brain damage. She's delirious, and she's had one seizure."

Inspired, Zref said, "Then treat her as if she had Ciitheen Fever! Ice jacket, brainwave modulator, the works. If she has more seizures, you may have to resort to a blood exchange or dialysis, but try this first."

"Zref!" cried Ley, as if betrayed.

Zref put a hand on Ley's shoulder, "Only as a last resort. And then, in a year or so, you can try again with normal venom." Talking quietly in that vein, he convinced Ley as the doctors worked to combat Jocelyn's fever.

In the end, he left Arshel there with Ley, and went to check on Khelin. Ley had just spoken to him on the comtap, and Khelin had insisted he was fine. "But," said Ley, worriedly checking the time, "he wouldn't turn on the visual."

Zref agreed that was a bad sign. Technically, Arshel, the only other one immune to Khelin, should have gone. "But," she objected, "he shouldn't see me like this—when he's like that!" She was perfectly correct, of course.

So Zref went, saying only, "Ley, come as soon as she's out of danger."

Face haggard, Ley nodded, "Sooner if I must. Call me, Zref, if that so-'n'-so is lying about his condition."

Zref didn't promise to do that, and later he wished he had, for then he'd have had no choice.

When Zref arrived at the suite, he found Iraem and Shui sprawled on the floor of the sitting room, absorbed in a board game. As Zref entered, Shui scrambled to his feet, looking from Zref to Zref's door. "But—we thought—"

Iraem sighed, disgusted. "They got away from us again."

Zref explained rapidly as he went toward the stairs to Khelin's door, finishing, "So you can tell Arai and the others, then check on Arshel in the infirmary." Zref paused, looking down at the two kren. "And tell the stewards they can do our room while Arshel is with Jocelyn."

Shui hesitated oddly before suggesting to Iraem, "You could stay here while I go to Arshel?"

It struck Zref, both these kren now had to be considered mates for Arshel. Shui would surely attract her, if anyone could after Khelin. "May I ask a personal question?" Shui tilted his head up, and Zref asked, "What did you mean when you said you wouldn't be mating during the Cruise?"

"Our contract with the Guild stipulates no mating. It's not an unusual provision." Then, guessing Zref's concern Shui laughed, "Iraem here hit on a perfect solution to the steward problem. He's attracted to the female who cleans our room and could easily have taken her except for the contract. I'm sure we'll both find Arshel attractive, but we'll get around to it another time."

Politely, Zref told them he was glad there'd be no more distractions now, but he'd welcome their attentions later.

As they left, he opened the door to Khelin's room.

The odor of molt venom struck hard. It was the first time Zref had perceived Khelin's body odors as different, but it underscored Zref's lack of personal immunity to Khelin.

The lights were dim. Zref peered over the balustrade at the pond and sandbed.

Khelin was prone in the sand, a dark stain spread about his head. He was scratching feebly after his beadstring which lay just beyond his grasp. As Zref gaped at this spectacle, realizing the stain must be from blue-voiding, Khelin cried out and grabbed at his head, whimpering like a child. Then he screamed.

Galvanized, Zref flew down the stairs and bounded across the carpet, and, heedless of the danger, scooped the kren into his arms to keep him from bashing his head on the rim of the sandbed as he thrashed in a seizure.

The instant Zref touched Khelin, the room shimmered out of focus and became an ochre and russet desert under a purple sky. They were among the tumbled ruins of a stone circle of ruddy stones scarred and pitted by countless sandstorms. Khelin's beadstring lay upon the horizontal central stone while he sprawled with one foot trapped beneath a huge fragment of a newly shattered monolith.

Beyond the central stone and the beadstring, an apparition stood amid swirling veils of mist. It was female, now feathered, now scaled, now furred or smooth-skinned. As Zref fixed on penetrating the apparition, it wavered and almost vanished. He saw Ossminid, Emperor of Crowns, then an opaque ebony statue that spoke. "One last chance. Tell me, and you can have your beads—and your life."

"No!" croaked Khelin. "I've died worse deaths than you can conjure!" He wrenched himself free of Zref's grasp and lunged toward the beads, crying out in agony.

Zref scrambled toward the beads to fetch them, but ran into a soft scorching barrier that threw him back. The apparition laughed.

A tiny voice in his mind announced, *"Orbit broken. Interstellar drive engaged. All secure."*

Abruptly, the desert vanished. Zref was sitting in the sandbed hardly arm's reach from Khelin's beadstring, and Khelin's leg was not pinned. The room seemed cold. His head was splitting. Using his jacket to keep from touching the beads, he pressed them into Khelin's hands, and withdrew from the sandbed.

Soon, clutching the beads, Khelin responded to Zref's presence. "Ley?" Suddenly aware it wasn't Ley, he raised venom, his fangs descending.

"It's Zref," Zref whispered. "I'll call Ley."

Khelin snapped his fangs back against the roof of his mouth, forcing them against reflex for his sack was clearly distended. "No! He's with Jocelyn. She's dying!"

"It's not your fault!" said Zref. "And despite those idiot

medics, I don't think she's going to die."

Khelin trembled with the effort to control himself. "Go away, Zref! Leave me. Ley will come—when it's time. Go!"

Zref edged away, knowing he had no business in this room now, but appalled at seeing Khelin irrational. Gently, he tried to explain, "Ley is staying with Jocelyn because he thinks you're all right. When I tell him of that hallucination we just shared, he'll come."

The kren's eyes flew open. "Shared? A blue-void hallucination?"

Zref related what had happened, wishing he hadn't told Khelin he'd call Ley. Khelin's negative held him from opening to signal Ley.

"It was real, then! But—how? Who could do such a—"

"The Enemy. You were alone, vulnerable. Let me call Ley! You can't expect to do this like the white priests do."

"What would you know—" The sudden rejoinder ended in a gasp. "You remember?"

Zref had to admit, "No. But even if I did, I'd still be compelled to call Ley. He asked me to."

"He'll come—at the right time."

"Maybe a kren would be able to," replied Zref, "but Ley's human, and he's out of his mind with concern over Jocelyn. He knows his judgement's off, so he asked me to call him. I'll just wait here until you're ready."

"Zref—no." It was a defenseless denial from the depths of misery, and Zref wanted very much to quit the room.

"I can't go, not as a human and not as an Interface—because Ley charged me with judging your welfare for him. He has to be there to order the transfusion, if she goes into convulsions again."

Khelin looked up, sack pulsing with new venom. "But she signed the order not to—we never expected . . ."

So that was it! No wonder Ley was nearly hysterical at countermanding that order. "How did you ever decide to do this before your molt? Relieve an Interface's curiosity?"

"She begged me. She told me what she suffered on Sirwin. Some of her visions were real past life memories, some just nightmares, and a couple were like that attack in Jylyd's chamber, and this 'hallucination.' Zref, it's partly my fault Jocelyn's

wide open to possession. I brought her consciousness to the
level of body fields. She went beyond that by herself, but it's
obvious she's been used this way before. She's even cultivated
it in her dancing.

"I judged we had to bring her deep into our aklal to protect
her. I didn't think it could wait, Zref—especially when Ley
told me she'd spent the whole night alternately crying hysterically and vomiting. In that condition, there was no way I could
teach her any self-protection. The medics insisted she was
physically well, so we—well, I decided to do what they both
begged me to do. If it hadn't been for you just now, I guess
it would have backfired! But Jocelyn is—part of me, of us. If
I've killed her—I'll—"

"No," denied Zref. Khelin was raising venom. Zref folded
his legs under him and sat on the floor. He was more than
arm's length from Khelin but any kren could move that far in
strike. There was a better chance he could survive Khelin's
venom if he had to, then there'd been with Arshel all those
years he'd tended her with only the general Vrashin Island
immunity the public venom clinic provided. "Don't blue-void,
Khelin, you're going to need that venom."

"You're not going to try to express me! Arshel would hate
you!"

"I won't touch you," promised Zref. He felt no urge what-
soever to get any closer. The emotions welling up from the
crack within himself, urged him to flee the room in panic and
scream for Ley. But he couldn't, under Khelin's injunction.
Ley warned me he's a so-'n'-so over these things.

"I'm not going to—do it. With you watching!"

The inability to use the phrase 'self-express' was an odd
prudishness to discover in Khelin, and it sparked an insight.
"I think I understand something now. The test for the purple
that defeated you time and again was self-expression. You're
blocked on that—from within." The crack within his mind was
open now, not by the imperatives of his bhirhir's need, but by
something else. He added with unintentional cruelty, "The talent you went to Mautri to tame is based on leftover fragments
of the Persuader's power."

"No!" denied Khelin, rising a bit on his haunches. His
venom sack pulsed once again, and Zref began to fear the

distention would rupture the skin prematurely.

As if feeling the pain of that swelling, Khelin reached for his venom bottle, but he stopped with one hand gracing the fine-tooled leather, self-conscious still.

"You've been afraid of that power all your life," persisted Zref, though he kept his voice low and gentle. He'd started this; he had to finish it. "I remember how it was with Ley—that at first you two were inseparable, and then he caught you manipulating his motives with your talent to see into people. So you went to Mautri, determined to *suppress*, not master, your talents."

Zref took a breath, trying to gauge how much more Khelin could take. The kren was poised, eyes closed, fingers wandering over the venom bottle which sat in the sand on the far side from Zref. But he was listening, Zref was sure.

"Khelin, I've seen you using your ability to make peace among people—as Persuaders were commissioned to. I've seen your ability to be in the right place at the right time—why, that's how we found each other on Eiltherm! It's a big galaxy out there, but I bet you could find me, or Arshel, just by wandering around. You think you learned all that at Mautri? No, you've spent lifetimes mastering those skills!"

Tightly, Khelin added, "And abusing them."

"Maybe," conceded Zref, "but it's taught you the ethic governing influence over others, and over chance. It's such a bitter lesson, you're terrified to remember you first learned it in the Maze I built! You walked the Maze again and again, and seated those powers deep within you. As long as your goal is to use Mautri to suppress those powers, Mautri will reject you. What you suppress, Ley must control. If you would be whole again, you must remember the Maze."

On impulse, Zref extracted the Glenwarnan case from his pocket. Moving with utmost care, he proffered it. "Here. Look. This will help you remember."

Khelin shrank away.

Zref encouraged, "I'm not going to touch you. I promised. I know you'd only strike me and lose your venom."

It was criminal, what Ley's absence was forcing Khelin to endure, and Zref knew he was making it worse. Yet if this worked, it would mark a crucial turning point for Khelin.

With infinite caution, Khelin reached to take the casing. Zref noted the ashen blisters of dead hide on Khelin's hands. At least the skin was parting properly there, but what about the areas of his body he, himself couldn't reach. But he put that thought aside as unworthy. Ley wouldn't neglect that duty, even if Khelin begged him to.

Before Zref could doubt his decision to show Khelin the innermost secrets of Glenwarnan, the kren held the holoscope up and looked within. With his hide stiffening, it was hard to read his face, but Zref thought he saw fascination, awe, and then dawning comprehension there. *What if I've truly read his past lives, and he was at Glenwarnan, too?*

Fifteen minutes later, Khelin lowered the instrument. He breathed, "I was praying for this—before you came in."

The emotion sweeping through the kren poured new venom into his sack, and in one convulsive movement, he clutched at the venom bottle, hooking his extended fangs over its padded edge as he held it himself. But he didn't brace the bottle against his lower jaw, as a bhirhir would.

With one lax, slow outbreath, Khelin allowed the stored venom to pour in twin yellow streams into the venom bottle.

In the middle of this, the upper door opened and Ley entered. He assessed the room with one flickering glance, and then strode across the landing and down the stairs, charging at Zref who was rising carefully to his feet.

"Out!" demanded Ley. "You—you—you—*out!*"

CHAPTER NINE
Stonehenge

"A kren," said Zref to Arshel, "would've struck me!"

"When he left here," she answered, "Ley was as distraught as any kren would have been that Khelin hadn't called for him." They were sitting in Jocelyn's room at the infirmary, Shui with them while Iraem ran errands.

After Ley had left, Jocelyn's fever had broken leaving her in a deep sleep. Zref had related Khelin's triumph over the purple degree's technique of self-expression, though not mentioning his holocase, which he'd left with Khelin. "I'm not sure Ley will ever thank me," said Zref. "But at least it wasn't what he thought when he walked in."

"Khelin will talk some sense into him," said Shui. "I remember all the years Khelin's suffered trying the purple expression, and now you've given it to him. If he's really a purple now—maybe—" His eyes flicked to Jocelyn.

Arshel said, "We have to tell him. But, Zref, remember I'm only a green and Shui has barely taken the light blue. This is really for Khelin or even Jylyd to judge—"

Zref waited, caught once more in the trap of the Interface who hasn't been asked a question.

"I think we've lost Jocelyn," said Shui. "Khelin warned her she might be open to unfriendly influences, and—"

Zref stared at Jocelyn, face pale against russet hair, and his private file conjured the illusion-shrouded image of the Enemy. At the time, the vision had no power over him. Now, his guts writhed, and it took all his courage to touch Jocelyn's face, as he'd touched Khelin. But this time, he sensed nothing. He related Khelin's battle, ending, "He's no mere purple; he's a white." Yet there was nothing they could do until Khelin and Ley rejoined them.

* * *

Two days later, Zref walked into the sitting room from a tedious day's work with students. Among their uninspired theories, he'd found some brilliant ones. Originality excited curiosity from which an Interface derived his sole pleasure in life, yet Zref also feared success, for the Enemy might grab the vital clue to the Object's location from the student's very mind, if not from the surveillance recordings.

Ley was sitting in Khelin's chair, imitating Khelin's posture—elbows on knees, hands drooping between his legs. As Zref crossed the room, Ley looked up, face ravaged by sleepless exhaustion, hands trembling with fatigue. "Zref."

At least he's talking to me. Feeling awkward towering over the man, Zref sat cross-legged on the floor at his feet.

"Zref, I'm sorry for how I acted. You were only trying to help—and you *did* help in a way nobody else ever could."

Helped him toward balbhirhir, thought Zref sadly. It was a path Khelin had long forsaken, to Ley's vast relief. To change the subject, Zref said, "I've done something for Jocelyn." She'd gone into a coma, and they didn't have the equipment aboard to test for brain damage. "We'll be on Earth in a couple of days. I've alerted Earth Comnode to meet us with an orbital ambulance. Where else in the galaxy could you get better treatment for a human?" They'd be on Earth for less than a day before making the long jump to Pallacin's Sorges River Valley where Zref had built the Crystal Crown to house Arshel's model of the Globe of Stars.

Ley smiled. "Thank you. It's handy having an Interface for a brother."

At that point, Khelin joined them, looking young and virile. The spring was back in his step, and his eyes seemed bright and healthy again. He was wearing his blue medallion. As he edged onto the arm of the chair Ley occupied, he said to Zref, "I owe you an apology. My behavior—"

"—was perfectly normal," interrupted Zref. "*I* should apologize. I was intrusive, and ralbhirhir."

Both of them recoiled at that near obscenity, and hastened to deny it, but the arrival of Shui and Iraem forestalled argument. Then Arshel came out of the pond room, her fluff still slightly damp, wearing a crisp, new, yellow outfit that made her skin seem to glow.

Zref heard all three male kren stop breathing as she went to congratulate Khelin formally. Everyone else chimed in, and then Arai, Neini and Waysjoff arrived.

When they'd settled down, Zref said, "This's the first time we've been together since before Jocelyn—look, I have news that may be already stale." He told them of the Guild's threat to have Shui, Iraem, Khelin and Ley removed at Earth. "So I wanted to know how public opinion of us is running."

Waysjoff's pink fluff wilted. "They hate us."

Neini and Arai were sharing the settee Ley and Jocelyn usually occupied. She said, "Waysjoff's too sensitive. Mithal Meguerian's out of favor. They don't know that's us."

"Nobody's been particularly down on you lately, Zref," said Arai. "People accept the bhirhir's duty, and you've caught up on your work."

Relieved, he told them of his arrangements for Jocelyn on Earth. "But she might have to stay when we leave."

Khelin said, "Of course, we'd stay with her. But—"

"It would break up the group," said Zref, as the puzzle formed a coherent picture. "Is that what the Enemy wants?"

Iraem said, "If the Guild fires us, we'll buy passage for the rest of the Cruise."

Oddly warmed by that loyalty, Zref said, "The Enemy seems to have two goals—to break up our aklal, and to make us find the Object for Her." He looked at Khelin. "Or tell Her where it is."

"She thinks I know where it is," said Khelin, relating the experience he and Zref had shared. "But I don't know where it is. We need the aklal intact to find the Object."

"And," added Zref, "together, we can destroy it!"

Khelin's eyes pierced Zref. "You remember?"

"No," answered Zref sadly. "And the curiosity is frustrating me, because the comnet can't help, except with logic. I got this from available data using a Sift&Sort program with intuitive lobes."

After they'd discussed how the Enemy seemed to have cut Jocelyn off from them, perhaps even prompting her to beg for Khelin's immunization, Zref asked, "But what if Jocelyn recovered tonight?"

Ley raised suddenly bright, hopeful eyes, and Khelin put

his arm around his bhirhir. Neini said, "The group wouldn't be broken up at Earth by losing Jocelyn, Khelin and Ley!"

At Zref's silence, Ley prompted, "But what can we do to make Jocelyn recover?"

Zref searched their eyes, remembering Sidenl's warning. An aklal wielded the power of Soul Dispersal.

Arshel had curled up beside Zref on the floor near Ley's feet. Now Khelin slid off the chair arm and took Zref's hands, whispering, "Forgive me." Aloud, he said, "Zref may Sift&Sort, but Tschfa'amin *remembers.*" Unveiling his eyes, he penetrated Zref's gaze. "Tell us your plan, Zref. You needn't fear us, and with us, you needn't fear the Enemy."

Zref had never before been the target of Khelin's talent. The Interface stored Khelin's speech as input, but the crack through which *caring* oozed up out of his former selves widened, and Khelin's words sank into that chasm. Zref's reluctance to speak evaporated into a relaxed acceptance. *Is this what it's like to be Persuaded?*

"Do you remember when Arshel was climbing the cliff, and almost fell?" asked Zref. "We all gathered, yearning to help, and she felt my hand guiding her foot. I'm certainly no telekinetic. Does anyone here have that talent?"

Waysjoff, who had made itself comfortable on the floor near Zref, said, "I do. Sometimes."

"Jylyd once thought I might develop it," confessed Shui.

Nobody else admitted to the talent. "However little trained talent we had, the group used it—apparently through me. For that moment, the nine of us were aklal, able to act because we knew how vital Arshel is to our common purpose. So we saved her. Now we know Jocelyn is also vital. I submit we must do the same for her. Once we've consciously joined in aklal, we'll be 'constituted' and indivisible."

Khelin said, "A good plan. When?"

Zref said, "We're all tired and hungry, and Ley's staggering. Let's spread out and go to supper while Ley gets some sleep. We'll meet in Jocelyn's room at midnight. And we'll help her. Somewhere among our lives we have the skills to do it."

They scattered through the dining saloon. Neini had hit on the scheme of "using" their connection with Zref to bring him querants with personal problems, making it seem friendly by catching him during meals or in the halls. Thus people came to lose their reluctance to approach him. So Arshel and Zref had a constant stream of visitors during the meal.

Even so, Zref had plenty of time before midnight to cultivate doubts, and he nervously resolved to file this entire matter in the part of his private file set to self-destruct upon his death, or kill him if it were breached.

When they gathered over Jocelyn's bed, Zref diverting the duty nurse with comtap access to a speech at a medical convention on Ciitheen, they were prepared. The kren priests had brought their beadstrings; Neini, incense and candles; Arai, his holocase. Khelin returned Zref's holocase and contributed a Mautri meditation chimes recording.

Diffidently, Arai said, "I've a suggestion for a visual—it's a universal that might speak to all our species."

"The white cube," guessed Arshel.

"Yes," answered Arai. "A pure white, perfect cube, sparkling in brilliant sunshine, glowing with its own radiance as well as reflecting perfectly."

"And on the cube," said Khelin, "a perfect sphere of ocean depth green."

Zref saw what they had in mind. To join those two symbols would be to call Mautri *and* Glenwarnan in aklal against the Enemy's untrained millions in the Lantern aklal.

"This is awfully unscientific," said Neini. "Somehow I wish that bothered me more than it does!"

Khelin held his spread hand over Jocelyn's face. "Science has failed to cure her. And, Shui, I think you and Arshel were right. There's—murk." He shook his head. "I'm out of my field. I shouldn't have tried to teach—"

"Khelin, you had to," said Ley. "And she wanted it."

"True," conceded Khelin abstractedly. He draped his beadstring over his hands, something he never did in public. On that signal, the other kren did likewise.

In a quiet voice, Arai said, "I suggest we start by adopting our own slowest breathing rhythm."

They consented silently and settled—Arai, Neini, Khelin and Ley on the vacant bed, Waysjoff, Shui and Iraem on the floor, Zref and Arshel perched on a table, leaning on the wall. Zref glanced at his holocase, now displaying the image of himself dancing in midair, wearing blue feathers. Holding that picture, he summoned the white cube and the green sphere from his private file. Never could the unaided inner eye be so sharp yet it lacked something. And then he understood, visualization was more than perfect visual reproduction. It had to be backed by the power that welled up from beneath the floor of his mind. In fact, it ought to come from there.

He moved closer to Arshel, thinking of all she'd come to mean to him. The faint scent of her new skin enveloped them. He understood how Ley was both devastated and elated by Khelin's purple expression. He knew intimately how Ley's love for Jocelyn didn't subtract from his bhirhir with Khelin. Through Ley, Jocelyn had become Zref's sister.

Arshel stirred, and then she did an unprecedented thing. She placed her hands over Zref's, the beadstring twined about the tips of her fingers. As their hands joined, she slipped some loops onto Zref's fingers, so the two of them were joined by the sacrosanct symbol of Mautri.

Dimly, Zref felt the other kren, disturbed, finally accept him. The room was totally silent except for the mechanical wheezing of Jocelyn's breather, backed by the Mautri windchime recording. The candlelight revealed a faint haze of incense, a strange odor yet hauntingly familiar.

Zref kept the cube and sphere image in the forefront of his mind, mentally projecting it over Jocelyn's bed. But another part of his mind was acutely aware of the beadstring, as if tendrils of warm, invisible light connected all the beadstrings in the room, penetrating his body, weaving a basket to contain his heart, drawing his mind down into the incandescence beyond the crack in the floor of his mind.

Suddenly, the crack shook the floor of his being, widening, crumbling his reality. Frightened, he disciplined himself to calm. *Anything to help Jocelyn.*

Welling up through that crack, came his old childhood certainty that help in any crisis could be had for the asking. He turned to the Creator of the Universe, and he prayed, wordlessly, helplessly, *knowing* that of his own will alone, he could not prevail, of his own judgement alone, he dared not say what was best for Jocelyn or the galaxy.

The Power suffused his being with brightness, and he experienced lifetimes lived wholly dedicated to this brightness, a unique gratification. He remembered neglected duties, and with consent in his heart, he reclaimed his responsibilities.

The unbearable brilliance faded, leaving him tingling, shaking, bewildered. The broad grasp of his lives had faded, and he knew not what he had consented to.

They were all breathing raggedly. Zref noticed with a bemused distance, that over Jocelyn's outstretched body, a zone of wavering light gathered all the drifting smoke in the room. Zref felt the automatic private file message that his eyes were in fact shut. Yet he could *see* a smoky tendril of thinning substance stretching up from Jocelyn through a veil of stars set in a sphere of glass.

Beyond the star-dotted barrier, Jocelyn's form struggled with the polished ebony statue which had come to represent the Enemy for him. The statue had twisted the smoky tendril connecting Jocelyn to her image, around her hands as if it were a leash. As Jocelyn's image dashed and lunged, battering herself against the impenetrable glass globe, the statue tugged her back, strangling the life from her as She demanded, "Tell me where it is, and I'll let you go!" Yet through it all, Jocelyn maintained her ineffable grace, as if she were dancing the tragic Ballet of the Lost.

Bemused by the outre vision, Zref watched until on one of her approaches, Jocelyn fell into the elastic barrier, her face stretching it, almost penetrating it. Her yearning and terror galvanized Zref. He stood, reaching up to the barrier but it was too far above him. Even weightless, he couldn't jump that high. He climbed onto Jocelyn's body, but still couldn't touch her image. Laughter floated down from the statue, and Jocelyn cried out. Then he remembered Arai's cube and Khelin's globe.

Instantly, the glowing white cube topped by the deep green globe—now searingly white as well—materialized on Jocelyn's chest. He climbed to stand on top of the globe, clad now only in feathers. On her next approach, he leaped upward clutching at the strange plastic substance, but it wouldn't tear and let Jocelyn through.

In desperation, he used the screw-like helix he found in his hand, twirling himself as he leaped, driving its point through the membrane. Once torn, it parted and vanished.

Jocelyn poured through the gap, slithering through him, through globe and cube into her body. The downwashing forces sucked Zref head first into a dark chute lined with stars. *Is this what it's like to be lost from a ship in orbit?* But only the unshakably rational Interface could think. The rest of him was terrified, for he fell forever.

The bottom, when he hit, was hard.

When he came to, the room was in darkness except for the bedside instrument lights. The incense had dissipated. The windchimes had ceased. People slumped and sprawled around the room. As Zref extricated himself from Arshel's beads, Ley pulled himself up, saw Zref and, awed, said "I saw you dancing on the globe wearing blue feathers, holding distilling coils in your hands—using them to—Jocelyn!"

As memory solidified, he jerked about to stare at Jocelyn's monitors. Something had changed. Zref consulted *Epitasis* for an interpretation, and then as everyone else came to, he assured them, "She's sleeping normally!"

Arai said, "I was right. You *are* who we thought you were— Sidenl and I. You remember now."

"I remember dancing on the green sphere, holding tools I used to break Jocelyn free. But that's all."

"But I *saw* you," said Neini.

"I danced with you," said Waysjoff. Shocked, it added, "On only two legs!"

Jocelyn stirred, and everyone gathered over her, hushed. She rolled her head a few times, fretting at the lines connecting her into the machines. Then her eyes opened. Ley turned up the nightlight so she could see them all—not just looming shapes in the darkness. Understanding dawned, and heedless of the cords and lines, she sat up and threw her arms around Zref, bursting into tears.

"Hey," said Zref coaxingly, "we're all glad to see you, too. Look, here's Ley."

She loosed Zref and hugged Ley. "Ley, I love you. But you don't dance the way Zref does."

Then she hugged Khelin, calling him her very own kren. But she fell asleep again in his arms. They put her down gently and stole quietly out of the room.

Over the next few days, they all managed to get enough

rest so the prospect of planetfall seemed inviting. When *Epitasis* first raised Earth comnode, Zref used it to check for possible pirate ships around them. He found none, and reported this to the Captain, who was now happy with his performance. Shortly after that, Rodeen congratulated him because Lantern had withdrawn its criticism of him.

Arai commented, "The Enemy's a graceful loser!"

Waysjoff commented sourly, "But I'll bet Lantern won't reissue our books! How are we going to make a living?"

"I'm not worried," said Arai.

"You've been technically unemployed all your life!" retorted the Jernal. As a Glenwarnan master, Arai had refused payment for his talents and had allowed Neini and Waysjoff to support him from the proceeds of their novels.

"Waysjoff," interrupted Zref, "do you realize Arai's the only one of us who has never taken a single credit from Lantern?" He looked around at the group assembled in the sitting room. Zref had to show them how companies they'd worked for were ultimately owned by Lantern.

"You're right," said Neini. "And all of us—except Arai— have been deeply infected with the dream of finding the City. When Arshel found it, Lantern replaced our dream with the dream of recreating that golden era—only we didn't go along. That's why we were fired."

"*That's* how the Lantern aklal swallows people!" exclaimed Shui. "Like a huge, tenuous soap bubble, touch it anywhere— read a novel, take its money—and it closes around you without your knowing because it's so big it's unnoticeable," said Shui. "Like the Globe of Stars itself."

The Globe of Stars was an artifact of the First Lifewave so big it went unnoticed until Arshel discovered it. It was a sphere of yellow stars each with a single planet from which a part of the galaxy was ruled. One of those planets, Pallacin, was now a member of the Hundred Planets. Another, across a diameter of the sphere from Pallacin, held the City of a Million Legends.

"What can our little group do against a power like that?" asked Waysjoff.

Zref answered, "We extricated Jocelyn from it! Big isn't necessarily powerful." He remembered the ebony statue playing Jocelyn on a tether, cruelly taunting Khelin. "The Enemy doesn't know how to handle the power she has. If we can discipline ourselves, we can succeed."

The respect focused on Zref since they'd fought for Jocelyn was rapidly turning to awe as they each assimilated what they'd seen and began to remember what they'd been. Zref found it awkward, but couldn't stop saying things that evoked their awe.

But this time, the ship's address system saved him by calling for the excursion groups to form up at the shuttle bays. They had arrived at Earth.

Zref had never set foot on the mother planet of his species, though many of the nonhumans were thoroughly familiar with conditions and customs, while all Zref knew were the details of Stonehenge. On the way down, phrases echoed through his head from students' papers—"Pembroke rocks from the Presely Mountains make up the smaller, less complete, of the two circles. It is now composed of twenty stones above ground, four of which are rhyolites, namely 46 and 48, and 38 and 40..." "...sixteen others are of a spotted dolerite known as Bluestone..." "...they are of five kinds: spotted dolerite, volcanic ash, rhyolite, micaceous sandstone, and a greenish-gray sandstone of which only fragments have been found."

Endless research papers proved by heavy academic reasoning and tedious laboratory reports that, unlike the Crowns, every single stone and fragment was native to the planet. There were hundreds of virtually identical stone circles found all over the planet, and all of them oriented toward the local solstice points, to function as calendars.

But it was Stonehenge itself which was famous throughout the galaxy. Of recent construction—less than ten thousand standard years old—it had been built in three, perhaps five, stages over a thousand years. Who had built it? Why?

The site itself was determined to be psychoactive, a place where the ground currents interacted strongly with the biofields of the native lifeforms. That effect, it had been determined, was enhanced by the minerals in the stones and their placement. However, how did the Builders know this?

The psychoactivity enhancement wasn't nearly strong enough to make contact with any Crowns, but the orientation of Stonehenge brought it into regular alignment with the several nearby Crowns. "As if," one scholar had speculated, "the Builder, perhaps a latter day incarnation of a First Lifewave Crown Engineer, had been *trying* to make a contact!"

Zref suspended judgement, as required of any Interface. He made the journey down amid the ever increasing excitement of the students. The faculty with them, having taught the dull details of the monument's history for the last weeks, was not immune to the anticipation either. Zref was kept busy by inquiries designed to settle bets.

Arshel, Shui and Iraem rode with him, but the rest of the group was scattered through the other shuttles. They had to land well outside the Park Reserve surrounding the monument, and ride in on ground vehicles.

Locally, it was early spring, the middle of a work period. They arrived in late afternoon, with the sun lowering through thick, black-bottomed clouds.

Their bus topped one final rise on this very flat, barren plain that blurred into mist at the horizon. To the right of the bus, well off the highway, yet clearly visible, stood the tight grouping of massive stones, etched with an impossible vividness against the colorless gray background.

It was as if living fire seared the image directly into Zref's brain, without going through the eyes. He gasped, breath suspended, eyes riveted on the standing stones.

Zref knew every minute detail of the site. Yet seeing it standing on this featureless plain like a brand new building— like a home momentarily left but not vacated—was a thrill that vibrated to the core of every cell.

At length Arshel began to breathe again, saying in hushed tones, "It's still alive! Zref—"

"I know. I see it." They rode the rest of the way into the paved and painted parking lot in silence.

Across from the site, the local tourist bureau had set up a cluster of restaurants catering to various species, public toilets, and a museum where one could buy imitation relics, photo souvenirs and tickets to the monument.

Zref had *heard* about Earth, but he hadn't really believed it until now. However, today at this hour, the official concessions were closed. Their group had a special permit which the Cruise Director presented to the two guards who admitted them to a tunnel which led them under the deserted eight lane highway and onto the monument grounds.

"We're permitted to enter the roped off areas for archeological observation," called the Director when he had them all assembled on the other side of the tunnel. "However, this is a Planetary Shrine. *No* samples may be removed. Have the Interface record anything of interest to you." Then he gave them their departure time.

The wind whipped Zref's clothing about him, an icy knife laced with stinging raindrops. But they'd been warned and had dressed for cold. The Jernal, however, all complained. Jernal, Zref had long ago decided, always complained.

As the group dispersed, Khelin, Ley and Jocelyn joined Zref, Arshel, Shui and Iraem. Soon, the three writers filtered through the crowd. Zref led the way toward a mesh-matted track that led around the outside of the site, which was as close as any tourists were allowed to the standing stones. Silently, they circled the monument. They knew it so well by now, Zref didn't have to point out the features, the Heelstone, the Altar stone, the so-called Slaughter Stone, and the post holes. They strung out along the track, individuals stopping to view the monument from different angles. Neini used a holocorder to make her own record.

At last, only Zref and Khelin were still moving around the big circle, squinting back into the setting sun as they moved between the Slaughter Stone and the Heelstone, on line with the central Altar Stone. The sun silhouetted the circle, outlining the stones in liquid fire.

In a distracted daze, Arshel tromped across the turf toward the circle, where all the others from the Tour milled about. Khelin saw and raised a hand, starting to object. "Let her go," said Zref. "She was never a Persuader."

Khelin looked at him, then at her retreating back. "But it's not a real Crown—yet I feel . . ." He trailed off.

The magic of the place reached out to them as lances of golden sunlight pierced chinks in the stones and—made visible by the mist—shafted outward in radiant beams as the sun set. Spellbound by an experience no Interface should even be able to perceive, Zref watched the sunset, hardly daring to breathe, fearing a student would interrupt the moment. At last, Khelin whirled in place, turning his back on the dynamism of the place. "It's *new!*" was all he said, but Zref sensed a shuddering pain opening within the kren.

He looked about for Ley. There was still a scattering of people on the outer path around the monument. Too far away to identify, they might all be others of his—he forced himself to use the word—*aklal*.

Khelin bent backward, looking up at the looming, tilted Heelstone, peering at its dirt and moss crusted surface, at the runnels and curves in its surface. Behind the stone, glowing in the gathering dusk, an energy fence marked the edge of the monument property. In the dense twilight, Zref could make out a very distant line of greenery beyond the bleak plain. The Heelstone, held Khelin as raptly as the monument circle had. Suddenly, he spun about, peering at the circle of stones. "No," whispered Khelin. "No." It was something between a statement and a plea.

Then he walked up the avenue toward the Slaughter Stone and the circle itself. Perforce, Zref followed him. The kren was raising venom slowly, moving like a puppet. When he came to the token barrier, a few cords strung between upright spikes, he stepped over it, oblivious.

"Khelin?" called Zref, scrambling after his brother. He felt a crawling discomfort as he approached the circle, but the thing, after all, wasn't a functioning Crown, nor was he a functioning Persuader. *If the Enemy's attacking Khelin again—* He banished the thought.

As they entered the circle, Zref felt as if he were penetrating to the heart of a cathedral. The sense of living power redoubled with every perimeter they crossed. Arshel was standing at one of the upright stones, both her hands spread on it, her head leaning between them as if she were listening to the heart-murmur of the world. Her eyes were closed, and she was breathing with her mouth open, her fangs hanging laxly from the roof of her mouth.

He didn't dare touch Khelin, but his own bhirhir he could rouse. As he passed her, he shook her to awareness. "Get Ley!" he hissed. Then he took off after the kren again.

Ley and Arshel caught up with Khelin and Zref as they reached the broken Altar Stone. It was a different substance than any other stone, but the color could hardly be discerned in the fading light. Khelin went to it as if drawn, knelt, spread both his hands on it, and froze, listening.

Ley pulled up short, looking from Zref to Khelin. Then he wrapped his coat tighter against the whipping wind, and used his body to shelter Khelin from the worst of it as he examined his bhirhir.

"Zref," asked Ley, "do you think I should try to distract him? He's not raising venom now."

"Arshel," asked Zref, "have you ever seen a blue or a purple act like this?"

"No, but maybe Shui and Iraem have. I'll get them."

She whisked away as if blown by the wind. Zref circled to stand across the Altar Stone from Khelin. Clearly, the kren was deep into some inner experience.

Could I have built this imitation Crown? Zref discarded that idea. According to Arai, Zref had stopped building Crowns after he'd built the Maze, because the two powers were incompatible. Zref still felt queasy being here but not enough to drive him away from his brother.

Arshel returned with the rest of their group. They spread out, examining Khelin. Then Arai knelt at the Altar Stone, leaned over and put his own Theaten hands onto it. He looked up at Zref and said, "I think he's remembering."

Immediately, Zref knew. "Let's help him," he called to his aklal. The nine of them gathered about, putting their hands on the stone as Khelin had, and closing their eyes.

Zref felt it then, like a tangible thing, a warm cloak gathering about him. It was a musical chord in full resonance, a rainbow at full circle, a forest in full bloom, a completion that could not be sundered once it had existed.

Time stretched. But the only image in his mind was of a deep well with black water lying still at the bottom. He kept the water still, but another gazed in its surface.

When they came out of it, Zref found himself standing atop the altar stone, his hands raised to the dome of stars.

Around him, the others stirred. Khelin fell back from the stone, folding down on his haunches and forward to bury his face between his knees as if he were in his sandbed. Ley went down beside him, not quite daring to put his arm around Khelin's shoulders in public, but almost in that position.

On a random gust of wind, Zref heard a shrill voice comment, "I suppose an Interface can get away with anything." He realized his position was tantamount to sacrilege.

He jumped down, nearly turning his ankle, and hunkered beside Khelin. "Rozdiben!" The word was out of Zref's mouth before he knew it was a name Khelin had once been known by.

Khelin's head snapped up, his eyes piercing Zref. "Tschfa'amin!" He threw his arms around Zref, whispering a short trembling sentence, "I know where the Object is hidden!"

CHAPTER TEN
Shattering the Crack

Khelin's announcement was torn away by the wind. The lights came on—rising on slim poles, casting wavering shadows through the harsh mist. Revealed by the light, Zref was soon besieged by requests for Interface services. Hours later, when everyone was thoroughly chilled, the Guards served them hot tea and cakes in the foyer of the museum, and Zref was dragged about the displays making entries and correlations with never a moment alone with Khelin.

Sixteen hours after they'd left, they returned to their suite, the humans shivering, the kren lethargic from the chilling, and Waysjoff complaining of the damp grit in its fluff. They adjourned to hot soaks and exhausted slumber.

Seven hours later, they reconvened over breakfast. The others were there as Arshel and Zref arrived. Zref sank into his favorite chair, Arshel beside him. They discussed the evening's experience, while Khelin's gaze rested on Zref, and he refused to answer queries. "Zref, I haven't even told Ley. It's up to you."

Zref double checked their security. "Tell them."

"When the Empire of Stars was breaking up," said Khelin, "and we couldn't protect the Maze, Zref delegated me to hide the Object. Then he went into the Maze and gave his life to extract it from its place and get it to me."

Gazing at Zref as if he'd never seen him before, Khelin added, "All these lifetimes, Tschfa'amin, I've blocked my memory of being Mazemaster so I wouldn't even know I knew the secret. But you showed me—yourself. And I knew who I'd been. Then you brought me to a new Crown—almost a Crown—and I couldn't keep the memory buried any longer."

Ley put both his hands over Khelin's, a bhirhir's gesture which Khelin welcomed, despite his purple's control.

"You mean," asked Iraem, "Zref built Stonehenge?"

"No," denied Arshel. "A Crown Engineer named Zuurlish was killed in a crash on Earth, so he reincarnated there. His sense of mission, to build Crowns for new colonies, drove him to work several lifetimes to build one."

The name meant nothing to Zref. He asked Khelin, "Do you want to tell us where the Object is?"

"You don't remember?" asked Khelin. "Even though you called me Rozdiben?"

"No," answered Zref. "I don't know why I said that."

"I blocked those memories," said Khelin, "because you ordered me to be sure the Object could not be located. You, yourself, particularly didn't want to know."

Zref thought about that. "Then maybe you shouldn't tell me until I remember why I gave that order."

"Zref!" exclaimed Arshel. "We have to destroy it."

"But I don't know how!" argued Zref. "Do you?" He looked about at them all. At their blank looks, he decreed, "Then let's drop it. We must concentrate on strengthening our aklal to protect Khelin from another attack by the Enemy, because now he does know what She wants to know. And I think we should start by comparing our dreams."

The discussion revealed they had each had dreams of the Maze, and later lives in which they'd been mate, child or parent to each other. Zref, correlating all the new details, including Jocelyn's claim to have been mate to the Enemy during Her first walking of the Maze, summarized. "We seem to have spent millennia repairing the damage done by turning the Persuaders loose on the galaxy."

"But it took this long," said Arai as if a puzzle had been solved, "because the Enemy has been working against us!"

"And we're finally strong enough to win," said Shui.

"One thing worries me," said Khelin. "If Jocelyn was once mate to the Enemy, that explains why she's an open channel into our aklal. But she was also once mate to me, and is now mate to my bhirhir, which means I'm open to her."

"But," said Iraem, "the Enemy has already tested you, and you gave Her nothing. Zref should be the next target."

Neini, sitting next to Arai, clutched his arm fiercely. "Then it's a race! Zref has to remember how to destroy the Object—and why he's not to know its whereabouts—before the Enemy finds out that we know."

"Maybe," said Waysjoff, "Zref is not to know because the Enemy believes he knows? Zref is drawing fire from Khelin."

"If anyone is drawing fire," said Ley, putting his arm around Jocelyn's shoulder, "it's Jocelyn."

She looked more exhausted than the rest of them, for the medics had allowed her out of bed only the day before the trip to Stonehenge, and she had insisted on going down. She said, "I wish I could analyze all those dreams. It was mostly delirium, but there might be a clue in it."

Ley shook his head. "Dwelling on such nightmares can threaten sanity."

Khelin said, "But there are safe methods for recalling such material to dissipate trauma. Shui is an expert."

"I could work with you on it," agreed Shui, but he looked at Zref, "if you think it's a good idea?"

"Unresolved conflicts can weaken resistance to the kind of attack the Enemy favors," said Zref. "It's worth the risk, if you all agree." They nodded, and Zref rose.

They had a long, long trip to Pallacin, their next stop, so the discussion adjourned, but as Zref was left alone for a moment with Arai, the Theaten gestured Zref to his chair.

"Do you know how to use the holocase yet?" asked Arai.

Zref took it from his pocket. "Every time it's moved, it shows a new image, repeating only in different sequences. Without communications, I can't read its program."

The Theaten deliberated, then said, "Zref, hidden in those images is a comnet code accessing the most private file of Glenwarnan, containing all the lore preserved from the First Lifewave. I believe you, yourself, gave it to us so you could now reclaim it. I'd tell you the code, but—unless you find it for yourself, it might be dangerous."

Zref fingered the holocase. Not so long ago, he'd have destroyed anything that offered First Lifewave ideas. He'd become an Interface, sacrificing so much to dedicate his life to preventing the mixing of past and present. But maybe he, like Khelin, had shunned memory to protect a secret. "This," said Zref, "is the Glenwarnan material under vow of secrecy?"

"Yes," agreed Arai. "But if you weren't an Interface, you'd have remembered it all by now. Since you are an Interface, you probably could crack the locked files anyway."

"Not without violating the Guarantees," said Zref, "which would kill me." He pocketed the case again, and agreed to study it. As he went toward the pond room where Arshel was waiting, he asked himself for the thousandth time which meant more to him: this half-glimpsed past binding his family/aklal who were becoming ever more dear to him, or his dedication to the Guild and its policy against First Lifewave research. He didn't know. Maybe he'd never have to choose.

He was convinced, for Guild or karma, they *had* to get to the Object first to prevent it from being used—even if that meant destroying a thing of such potential value. Maybe the holocase would show him another way to stymie the Enemy.

Arshel was scrolling something across the deskpad. He peeked over her shoulder, seeing the inscription from the plaque at the gate to the City. She said, "That last sentence. They've never translated the middle section."

It read: IF THE MAZEHEART IS FOUND—(some untranslatable and illegible words)—DESTROY ITSELF.

"Zref, this may tell how to make it self-destruct!"

"I've watched the archeolinguistics journals, hoping for that. But—nothing. We don't know the Object will destroy itself. Maybe it makes something else self-destruct."

"You don't want to destroy it!" she accused, glaring.

He couldn't deny it. "It might be impossible to replace it, if someday it's needed. Yet destroying it may not *prevent* another from being made. In fact, if someone tried and botched it, it might cause more harm than this one has."

"Do you really think this one wasn't botched?"

He shrugged sadly. "I believe it's a good thing, but not to be *unearthed now*. Jylyd said I've got to convince you of that." *And Sidenl said she's my key*.

"Yes," she said, also sad. "But I reject that. I just hope your vow won't bind us even after we've destroyed it."

"Maybe, it's already been destroyed." But they couldn't live on such a tenuous hope.

As the study routine set in again, Arshel gave a seminar on the early days at Pallacin and her key discovery there—the Globe of Ossminid, the solid gold sphere in which was embedded, in different gold alloys, a model of the Globe of Stars from which the Empire of Stars had been governed.

Either Shui or Iraem was always with Zref, but the general tenor of public opinion aboard was lighter. Arai, Waysjoff and Neini disappeared into their suite for days at a time. Jocelyn got Ley and Khelin involved in her dance exercise course which the Captain emphasized as important during this long jump. Iraem and Shui dragged Zref to the dancing, insisting his physical fitness was as important as his safety, but they danced with Arshel.

Once, though, when Jocelyn chose Zref to partner a demonstration, he saw Ley leave the room followed hastily by Khelin. After that, Jocelyn started pairing him with Neini to show form. But soon, Arai withdrew into a tense silence, and Neini's temper became ragged. Even an Interface could see what had happened, so Zref drew Arai aside one evening.

"What do you want?" asked Arai tensely.

"You must understand, Interfaces don't mate."

"You're not exactly typical of the breed," he retorted, then sighed. "Look, Zref, Neini can't be any sort of mate for me. You're at least of her species, and she feels for you. If it works, I'll be happy."

"No you wouldn't. And neither would she. Because there just isn't anything there."

"If you're sure of that, you'd better talk to her!"

Zref caught her over the punch bowl after dance class. "I think we've a misunderstanding to clarify."

She looked up at him, eyes limpid. "I've been afraid of that. You mean there's no hope?"

"Neini, the man I once was wants to tell you you're very attractive, and could have any human male in this ship for a smile. The Interface *remembers* but doesn't feel it."

She looked down. "I knew. I just couldn't believe—"

"I'm flattered," answered Zref. "But remember, if a bhirhir is ever interested in you, his bhirhir will approach you—or possibly Arai. It's clear how you two are."

She stared after him with wide eyes, but a few days later, Zref caught Neini, Jocelyn and Arshel laughing in intimate friendship, and he flushed with inward *caring* for his new family. How could he ever give this up? But if keeping it violated the Guarantees, it would kill him.

One day, Zref was in his office waiting for a student who

was late for an appointment, and pondering the holocase trying to divine the hidden comcode when Neini came in.

"We've just written a new novel. We've decided to go amateur, and put it into the Open Catalogue to see if anyone will read a Meguerian without the Lantern imprint."

Zref thought it over. "The Meguerian reputation will sell it, but are you sure Lantern can't sue you for this?"

"It's new material, but it's pure Meguerian."

"You don't need an Interface to enter an Open title."

"No. But first we wanted to put it into the *Epitasis* library Open. Only we couldn't figure out how!"

Zref averted his gaze, found the price list, and put it on his desk monitor for her. "You're right, they've made it ridiculously complex. What's your title? I'll do it."

"No," she said, "that was the other thing I have to talk to you about. This is a book Lantern would never let us write—about the evils of Ossminid's reign, and how he destroyed both Crown and Maze by trying to master both. If the Enemy was Ossminid, maybe you should read it first?"

She had a point. "Maybe we should all read it first?"

The whole group had rarely met during the first weeks of the Pallacin leg. Now Zref called a meeting after dinner.

"A new Meguerian?" grinned Ley. "When do we get it?"

A chorus of cheers went up, and Zref cheered with them, then added, "This would be our first aggressive move."

"What will the Enemy's counter move be?" asked Iraem.

"Depends," said Shui. "What could this book do for us?"

Neini said, "Thumb our noses at Lantern, that's all."

"I wouldn't put it that way," said Waysjoff, and everybody laughed, for it was a moot point whether a Jernal had a nose. "We wrote this book because we need the money."

"And because we have faith in it," added Arai. "If it's read widely enough, it might erode the Enemy's aklal."

Zref said, "But this book is the only progress we've made these last few weeks. I seem no closer to memory than ever. Jocelyn still shrinks at the mere mention of what was done to her. Does anyone have anything else to offer?"

A resounding silence filled the sitting room. Zref said, "Then let's read it, and try it out onboard. These people seem totally enamored of the glamorous view of Ossminid Lantern's selling now. It should be a real test."

Ominously, Waysjoff said, "Then we should get set for a real attack. Zref says we've 'constituted' our aklal, and that should protect us, but I don't feel any different."

"I know why," said Khelin. "When you write together, you spend days in your own triune aklal state. You're so used to it you don't notice when the larger group forms."

Arai's ruddy complexion paled. "We do not—"

Khelin just stared at him until the Theaten crumpled. Zref said, "You've constituted them, Arai. I thought you knew."

Neini moved to comfort Arai. "We've never abused it!"

Khelin lectured, "We're all members of groups which are in turn members of other larger groups so each of us is tied into all life everywhere. An aklal is a group of people with common emotional responses to a common experience—such as dreaming about a novel's characters. The stronger the emotion, the more powerful the aklal. If every member feels the same thing at the same time, the power of the aklal to affect events is increased orders of magnitude. An aklal of individuals, in physical contact, trained to focus all levels of consciousness coherently, acting in emotional synchronization, can achieve—miracles."

"Individuals have performed miracles," said Waysjoff.

"True," answered Khelin. "It's the difference between dancing a solo and dancing in a chorus. It's all dancing."

"But," said Jocelyn, "a chorus of soloists would be ever so much more powerful. If you could get them to cooperate."

Neini agreed. "And Zref calls us to cooperate." He looked about at them, sprawled over chairs and floor in various exhausted attitudes. "But I don't think Zref can remember alone. After he's read our book, we're going to have to convene to do for him what we did for Khelin."

Read their book? But her cryptic remark became clear the moment he opened to the novel. It was titled *Phailan Atrocities*. Chilled, he forced himself past the opening, and became engrossed in the realistic dimensionality of the story. It hummed through his unremembered dreams, and in the morning, it seemed everyone else had felt the same. They voted by acclamation to release the novel onboard, though Neini had a hard time convincing Arai he hadn't abused power.

For the next two days, the three writers were unapproachable. Neini's ordinarily well groomed fingernails became raggedly bitten, Waysjoff took on an unkempt look, and Arai withdrew to his own room refusing to speak to anyone.

Iraem thought of leaving various public screens tuned to scenes from the novel, and then it was quickly discovered. Responses began to come in. Soon, mealtime discussions revolved around this new amateur writer who'd usurped the Meguerian byline. But even those who adamantly preferred the new Lantern utopia novels to the black tragedy, agreed this new amateur created Meguerian's haunting aura of reality.

Gradually, a swelling wave of argument rolled through the ship, regarding Soul Dispersal as pure fantasy, but arguing pragmatically. Ossminid's wishfulfillment utopia was one thing, but uniting Crown and Maze would have rendered all Crown communications untrustworthy—as once Interfaces were disturbed because a Wild Interface could read Guild private files and betray commercial, and personal, secrets. Distrust would have paralyzed the First Lifewave just as it had the Hundred Planets. If Persuaders used the Crowns to force people to trust the Crowns, it would sow wider distrust of the Persuaders who were mortal and could be killed. Without Persuaders to keep the uneasy peace, the galaxy would have dissolved in war. Which it apparently had.

The *Epitasis* aklal gradually wakened from its romance with Ossminid's utopia, and talk of recreating it subsided.

"I told you so," said Waysjoff at breakfast in the privacy of the suite on the fourth day. Its fluff was now meticulously groomed. It looked every inch the celebrity.

"I never doubted the power of the book," replied Arai, rejoining them. "I just hadn't let myself realize where that power came from."

"I'm amazed," said Neini, "the Enemy has allowed it to infect this Lantern sub-aklal without retaliating."

"Maybe She doesn't know," said Zref. "We're skirting the edge of the comnet. I can barely sense my private file. If this Captain wanted to kill me, she could simply head for a frontier planet such as Laleen. Without the comnet, I'd die as my autonomic nervous system ceased function."

Arshel, hearing this for the first time, came to sit closer to Zref, alarmed. "When will you regain contact?"

"Forty-three hours," answered Zref. "By midnight we'll

have reached the farthest point."

Pleased, Khelin asked, "No strain in answering?"

"I still have *Epitasis*," said Zref.

Arai said, "Could the Enemy have planned to kill you by running the ship too far after we'd located the Object for Her? And now She can't because you have *Epitasis?*"

"Null speculation," answered the Interface flatly.

Khelin prompted, "Did you call us here because you're losing the comnet?"

Arshel was tense. Zref squeezed her hand reassuringly. "Yes," he answered. "I've no new memories. If the aklal can help me, it will be while the comnet's influence is least."

They agreed to make the attempt at midnight.

"Zref, you're scared," accused Arshel that night after he'd expressed her and they were dressing for dinner. He let the Interface's nonresponse to statements keep him silent. She rephrased, "Can you tell me you're not scared?"

"No," he answered.

"Zref, don't treat me this way."

He hadn't been Interface with her for a long time. Her presence opened the crack in the floor of his mind, letting him draw on a human self. "I don't know what I feel, Arshel. Maybe the aklal will have to overcome my resistance. I don't know what that'll do to me, but it may have to be done."

"Don't pretend clinical detachment with me!" Her venom sack throbbed with emotion. Then she threw her arms around Zref, the fine scales of her face scratchy against Zref's chest. "Don't you dare die! You hear me? Don't you dare!"

He smoothed the fluff which now stood out about her head in all its silver glory. It felt like soft feathers, not stiff and brittle as before molt. "I'll survive if you do."

Arai came early, and signaled at Zref's door, taking him out into the sitting room while Arshel was meditating over her beadstring. "You haven't gained the Glenwarnan access yet, have you?"

"No," admitted Zref. "And that's a puzzle, for I've used the *Epitasis* logic units shamelessly. Any Interface would declare there's no code here." He waved the holocase.

"Of course. Did you use logic on a nonlogical premise?"

"No. Such a premise would be part of the Glenwarnan

teachings—which I don't have. This," he brandished the holocase, "is only a mnemonic, not meant to teach the code."

"Oh, no," said Arai. "Each one who finds his holocase, has to decode it. We're sworn not to give it."

"I see," said Zref. "And how was it protected from the Wild Interface?"

"During that time, the file was wiped clean, and ... ly in writing. The reentry was completed only recently. It's . very long file."

"Arai, could the contents of that file have been given to someone unauthorized, before the Wild Interface?" The Enemy might have gotten the First Lifewave technology used to create the Wild Interface from the Glenwarnan files.

"No," answered the Theaten flatly. "It cannot be given. It can only be discovered."

Before Zref could pursue that, the others began to arrive. In moments, the room was transformed into a temple evoking every devotional impulse known among them. They had never discussed deity. As far as Zref knew, the Mautri ignored all concepts of deity. The others brought their symbols with them without embarrassment.

When Neini suggested a formal invocation of the Creator, the kren consulted each other by glances, and Shui asked Khelin, "Should we retire while they do that?"

Khelin looked worried, then caught Zref's eye. "I believe it'd be more dangerous, but if you stay, we'll stay."

Zref asked, "Why do you say it'd be dangerous?"

Khelin answered, "Deity can be approached only in the extremity of terror, with soul-shuddering awe, and utmost preparation, without intention to remain mortal thereafter. One doesn't call upon Deity lightly or involve Deity in mortal affairs such as this. We are called priests, but we are not priests of Deity. We are priests of mortality."

In the ensuing silence, Zref said, "May I suggest a compromise? Before we convene as aklal, let those who wish to, invoke. But after we unify, let's dismiss such thoughts and concentrate on perceiving the shape of our mortal lives."

"Well spoken," said Shui, much relieved.

The others agreed, and so they took time to work privately before Zref suggested the white cube and green globe image.

Khelin interrupted him. "That might be too powerful for this first try. Let's have Arai convene—"

"No!" The Theaten burst out, then said more softly, "I admire Zref's courage, but I can't—won't—emulate."

Zref could see Arai's fear as a throbbing mist about him. "Khelin, it'd be better if you convene us. Tell me what to do." *Will they ever write together again?*

Khelin sighed. "We need an image of our own which will be to us the centering talisman of this aklal. Zref, you showed me once an artist's reproduction of the Maze as seen from above. Do you have that on board?"

"A moment," replied Zref. "I can fetch it." Khelin had been distracted in mating when Zref had found the drawing, but Zref had kept it in his private file. He opened now, and called the image to the comtap screen in the sitting room. There was a time lag since they were so far out now. Then the screen lit the whole room with a desert-colored light.

"Does that look familiar to anyone?" asked Khelin. The view showed high walls outlining a precinct divided into winding hallways by curving walls. In the center of the maze a roofed area must have housed the Mazeheart Object.

"It's the wrong color," complained Arshel.

"What color should it be?" asked Khelin.

"Blues and ocean-greens, pinks and yellows, and a little purple. The central roof should be a rust-red. Like the colors of our body feathers—I mean, their body feathers."

"Zref?" asked Khelin.

"I—don't—know..." said Zref, thinking he'd been asked to comment on the rightness of the image. The shape of the paths through the maze was much too easy to see from above like this, making it too easy to walk it.

"I mean can you tint the picture for us?" said Khelin.

"Oh." Zref played back what Arshel had said, coloring the portions of the maze as she made critical comments.

"Now," said Khelin, "is there any way you can make that picture stay there without yourself exerting influence?"

"Certainly," replied Zref, and inscribed the image in the *Epitasis* memory he used for his own purposes.

"Good, then also arrange whatever you must in order to close as completely as you can. Forget you're an Interface."

That command sent a shiver through Zref, but he turned over his routine scanning duties to an *Epitasis* program and said, "I'll be alerted only in a major disaster. I'm essentially out of the system now."

Then Khelin placed Zref and Arshel at the center of a semi-circle the rest formed facing the comtap screen which now cast a blue-green hue onto them. He made them lie supine so they couldn't see the screen. In a low, relaxed voice, he coached them through a long sequence of slow breathing and relaxation as they recalled every detail of the image, "Until you can see it with your eyes shut, with your mind shut."

As he spoke, Khelin moved about the room, like an instructor marshaling a class. Zref felt Arshel relaxing as Khelin continued, and he guessed this took her back to Mautri when Khelin had been her instructor.

Eventually, Khelin worked around to the center where Zref and Arshel lay. The first time by, he ran his open hand in front of their faces, and then all down their bodies. Zref was aware of the movement, but didn't care enough to focus on it. The second time around, Khelin took Zref's hand and placed it on Arshel's, pulling Zref's arm straight out from his side. Then he removed Zref's slippers and put Zref's right foot against Arshel's.

The kren rearranged all of their limbs until they lay on their backs, arms straight out from their sides, legs apart, feet everted. In the warmth of the suite, Zref relaxed, even ignoring the languorous memories of Sudeen flickering up through the crack in the bottom of his mind.

Khelin seated himself between Zref's head and Arshel's, admonishing them to hold the image of the Maze. Zref could have called that image up, but remaining closed, without access to his mind, he couldn't even remember Khelin's description of it, but by this point he didn't care. He was floating, and it was too nice to disturb. The crack in the floor of his mind was oozing random memories.

Khelin's soft voice evoked the visual image of Zref as he'd appeared to them several times, in feathers. Zref could not track it because the words evaporated from his mind as soon as they were uttered, as if he weren't recording them.

In a distant panic, he wondered if the ship had gone out of range of the comnode. But the panic couldn't penetrate the delicious peace engulfing him, and it subsided.

Dimly, Zref recognized Khelin's use of his name, Tschfa'amin. Khelin was sharing with them his memory of studying under Zref at Mautri. Some images resonated in Zref's consciousness. A lifetime before he was called Tschfa'amin, he and Khelin had been bhirhirn studying at Mautri together, until Khelin had fallen behind.

Delicately, in words meaningless to non-bhirhirn, Khelin related a potent memory of Zref taking the dark purple degree then striving for the white, to molt without a bhirhir's assistance. Khelin was in the dark blue degree feeling all the terror of a bhirhir abandoned.

Arshel's hand turned under Zref's, and gripped him hard. He felt her tremor of fear as if it were his own.

And the fear was his own, billowing up from under the floor of his mind as the crack shook and widened as if a volcano were pushing upwards. That floor had been laid by the Guild surgery, and the Guarantees had been set into the very cells of his brain in order to protect that floor.

He heard Khelin regressing yet another lifetime, calling upon others to remember their encounters with Zref in distant lives, evoking from each of them in turn a memory of Zref. Echoes filled Zref's consciousness, as if he'd accessed a snarled repeater circuit between two comnodes. Khelin's words touched off violent spasms of swirling echoes underneath the crumbling floor of his mind.

None of this had quite the power needed to shatter the bottomless peace that held him bemusedly elsewhere. But then Khelin began to conduct them through the Maze.

The Maze sprang into his mind, newly fashioned and gleaming brightly in the sun—gleaming with more than light, set in place by more than mortar on stone, trapped around on every plane of existence with more than ordinary guardians.

Momentarily, the image lived within his mind, and then the inner gravity that kept his thoughts in order failed. In a swirling whoosh, he fell into the glowing magma upwelling from the bottomless chasm beneath him. Panic seized him, and he convulsed. With a roar, he sat up. "No!"

Dizzy-starred blackness whirled about him, flowed over him and into him, detaching consciousness.

I really am dying.

CHAPTER ELEVEN
Glenwarnan Secrets

"Maybe he lost touch with the comnet."

"If that were so, he'd be dead. He's breathing."

"Khelin, *do* something!"

That last was Arshel, clutching Zref's hand tightly, her barely controlled panic penetrating him, surging up through the loosely reassembled fragments of the floor of his mind.

With a convulsive twist, he fled the threat.

Rough kren hands caught at him. Human hands pushed him down again. Khelin. Ley. He smothered a whimper.

"Wait, Arshel," Khelin warned her off. "Zref?"

Panting, Zref opened his eyes. Shui and Iraem were kneeling at his feet, Khelin and Ley at his shoulders. Shui said, "He used to have seizures like this."

"No," gasped Zref, as panic subsided. "I wasn't open. I think—Guarantees—triggered." The image of the Maze floated into his mind—not from the comnet, though.

Khelin's hand spread over his forehead, the membrane connecting thumb and forefinger across the bridge of his nose. Khelin removed his hand, saying to Arshel who reeked of fear-venom. "A memory came."

"Yes," agreed Zref, struggling to sit up and tend Arshel. Ley supported Zref's back. Arshel had both hands plastered to her face, half hiding the pulsing venom sack, and she seemed afraid to breathe. The sight stirred the unsteady floor of his mind, making him queasy. He drew her close and whispered, "My memory changes nothing between us. I saw only the Maze—just as you described it."

She began to breathe again, and with relief Zref let her go and crossed his arms over his middle as tension drained from him, his body shaking until his teeth rattled.

Khelin issued orders, and within minutes the room had been transformed back into the sitting room, with soft lights, comfortable chairs, and the aroma of hot drinks.

Ley massaged the knots out of Zref's shoulders, then lifted him into a chair, Arshel hovering helplessly when Zref begged her not to touch him yet. Finally, when they'd all settled again, he had to describe what had happened to him.

Neini and Jocelyn nodded amazed. "Yes, that's what I saw, too!" said Jocelyn. "The whole thing *glowed*, not with color or light, but like Stonehenge—vivid!"

"Yes," said Waysjoff. "I don't perceive color the way you do, so Arshel's description wasn't real, but Khelin's was. It may have been a memory."

The Theaten nodded in practiced imitation of the human mannerism. "You were there with us."

Zref asked, "Arai, what do you know that you're not telling us?"

"Nothing. Sidenl might know more than I about us, but I think he told us all he was sure of. And much of what I seem to know is only personal interpretation, easily misleading."

"This," said Shui, "we learn also at Mautri. Very few fragments of the past pertain to the future. But I think Zref's memory of the Maze does."

Iraem added, "I think it's the most hopeful sign we've had because it means, Zref, that you can remember."

Cautioning them that his imagery was only a metaphor, Zref described how Arshel's emotions broke up the floor of his mind. "So she triggered my reaction. Closer to the comnet, it might have killed me." He touched her gingerly.

Khelin agreed. "If we'd used the immensely powerful techniques you advocated, we'd have destroyed you. Now I say that's enough. We must all sleep, and recuperate."

Alone with Arshel, Zref was surprised when she asked hesitantly, "Do you think you could manage to express me?"

He flung aside his jacket and came to her sand bed. "Of course. I'm not rejecting you." He tried to explain. "We are bhirhirn, but I don't claim proprietorship over your talent any more than you do over the Interface. You didn't mean to interfere with the Guarantees that bind me!"

He worked with her, tentatively permitting himself the rich, real sensations of true human emotion, yet torn by the memory of the price exacted for a full contact with those emotions. Yet he knew he couldn't ever give this up. He tried to communicate only that through his touch.

Later, as he lay awake deciding not to do Khelin's reverse memory exercise tonight, he was aware of the floor at the bottom of his mind surging like the surface of an ice-bound sea. Shunting aside fear for his sanity, he slept.

By noon, there was no more time lag with his comnode contact, and he felt much better. He enjoyed doing the backlog of student requests, then, before supper, found himself in his office reviewing the Glenwarnan dioramas.

Memory of the ones he'd seen in person overlay his private file recordings of the holocase, so even the ones he hadn't seen in person gained a dimensional reality. Entranced by that inward display, he became Sirwini.

The monotonous blues took on a multi-hued texture. Coloring details that had seemed accidental gained profound meaning until he seemed to walk amid the life-size figures and into the holograph like a child in a wondrous daze.

It was an arduous test, yet it was sheltered and apart from the unimportant. It was a journey such as the Cruise should have been—from point to point simply to marvel at life, searching for its meaning, nature and purpose.

He had neglected to program a timer before entering the meditation, so only when his watchdog program told him someone was speaking to him did he come away from the image of six chain links assembling themselves in midair.

". . . if you're too busy to go, I'll—" said Arshel.

He held up one hand to stop her as he played back the first thing she'd said. "A new sensodrama that just came with the mail is being shown right now. But if you're—"

Mail? He accessed a peripheral file he kept updated in *Epitasis* and found a title: The Lantern sensodrama, *Healing Day*. There followed the list of credits, release dates across the Hundred Planets, and promotional copy.

"Arshel, do you know what that drama is about?"

"Just one of the Lantern novels. We ought to see it."

"But not together with everyone else aboard, and not at the same time. Where's Khelin?" As she denied knowing, he scanned *Epitasis* and discovered Khelin and Ley had entered the suite. He flashed notes onto the deskpads and comtaps in the rooms of every one of their group while searching for the rest. Jocelyn was finishing a dance class. Iraem was in it, but Shui was auditing a seminar across from Zref's office.

The three writers were standing in a lounge watching the promotional excerpts from the sensodrama. From Waysjoff's gestures, Zref surmised that it was criticizing. When nobody else was watching the particular display the writers were, Zref overprinted a message to them to come to the suite.

"Come on, Arshel, this could be serious." They sent Shui after Jocelyn and Iraem and headed for the suite.

Soon, they'd all gathered in the sitting room. Zref explained his intuition. "This's the first Lantern novel dramatization in years," he finished. "Why not?" He turned to Khelin, "If reading books can create and manipulate an aklal, create a psychic vortex so powerful it can draw the unaware into it, how much more powerful is a sensodrama?"

Thoughtfully, Khelin answered, "Orders of magnitude more powerful. The measure of that power is that when the first showing was announced, we were all set to run to see it."

Neini said, "As professionals, we have to see it."

"We all have to see it," said Shui. "But Zref is right, not together with the others. Can we arrange that, Zref?"

"Certainly. The apparatus is run by *Epitasis*, so I can operate it. But we shouldn't be in any hurry—"

"True," said Arai. "Zref, show us the release dates."

Zref threw the listing onto the comtap screen saying, "I could be paranoid to think this is the Enemy's countermove."

"No," denied Khelin. "It's a perfect move to protect the Lantern aklal from the new Meguerian title."

Arai asked, "Were these dates changed recently as a counter to our publishing? And how did the Enemy find out we'd published? We've been out of touch with comnet."

"We're still a little far out," said Zref, turning aside to open and query distant comnodes. When he came back to awareness, Khelin was speaking.

"... every event in the cosmos, leaves a—'kyralizth tracing,' a kind of etching on the substrata of reality. Anyone who can read kyralizth tracings can discover happenings anytime anywhere—at a price, of course."

Arai agreed, "We, too, have this theory. But only a few

legendary people have had such access—Zref?"

The bizarre contradiction to accepted theory they were discussing didn't sound so preposterous. Zref said, "Yes, the release dates were moved up by an edict which came down the Lantern hierarchy. I can't trace the order to its source, though. Lantern works through too many panels, boards, committees and commissions. The edict was issued two days after we published."

"Zref," asked Neini, "could the Enemy have read our book and predicted the onboard aklal's reaction?"

"Ordinarily not," he answered, "but Star-Treader Lines ultimately belongs to Lantern. *Epitasis* would respond to their override code, and if such a code was used to call out the book, given time, I might be able to trace it. Is it worth the search?" There were ways to follow a transmission across the comnodes. Only a Wild Interface, not bound by the Guarantees, could have erased all traces.

Khelin said, "That's your judgement. But if we assume the Enemy read the book, we can also assume the Enemy feared it'd undermine Her aklal. The sensodrama is a logical counter— but it was begun a long time ago."

"Which makes sense. The Enemy has been planning this cruise—and the battle with us—for years," said Ley.

"Perhaps," agreed Shui, eyeing the comtap. "But notice *Healing Day* premiered in Firestrip four days ago. When was the last time any sensodrama made its HP debut in Firestrip?"

"And the second showing was on Sirwin," added Arai.

Waysjoff voiced their common thought. "Near aklal Mautri and near aklal Glenwarnan."

They looked at each other in cold surmise. Zref said, "Simple enough to check what's going on at home." He sank into a lounge, prepared for a long opening, and dropped to Youta who was still at the Guild office in Firestrip, *"Have you any news of the MorZdersh'n family or of the city? We've been out of touch for days. Zref."*

Simultaneously, he queried Cheurlin, an Interface he knew only slightly, but who was stationed on Sirwin. The replies arrived staggered by the distances.

"I'll query your family. Firestrip is in the grip of a new, virulent epidemic, dubbed Firestrip-A. It propagates across

*species. No vaccine yet. Mortality rate about 30 percent—
mostly the young and the elderly. We'll be under a planetary
quarantine as soon as it's announced. Youta."*

And from Sirwin: *"We've had an outbreak of Firestrip-A.
We're the second planet to succumb and be quarantined. Here's
the local news summary. If you need more, ask, but I'm not
feeling too well. Cheurlin."*

Zref dropped thank-yous and related what he'd found.

Jocelyn clutched at Ley's hand. "There can't be any connection between a sensodrama and a pestilence!"

Not in the world Zref had once inhabited. But lately, reality
had changed its shape.

Deliberating, Khelin said, "A question to the Interface. Can
you access Public Health and determine if the first to succumb
attended the first showing of *Healing Day?*"

As Zref agreed, Ley muttered, "What an ironic title!"

Stoically, Shui said, "Maybe it's only a coincidence. What
could She gain by creating an interplanetary epidemic?"

Neini said, "I never expected to defend this monster that's
after us and the Object, but—to suspect *anyone* of such a
thing—the people who'd flock to that sensod, paying premium
prices for the first showings, would be the core of the Enemy's
own aklal. No, I refuse to believe—"

Her disjointed defense ground to a halt as Zref threw his
research results onto the comtap screen. Clearly, the epidemic
had started in the theaters showing *Healing Day*.

"I could see if those not attending first showings but suc-
cumbing early were relatives of those who did attend," Zref
added. "I'm reluctant to, though. Neini's right. I don't want
to *know* what kind of a thing is after the Object."

Arshel was shaking, but not raising venom. She put her
hand over Zref's in the bhirhir's gesture she'd avoided since
his collapse. "You've got to check it. We've got to know. Can
you be just Interface and work out the figures for us?"

It was the first time she'd wanted him to suppress his hu-
manity. He steeled himself and sent the query, the answer
bouncing right back onto their screen. Yes, the other recorded
cases were close associates of the attendees.

Zref dropped the data into the private file of the Interface
working with Public Health. *"Is there something unsanitary*

about the sensory contacts in theaters? Zref."

A few moments later, while Zref was relating his action, the answer came from the Interface—a human from Earth whom Zref had never met in person. *"Dear God! Jules."*

While they'd been talking, the shipboard theater showing had commenced, to a capacity crowd including the Captain and most of the bridge crew.

"We could become a plague ship, banned from Pallacin! Or prevented from leaving," said Jocelyn.

Ley said, "But Public Health will have a vaccine soon."

The conversation swirled away from Zref's consciousness as a message arrived from Youta. *"MorZdersh'n has been especially hard hit by the epidemic. The Elder MorZdersh'n has died. Three other humans in the family are hospitalized. Venom immunization seems to undermine human ability to fight this virus. The MorZdersh'n nursery is now an intensive care ward. They're asking Ley to come home. A letter and four tickets are waiting for you at Pallacin. Zref, you can't abandon a Guild commission! Youta."*

Zref could not speak. He waved Youta's message onto the comtap screen. Arshel looked from his face to the screen, and then read it aloud. Khelin and Jocelyn seized Ley's hands as the blood drained from his face.

But Zref was being Interface. Despite the reverberation of dread for his family trapped beneath the floor of his mind, he said, "So that's what the plague is for—to break up our aklal by taking us away from you all."

As if he hadn't heard that, Khelin, raising venom in slow pulsing throbs, asked, "Zref, can you fetch their letter from Pallacin for us? Please. Bill it to MorZdersh'n."

"Forget the billing," said Zref, fetching the letter. "Do you want this on your deskpad? It's addressed to Ley."

Ley was in no condition to decide, so Khelin said, "No. Here. And translate it, Zref."

Jocelyn got up. "I'm going to get him one of those tranquilizers they gave me. Can you hold him, Khelin?"

"Yes. Do that."

Zref could see Khelin's muscles bulging as he restrained Ley, whispering to him that he could do nothing from here, and if necessary they would go right home.

Zref put the letter on-screen, and drew Arshel close. He wasn't feeling the uproar of her emotions now, but he knew what she was going through. Kren felt little for their children given to the fosterage of a surparent. The surparent bonded to the child, and invested their life in the young one as a future of their own.

Yet Arshel felt strongly for Khelin in a way most unusual for a kren. And Khelin returned her affection in a way Zref could only call love. Arshel was relieved Ley was as concerned as any surparent could be; yet these were the only children she had, and the only ones Khelin had, too.

As Jocelyn came back with water and a capsule, they were reading the letter. Arshel said, "At least Skanqwin is safe at Mautri." All their other children, among the youngest in the house, were ill and in gravest danger.

"We know what we're asking," the letter finished. "But you two have duties here. Bring Zref if you can—and Arshel. But warn him of the quarantine."

Ley shuddered, and forced out his first words since the news. "You can't go, Zref. You carry freshwater and saltwater immunity. This plague could be deadly to you."

Khelin, anguished, whispered, "I could wish I'd hidden the Object on Camiat. But—no. We can't go there. Ley must, and we can't. Zref, what are we doing to do?"

"We must understand this move before we reach Pallacin," said Zref. "Are the children being attacked? What's going on at Mautri? Could the Mautri aklal protect them as well as we could? What can an aklal do against a virus?"

Khelin straightened. "Viral disease is a statistical process since it involves so many billions of viral individuals. An aklal can affect statistical processes. I'm sure Mautri is already working on this.

"But immunity is the other factor in disease. That's where the aklal mechanism can be most effective. Under a true master, an aklal can bolster or destroy the immune responses of individuals—or of large numbers of people. I've never heard of an aklal turning on itself, though . . ."

"I have," said Neini. "A mob is a temporary aklal, and among humans at least, the mob can turn on itself."

"Yes," agreed Shui. "Humans are versatile. Pack hunters as well as loners."

Shui's distracted air reminded Zref of Jylyd, who had been Shui's bhirhir. Surely the kren was worried about him. Zref asked Youta to set up a direct relay with Jylyd.

Ley turned haunted eyes away from the comtap screen. "If we refuse to go, will the Enemy kill them anyway?"

Khelin said, "From Pallacin, I'm going to call home."

The Elder MorZdersh'n had been Khelin's favorite uncle. If no others died, Khelin's surfather might end up running the family, or even Khelin himself. Some of the elders were people Zref had loved as a child. Some of them, he'd never cared for very much. But they were his family, too. They'd even accepted Arshel.

That's nonsense. The Guild is my family.

"Khelin's right," said Zref, as the sensodrama equipment went dark while the kitchen geared up for a late supper. "When we get to Pallacin, we'll have enough data to decide what to do. If Ley has to go to Camiat—perhaps we'll all go. Then would the Enemy think the Object's on Camiat?"

Without warning, all the *Epitasis* asteroid deflectors snapped up. The ship took evasive action, squirting signals at the nearest astrogation node.

Automatic overrides diverted power from the interior gravity to the engines. The floor tilted, throwing Zref and Arshel into Arai's lap, and tumbling Waysjoff onto Neini. The forcefield containers over the ponds and sandbeds held, but loose articles tumbled about.

Zref, diaphragm paralyzed, twisted to put himself between Arshel and the Theaten who wasn't immune to her. The shock had brought her fangs down to strike position, though her sack was not full. Zref got a hand into her jaw reflex point and coaxed the fangs back into place, simultaneously rolling them both off the Theaten, and onto the floor.

With Arshel under control, Zref, trying to force his diaphragm to move, looked to Khelin. Ley had diverted Khelin's strike into a mid-air voiding by pushing the kren onto the floor. Khelin's sack had been more than half full from the Camiat news, and Zref could still see the droplets in the air as the gravity failed in spots around the room.

Finally able to talk, Zref called out what *Epitasis* sensors showed him. "We're being attacked—a black ship very like the first one. Escort is taking the brunt of it."

As the Escorter fired on the pirate, Zref sent a note to the Escorter Captain's conning screen via *Epitasis*. "At your service. Zref." But he received no reply.

Meanwhile, he noted Shui and Iraem were clinging to a lamp stanchion, and had each other under control. Neini was now holding onto the Theaten, who had anchored himself to his chair with both his large, bony hands.

He turned back to the battle. "Our Escorter is giving chase to the pirate. *Epitasis* and astrogation show no other ships in our vicinity. Gravity coming on—now."

Zref called it to the second, and they all settled back with a sigh as Zref read out the damage reports. They'd lost one receptor antenna, the rest was cosmetic.

Personally, their group had sustained no injuries except for Khelin's embarrassment. But one of the kren stewards caught off guard among the sensodrama crowd had struck a passenger. Zref reported this, and only moments later was able to say, "Luckily, the passenger is Ciitheen. He won't die from it. Right now he's hallucinating happily!"

Khelin's embarrassment was nothing to that of the hapless steward who may have created another Ciitheen venom addict. They crowded around the comtap where Zref showed them the view in the bridge plotting scope of the two skirmishing ships hurtling into the far distance.

Zref put the same display on screens all over the ship. Chances were good the Captain could see the display, as could the other bridge personnel who would now be scrambling back to their posts. Zref ran a message onto all the screens. "Captain, pick up any comtap or deskpad and I'll make it your Command Station. Zref." *Epitasis* was so well designed, Zref wondered why that provision had not been built into her.

Soon, he was reading the Captain's voice through *Epitasis*. She was at a comtap outside the theater. "Zref! Good work, Master Interface." And she began issuing orders for course changes and attitude rolls to compensate for the missing sensor dish.

Zref executed her orders directly, then put her voice onto the bridge speakers so the crew could hear her.

On the bridge, several officers sat with their hands in the air watching the Captain's orders appear in words on their screens—translated to their native languages—as their boards executed the orders.

"Zref, give me shipwide address," she ordered at last, and in polite and urbane phrases, she begged the passengers' indulgence over the inconvenience, and promised all would be put to rights within hours. Though they couldn't now serve supper, breakfast would begin three hours early.

Just as she was concluding this speech, the plotting scope flared incandescent. When it cleared, there was nothing to be seen but an expanding globe of hot debris.

Gravely, the Captain commended the bravery of the Escorter Captain and crew and announced a memorial service to be held in the ship's theater at noon the following day.

She touched the tab Zref had designated to terminate the shipwide address, ordering, "Get me Eiltherm. Pipe it to my cabin. And send the ship's log directly to Star-Treader Lines. Then take the plotting scope off the comtap!"

Zref managed all three simultaneously, turning the Eiltherm contact over to the Captain as she arrived at her private tap. "Just tell Eiltherm who you want to talk to. I'm out of the circuits now. Zref." He had to use the astrogation antenna to carry this message because the standard mail antenna had been lost.

He came out of it slumped in a chair before the comtap. "Are they all dead?" asked Shui.

It took Zref three blinks to realize he referred to the people aboard the Escorter and the pirate. "Yes. No point in looking for survivors. There isn't a molecule intact."

Silence stretched as they all absorbed the shockingly swift loss. None of them had known the people aboard the Escorter. Yet they had given their lives valiantly.

"There's a leak in the Enemy's organization," said Shui.

"So She's fallible, therefore defeatable," said Iraem.

"The leak," said Neini, "must say we've a good chance to succeed. Those pirates don't want Her to get the Object."

Waysjoff, whose fluff had doubled its volume in fright, said, "Which means the pirates will surely try again."

Khelin, standing behind Ley, who'd collapsed into a chair, dazed by the tranquilizer, asked with tense dispassion, "Pirates—or privateers?"

If the real sponsorship of the Cruise had leaked, many planetary governments might fear the HP getting the object. The interstellar government called itself the Hundred Planets after its founding alliance, but it actually governed several hundred planets, and more than a hundred species.

"Zref," asked Shui, "when do we get another Escorter?"

"Probably before we enter Pallacin's orbital control," answered Zref. "The Captain's talking to Eiltherm now."

Neini asked, "Zref, can you determine if there has been a security leak about this Cruise?"

"The entire Guild is aware of the security blanket and would automatically report any breach," answered Zref. "But I'll see if anyone has a clue." He sighed, opened and dropped an "all-Interfaces" bulletin with the query.

They talked until the silences stretched wearily. Finally, Zref said, "We're exhausting ourselves getting nowhere. The Captain has ordered us hyperlight. We'll come out near a well-traveled approach to Pallacin. Let's all try to get some sleep. I'll flash you if there's any news."

As Zref took Arshel to their pond room, he dropped a note where the Captain would see it when she opened her log, giving the news of the epidemic.

"I don't think I'm going to sleep," warned Arshel.

"On this occasion, it would be reasonable to take something. We're going to have to make some difficult decisions soon. We can't afford to be exhausted."

While they were trying to soak out some of the tension, Arshel said suddenly, "All of this would make great sense if the Enemy knows we know where the Object is! The children are hostage to keep us from destroying the Object! Zref, She might even know you're regaining your memory!"

A horrifying vision. Zref replied, "If the Enemy were omniscient, She'd just read kyralizth tracings to find out where the Object is—or how to make another one."

"It doesn't take omniscience to read Tracings. Both yours and Khelin's regaining memory has certainly left clearer Tracings than any event of over three hundred million years ago!"

Zref's curiosity was engaged, and he wanted to ask, *How much of this theory do you understand?* Surely her training at Mautri included it as part of archeovisualization. But if he started that, she'd never get to sleep. So he suggested they sup on the fruit and Ciitheen klab left from breakfast.

She meditated while Zref contacted the Interfaces who'd helped him identify Balachandran as the person behind the modern galactic criminal known as 'Ossminid,' this time looking for the identity of the Enemy, the true reincarnation of Ossminid, whom Zref suspected had been the force behind Balachandran. He couldn't explain how he knew all this to the pragmatists of the Guild, so Zref set them to look for a Lantern Officer with an abiding interest in the Cruise, who was also behind the sensodrama *Healing Day*. He didn't expect results in time to help—but he had to try.

Zref stretched out on his own bed, on top of the covers. He didn't want to sleep. He felt that his own children lay dying, which frightened him because it wasn't an echo of Arshel's emotions, but his own, genuine feeling. If it got too strong, would he be blown out as he'd been during Khelin's memory experiment? He didn't dare ask the comnet.

Unfinished thoughts burbled up around jagged spikes of curiosity. Finally, he gained control by sweeping through *Epitasis*, aiding the clean-up crew. The monotony lulled him until he saw recent events from a distant perspective.

At the edge of sleep, he was aware of the images of the Glenwarnan diorama as they'd seemed to him in his office, and simultaneously, he beheld the Maze as Khelin had evoked it. Sirwini eyes, kren eyes, Kinrea eyes, and human mind all overlaid into a simultaneous truth about himself. Never, even after his surgery, had he lost the ability to see through the eyes and emotions of other species. That, in itself, was a form of past-life memory. Perhaps he'd been afraid of his ability to remember as Khelin had been of what he might remember?

In this perspective, Zref saw the images of the Glenwarnan diorama imbued with the same invisible light that had etched the Stonehenge monument and the Maze itself. The source of that energy: *conscious intent*.

He was still open to *Epitasis*, all its traffic flowing through him, and he was open to the general traffic of the local comnode, though he was transparent to it, not shaping or drawing upon it in any way.

At the concept, *conscious intent*, the comnet responded as

his own mind, accepting the phrase as a cued command.

And the Glenwarnan Guarded File was laid open to him.

It was huge. It took him a while to grasp the Sirwini method of displaying original text against later footnotes and modern arguments-in-progress. But it was clear that here was set forth a view of the mechanism of reality very different from that taught by modern science.

If Zref had not possessed the clue that in this view of reality the more important variable in estimating results was the intrinsic nature of the actor, not the nature of the action, he couldn't have followed any of it.

He became lost in the vision of a reality responsive to *intent* as well as *content* of actions.

He was certain now that he had the solution to one of the problems posed to the students on the Cruise—and perhaps he was able to see it because of all their research traffic he'd handled. These edifices were charged with a kind of energy generated by their builders' conscious intent to build to last. That energy was renewed by future generations in some cases—in others, works of the First Lifewave, the original charge had held. The Crystal Crown on Pallacin was probably the most spectacular case.

When his message drop filled with Youta's answer to his query about Mautri, he was shocked that hours had passed.

As he read that message, he felt as if he'd wakened from dream into nightmare.

CHAPTER TWELVE
Lifereadings

Without bothering to dress, Zref charged out into the sitting room, ignoring the stewards who were tidying up, and climbed to the door leading to Shui and Iraēm's room.

Triggering the door signal, he flashed their deskpad and comtap screens. Shui opened the door, glanced at Zref then back into the darkness, as he stepped out, closing the door. Zref sensed the two had been discussing what they feared most, being separated by death, or aspiration to the white.

"News from Mautri. They're as hard hit as MorZdersh'n. Jylyd's too sick to use a relay patch to talk to you."

The kren donned the intensified calm of a blue priest. "Thank you, Zref. Give me a moment to tell Iraem."

He went back inside. The stewards had finished, so Zref went down to get something hot to drink while waiting for Arshel to waken. It was almost time for the early breakfast they'd been promised, and Zref was about to order it brought in so they could discuss yesterday's developments when Iraem and Shui came out of their room dressed for the day.

They walked the mezzanine to Khelin's and Ley's door, not noticing Zref. When they'd rousted Khelin, half-dressed, and appraised him of the Mautri news, Shui said, "It's up to you, but I think *now* it's time to invoke."

Khelin considered, then bent over the railing to glance at Arshel's door and spotted Zref. "Is Arshel awake?"

"Probably," answered Zref, setting his steaming mug aside. He went in and found Arshel stirring. Waking her, he told her the news. "Khelin wants to talk to you."

"Of course," she agreed. She dressed swiftly, but tied on her green cape and collected her beadstring, asking, "Do you have any news of Skanqwin?"

"Youta couldn't get details on everyone, but he's not in any of the Camiat hospitals—which are quite full."

They met Khelin just coming from his own room, now dressed. "Jocelyn says we can use her room. Ah! Arshel, you'll sing the primaries. Shui has his tlient..."

The kren went on, totally incomprehensible to Zref, but with the air of a competent organizer suddenly given an improbable job. At length, he turned to Zref, "Does Youta know if the Sundown Ceremonies are still being held?"

Zref had never known the Ceremonies to be suspended, but he said, "I'll ask," and dropped the query to Youta.

"Also what time is it in Firestrip now?" asked Khelin.

That was easier. "Almost sundown."

"Good, then we're ready."

Jocelyn came out beside Ley who was explaining, "The Mautri consider the threat to Firestrip and the HP a proper reason to invoke Deity, but it's a private ceremony. Since they don't have mutual pond privileges, they need your room."

"I see. Actually, I think it's about time."

Zref said, remembering that Mautri invoked Deity with no expectation of remaining mortal, "The rest of us should pray in our own ways, then we can all have breakfast here." He sent in their standard order.

At that moment, the three writers appeared, Neini gazing curiously at the retreating backs of the kren.

As the newcomers were being brought up to date, two messages arrived simultaneously. The Mautri sundown ceremony had not been held now for three days, and was suspended for the duration. Zref flicked this onto the screen in Jocelyn's room, while motioning Arai aside. Relating his success with the Glenwarnan File, he added, "And this is the bad news. Glenwarnan is as hard hit by the epidemic as Mautri. Sidenl is still well, but he sends word his aklal won't be able to help us again soon. Apparently, they were aware when we evoked the cube. Now I understand how that works."

In Zref's expanding concept of reality, the entire universe was one huge comnet—every point connected to every other point, with every sentient mind like an Interface.

When they rejoined the others and brought them up to date, Zref adding that he'd set up a search for the Enemy's identity last night, Arai announced, "I'm going to pray for the enlightenment of the Enemy—being willing to give my life to accomplish that without abusing power."

Neini and Waysjoff agreed, but Zref said, "My life isn't mine to offer, but otherwise, yes, that's my prayer. I'll add, however, the vision of health among the ill, asking how to use our aklal to retard the growth of this virus."

Ley and Jocelyn agreed with Zref and they settled in their favorite chairs. Zref composed himself to allow the magma of emotion beneath the fragmented floor of his mind to rise, knowing only that self could pray. But it frightened him. He could stay open to it only a few seconds.

The prayer he'd spoken exploded into his consciousness, flashing a vision of the MorZdersh'n nursery before his eyes: the kren infants, usually actively demanding, lay quiet, some surrounded by sterile tubes and pumps. The silence was frightening, but even more so was an insubstantial, black dome stretching over the house, leaching away all vitality.

Offended, Zref flung the white-hot magma of his emotions at the blackness, scorching holes in it to let the health-giving sun of Camiat shine in. He was a viewpoint without body, but he seemed to turn in midair and look downward into the house. He bathed each of the children in pure radiance.

At Mautri and Glenwarnan he did the same—washing the ill in beautiful light, washing away the dark sickness.

When it came to the Enemy, he couldn't frame a request to Deity. Lifetimes, he'd assimilated the Mautri idea that it was an insult to imply, by supplication, that Deity wasn't already performing at optimum. Instead, he simply accepted responsibility for all he'd done, in whatever lifetime.

His meditation was interrupted by a scanner echo, and another and another—ships behind and around them.

They were sublight now, so he used an astrogation relay to identify those ships—but they were unregistered. He alerted the Captain seconds before the watch officer did, then added fresh news from the Guild Astrogation relay. A squadron of Escorters was approaching from ahead of them, assigned to them for all five remaining stops on the Cruise.

The Captain was on the bridge within minutes of Zref's first message, and she surveyed the scopes carefully before asking Zref to relay her orders to the approaching Escorters under Guild Security Seal so the pursuit couldn't intercept.

The Captain then dictated a series of rapid course changes, cutting days off their travel time. "And notify Pallacin Orbital Control we're coming in on an emergency approach. Use our missing dish as an excuse."

Zref handled the traffic swiftly, and then monitored the maneuvers. Once he relayed a refinement of trajectory to one of the Escort ships. The unregistered ships disappeared from the edges of their screens, and all breathed a sigh of relief.

By the time the kren rejoined the group, breakfast was ready. But almost immediately, Zref was called to the bridge to act as Ship's Interface on the approach to Pallacin. Orbital Control was worried about the missing dish and didn't trust *Epitasis* without a "real Astrogator" working her.

"This time," said Zref, "come with me, Arshel. It should be quite a show." He apologized that he couldn't take the rest of them onto the bridge during a planetary approach. "But I'll put the view onto the comtap here for you."

The approach was as routine as possible, considering they were one of the largest passenger ships in space, coming in almost two days early, encircled by armed Escorters. Zref worked with the local Interfaces to part the traffic before them and coordinate the movements of the squadron.

But then, since they were early, they had no ground accommodations. It was decided to start work on the exterior repairs immediately, with the excursion to the Crystal Crown to be on schedule, not early. The passengers, claustrophobic after such a long trip and anxious after the attack, were loudly disappointed when the Captain announced that.

At the early supper shift, Zref was shunned by some of the faculty and students. But others came to thank him for his work during the emergency and to apologize for those who were rude, believing the new rumor that they were in danger because the mysterious pirates were really after Zref. The Enemy, Zref concluded, was trying to repossess Her aklal.

Later, Khelin and Ley joined Arshel and Zref, bringing their desserts from the distant table where they'd been sitting. "There's no way to get down to the surface now," complained Ley. "We can't just sit here for two days—"

"There's a small ship leaving tomorrow to bring medical supplies to Camiat," said Khelin. "Could we get onto it?"

Zref had spotted that departure. "That ship will take six days to get to Camiat," he started when an item dropped into his file from his contact at Public Health. *"You were right, the theaters are unsanitary. Public Health is closing all senso-drama theaters for tests. Good work. Jules."*

He related that and said, "That will tarnish the effect of *Healing Day* on the Lantern aklal."

"But the damage has already been done," said Ley. "Zref, I only want to go home!"

"Considering that's what the Enemy wants you to do, do you really want to?" asked Neini, joining them.

Zref looked around and found Arai and Waysjoff standing behind him. "We're becoming conspicuous," he said.

Khelin asked, "If we can't get down to the surface, or even over to the Interchange Satellite, can we at least get a transtellar vidphone hookup?"

Waysjoff said, "Do you know what that costs?"

"The family needs to hear from us," declared Khelin. The strain of the last few hours was visible only in Khelin's mildness of tone and fluidity of movement, transforming him before their eyes into the model purple priest.

"Unfortunately," Zref answered, "that traffic is normally handled by the dish antenna that's missing."

"Isn't there any way?" demanded Ley.

Zref had never fathered a child, but he felt the surfather's desperation as a palpable force churning the floor of his mind. And an idea occurred to him. He shoved his half-finished dinner away. "Come on up to the suite, I want to try something."

On the way, Neini fell in beside Zref, and said, "Now we're back in civilization—should we publish our book?"

Waysjoff scuttled out of the path of another Jernal, brushing against Zref as it said, "With sensod theaters closed, the public is going to be hungry for new books!"

Shui and Iraem caught up with them at the lift cages. In the privacy of the lift, which their group filled, Neini consulted Arai and Waysjoff, then authorized Zref to put the book in the general galactic catalogue.

As the lift stopped near the suite, Waysjoff led the way muttering dire predictions of being left destitute on Camiat.

Jocelyn, together with one of her best students, a lanky

Almurali male, was approaching from the other direction as Arai answered, half joking, "We'll all join Mautri, then!"

Waysjoff fretted, "They wouldn't accept a hatchling!"

Jocelyn didn't hear because she was adamantly denying she'd ever said the pirates were after Zref. The Almurali's parting remark was drowned in kren laughter at Waysjoff's pessimism. Peripherally, Zref wondered if Jocelyn had started the rumor at behest of the Enemy, then forgotten. But then they'd arrived at the big comtap in the sitting room, and Zref was pre-empting circuits for his experiment, and running the catalogue entry for Meguerian. "While I'm at it, I'll set cross-indexed and run you a full ad in the New Books random flasher. You may make the main news index!"

When Waysjoff complained of the cost, Zref explained. "It'll cost, even with the Guild fee, the same as entering by hand into the general catalogue alone. An Interface is extremely efficient on large jobs."

The Captain's permission to monopolize *Epitasis* went on record, and Zref began patching transtellar circuits.

An Interface on the Interchange Satellite studied Zref's work critically, and began helping. Soon Rodeen and two other Guild supervisors were observing.

"Whose idea was this? It's brilliant. There must be hundreds aboard Epitasis *anxious to call home in the midst of this epidemic. Rodeen."*

Half a dozen Interfaces named Zref as the originator of the scheme to bypass the ruined dish antenna and transpose the frequencies to use the *Epitasis* tracking scope.

As Zref put the announcement of special transtellar vidphone service onto all the comtaps in *Epitasis*, Rodeen dropped to him. *"A request has been made for your presence at the offices of the MorZdersh'n Contracting Corporation on Camiat. Since they're a preferred customer, we've tried to comply. However, Public Health is using all of us who aren't ill. We can't replace you there, and Lantern intends to continue the Cruise despite the emergency, since the next two stops are clean. Your contract binds us. Rodeen."*

Zref came to awareness with the screen before them showing the MorZdersh'n family crest. While they waited for someone in the house to answer, Zref told them the bad news. "I must stay, and you must go. Khelin, is there any way for an aklal to join and work at a distance like that?"

"Yes, of course," answered the kren abstractedly. "Did we not engage Glenwarnan and Mautri? Ask not whether it can be done, but whether we are yet able to do it."

They waited an inordinate time for an answer, with Ley becoming more fretful by the second, no doubt imagining the house littered with untended dead bodies, kren in molt with no bhirhir to help, infants dying of neglect because all the adults were dead. The instant the pattern wavered, Khelin said, "Khelin calling from Pallacin. I need information."

The screen cleared to show a very young kren male, very handsome, but with an off-color cast to his skin tones that clashed with the yellow Mautri cape he wore. Thin and haggard, it hardly seemed to be Arshel's first son, Skanqwin.

"What are you doing there?" demanded Ley in the tones of a parent offended by a child's irresponsibility.

"Forgive me, Surfather. Jylyd ordered me here because I brought the disease into the house. My bhirhir is also ill."

"Bhirhir!?" exclaimed Ley. The child had been on the threshold of an early maturity, but—"Who? Inzin?"

"Yes, of course, Surfather. I thought you approved."

"Everyone approves of Inzin," Khelin reassured his son. Aside to Ley, he muttered, "He's not really too young!" And to Skanqwin, he said, "You don't look entirely well."

"I will not be unwell until my bhirhir can care for me."

That staunch bravery brought tears to Ley's eyes. But he ordered steadily, "All right, brief us on the situation."

"Sranther's funeral was yesterday. That put father's surfather Senior. He's too sick to work, but Trien thinks he'll survive. Finseni's on the desk, but building in the city has halted. Vital services are running, mostly understaffed.

"We're managing. Bhirhirn are caring for each other, and those well enough to move are providing food and medicine to the pond-bound. Six bhirhirn pairs are coping with the nursery, though there'll be another funeral tomorrow."

He listed off the parents of dead infants. "But all my brothers are better now. Trien, the medic who moved in to mate with Disden, thinks we've turned the corner. There've been no deaths today. I've been sick for three days, but I'm on my feet.

Something happened last night—at the Sundown—Father, has climbing ever been suspended before?"

"Once or twice," answered Khelin. "Arshel, Shui, Iraem, and I invoked last night, when we heard about it. I want you to tell Jylyd that. Also—"

Noting the dullness of Skanqwin's response, Khelin commanded Skanqwin to record, and then addressing Jylyd, he told of the events of the last few days, and their surmises, ending with an introduction of Jocelyn explaining they'd formed a tenaklal, nine of whom had created the Object.

Skanqwin said to Jocelyn, "I thought I recognized you, but I'm never sure with humans. I saw you in an aklal cell."

Khelin agreed, and told of having drawn Mautri and Glenwarnan together to help Jocelyn, who was now full wife to Ley, and thus a MorZdersh'n. Before the boy could register incredulity, Khelin pressed on describing their situation.

He used the Mautri technical vocabulary which even Zref couldn't follow. When Khelin had finished, admonishing Skanqwin to rid the house and Mautri of every item remotely connected with Lantern Enterprises—even things in their private pond rooms—Ley added, "I know you're awfully young to carry such a responsibility, but while you can, you must."

The delayed reaction was finally surfacing, and the boy was raising venom. He looked to Ley. "Surfather—"

"I will come home, Skanqwin. For you—for the children. Count on it. I'm counting on you."

"When? If you're on Pallacin now—"

Khelin clamped a hand on Ley's elbow, and without really consulting his bhirhir, said, "We can't come now. Jylyd will explain. Zref's been ordered to stay here, so we must stay. We have invoked for you, and we'll continue to fight for you from here. We couldn't do more if we were there."

Skanqwin wilted, then gathered the indomitable MorZdersh'n courage. "Don't worry. We'd probably all be well by the time you got here. Concentrate on your tasks."

Ley wiped the horrified look off his face before he turned from Khelin to the screen pickup. "No MorZdersh'n was ever prouder of a son than I am at this moment."

"Now listen carefully," said Khelin in his blue priest's command tone. "Find the ranking priest at Mautri. Show this recording, and have those who are well enough function in aklal. Join them if you can, to pull the energies into the house. If we can whip this at Mautri and MorZdersh'n, the city will also find the siege lifted. Understand?"

Khelin, aware of the cost of the call—as well as the enormous financial disaster represented by the epidemic during the short building season—started to say good-bye, but Ley edged him aside, to let his own be the closing remark to Skanqwin, the first child Khelin had given him.

"Skanqwin. This is an order. You will not, repeat *not*, blame yourself for this. We love you; we'll always love you; and we commend you for how you're handling this. Now, do as your father said, then go to Inzin, and welcome him for me."

When the screen blanked, Arshel leaned on Zref, venom sack heaving. "He was so feeble at his hatching. I was so afraid we'd done the wrong thing. I'll *never* regret it!"

Dennis had been her bhirhir at that first mating with Khelin. She'd never had a living child by any other mate.

While Zref soothed Arshel, Ley collapsed into the chair. "Do you realize we could be grandparents this year!"

Khelin said, "Oh, it'll take longer than that. But not much longer. Did you notice how he's changed?"

Arshel pulled herself together. "Yes. He's become so virile—so attractive. But his heritage is so visible."

The salt/freshwater crossbreeds seldom survived to maturity, and when they did, faced such enormous prejudice, Zref could understand Arshel's fears. To change the subject, he said, "You said we'd fight from here, but I don't see how. Every attempt I've made to remember has nearly killed me, and I suspect if I *do* remember, it *will* kill me. Then how will we destroy the Object?"

"I've been thinking about that since our session," said Khelin. "Great, powerful forces are compelling you to remember. With or without help, it's going to break through to the surface soon." He looked to Arai. "Zref's lives at Mautri have got to be the key to his surviving the upheaval of memory without bringing down the whole comnet."

"You want me to do another lifereading?" asked Arai. The Theaten folded his tall frame onto a rack before Zref. "The first time I got deep into him, I almost died with him in the Maze. Some people tend to die stronger than others."

"No lifereading," said Khelin, ruminating. "But could you bring up a symbol from his lives at Mautri? If I were *really* a purple, I might be able to do it. But you could pick up a symbol rife with associations meaningful to Zref."

The Theaten heaved a great sigh, and his eyes went unfocused. It struck Zref how much Arai seemed like an Interface opening when he did that. Everyone else in the room stopped breathing. Zref felt like a specimen pinned live to a board, examined with a microscope.

Suddenly, Arai folded in half and toppled forward, his face gone lax. Zref lunged, catching the surprisingly light form by the shoulders. Neini scrambled across the room to help Zref ease the Theaten to the floor, unfastening the Theaten's collar and feeling for a pulse.

Arai's eyes stared blankly at the ceiling, and Zref was certain he wasn't breathing. He summoned the first-aid instructions for Theatens, found the respiration rhythm and began yanking the stiffly curled body out flat. "Grab his arms," ordered Zref. "He's got to breathe!"

They pulled and pushed the spasming muscles until they could get at his ribcage, and then, clearing the air passages, Zref began pumping air into his friend. "Medic should be here in a couple of minutes," gasped Zref.

But already the stiff muscles were melting, and breath wheezed in and out. The ashen pallor faded until the Theaten was his usual, ruddy color again.

Waysjoff fretted, "This only happens with Zref."

The eyes fluttered shut, and then Arai began to struggle against their efforts. Zref let up. When the medics he'd called arrived, Arai convinced them he hadn't had a heart attack. They insisted he come down for a complete physical before going down-planet, and wouldn't leave until they'd extracted a waiver of responsibility.

Khelin shut the door behind the medic team, and leaned against it. "I'm sorry, Arai. I shouldn't have asked that."

Arai was reclining now on the longest settee in the room, his feet hanging off one end while his head was propped up by the arm at the other end. Neini was plying him with a Theaten soup that filled the room with a rank, vile smell.

"Don't you even want to know what I found?"

Khelin crossed to Zref and Arshel. "Yes, of course." But Zref disliked the kren's speculative look.

When Arai was silent, Khelin turned to eye him quizzically. Arai admitted, "Well, I was climbing the kyralizth—with the first rank, so I suppose with the whites. And there was this huge—white—fire. Then—"

"No!" said Khelin. Arai paused, comprehension dawning as Khelin buried his face in his hands. Ley moved to Khelin's side, but oddly, Khelin took a tiny step away. "That's only for the whites. Like Tschfa'amin."

"Or Rozdiben," answered Zref.

"Yes," said Arai. "I hit an aklal barricade—Mautri, I suppose. I have one image from beyond it. It won't be spoken." The Glenwarnan ethic was as reliable as sunrise. The Mautri secrets would be kept as if Arai had pledged.

Khelin settled beside the reclining Theaten. "If Zref must be read again—I will do it."

"Are you sure you know the image of which I speak?"

"You will tell me—and Zref—in private," said Khelin.

Shui stepped to the center of the room. "They're reaching now for a potency Iraem and I refuse to touch in this life. Perhaps we're cowardly, but we've chosen not to face surviving the breaking of another bhirhir. Since we aren't going to Camiat today, I suppose tomorrow we'll be going to the Crystal Crown. Let's study up on it. Arshel? Will you help us?"

Arshel moved reluctantly. "Yes, if that's what you want." But she was looking at Zref.

He considered Arai and Khelin, distractedly chewing his lower lip—a most non-Interface mannerism. He hitched one hip onto the back of the settee, propelling Arshel toward the bhirhirn. "I'll see you later."

The other two writers stood, Waysjoff saying, "May we sit in on this seminar?"

Jocelyn pulled Ley after them. "Come on, we can use my room. It's neutral ground, as Khelin says."

As they went out, Zref heard Arshel start by reassuring them the large predators could easily be avoided.

When the door closed, Khelin inched back from Arai, hugging his knees as if to keep from shaking.

Looking at him, Zref said, "If I were kren, I'd be raising venom uncontrollably, and wishing Arshel could stay. As it is—well, anything that scares Khelin, scares me."

"Khelin has good sense," agreed Arai.

"I'm not so sure," said Khelin. "But sometimes I remember what's at the top of the kyralizth. Do you, Zref?"

"No," he said, but the floor of his mind was heaving again. He took Arai's empty soup cup to rinse the nauseating odor away. "I'm not at all sure I want to."

Khelin ran his fingertips through his headfluff in a gesture vaguely reminiscent of Ley's. Then he pulled a chair out near Arai and another for himself, urging Zref to be seated while he adjusted the lighting behind Zref to a glow.

As he took the seat facing Zref, Khelin said, "I'm not anywhere near taking the purple yet—I still prefer to have Ley express me. But, I'll try, Zref, because if you go down unprepared to the Crown you built, and real memories waken, you may not be able to handle the trauma."

"Khelin," said Arai, "try this. Focus your eyes on the light behind Zref. You can do fractional relaxation. Selectively, let your eyes relax into nonfocus."

The Theaten coached, his voice hypnotic, evoking visual impression for Khelin. He described the nimbus around Zref's body in colorful detail, along with each of the odd shapes swimming in it like sunspots in a corona.

Distracted, barely able to speak, Khelin agreed the colored fields extended way beyond the reach of Zref's arms, almost too bright to look at when Zref was relaxed.

Arai then led Khelin around some unimaginable corner, and began describing his previous life at Mautri. Khelin picked up the images, described, with casual familiarity, Zref taking the purple—a bizarre exercise Zref could never have imagined. But as the two lifereaders talked about him, Zref began to see himself as a kren within precincts of the temple forbidden to outsiders. And he walked with the line of priests, out the private door toward the kyralizth.

He was wearing the dark purple robe, ready to take the white. He was in molt, his skin stiff, his glands in riot. He wasn't sure he could make it up the side of the blunt-topped stretched-out pyramid. But he was determined to try.

The climb seared his heart. His dry mouth tasted of molt venom, and all he wanted to do was snuggle down in a warm sand bed—safe under his bhirhir's hands. But his bhirhir stood on the sidelines now, watching the line of priests splitting to surround the kyralizth, and ascending along each edge to converge at the top.

This time, he had the honor of leading the climb up the eastern edge. But when he got to the top, instead of the smooth ramp leading up to the firepit, a huge black hole was at his feet, and a staircase leading down into darkness.

He started down the stairs. What was below called to him, welcomed him, a home in exile—but he tumbled forward and fell head over heels into black space.

CHAPTER THIRTEEN
Crystal Crown

Zref came to with Khelin's hands on his shoulders, holding him upright in the chair. The floor of his mind was an incandescent quagmire, heaving threateningly.

Arai lay prone on the settee, huddled around pillows, back hunched against the threat of the room. But he was breathing—sobbing out some Sirwini poem.

"Zref?" Khelin's venom sack pulsed once.

Zref tried to answer, but his skull was filled with white-hot lava that wanted to pour out of his eyes and ears. He couldn't breathe through the searing pain.

"Can you hear me?" demanded Khelin.

Zref tried to nod, to reach his brother. But volition was paralyzed by Guarantees trembling on the brink of killing him. The question he had not yet faced erupted afresh. *What's more important to me—being Interface, or being Tschfa'amin?* He remembered his prayer, his surrender to responsibility. But how could he shoulder all that while every memory he resurrected threatened the comnet and the HP?

"You remembered dying in the taking of the white. A genuine memory. Right here within reach of the comnet."

The memory surged freshly, as bright and real as if it had just happened—but not coming to him through his private file. It was real in him, not the comnet.

He couldn't force breath into his lungs. Sweat started out all over him, running down his face. Tears and saliva flowed unchecked, every muscle in his body knotted against the searing pain from nowhere and everywhere.

"Don't repress it!" commanded the Mautri teacher. "Let the lava break through the floor that Interface surgery built into your mind."

Zref had related that image to Khelin in a vain effort to make him understand why he'd die if he remembered. He was dying now. He couldn't even nod.

"Remember the pond room. The sand. Part of the floor surfaced with cool, surging water. The door to the room without walls stands free. Walk into the pond room. Walk through the door. You're within eternity. You stand upon sand. Before you laps the water from which futures emerge.

"This is your mind. Part of the floor is solid. Part fluid. You stand within the door to the room without walls, on solidity. You've been invited to immerse, and have accepted that privilege. But now you may choose when to go down, when to emerge anew. You needn't choose to be Interface or Tschfa'amin. You can be either, as required."

As Khelin spoke in a low, urgent whisper, commanding, reverent, Zref felt a solid floor rise up—a floor tiled with neat, even black and white squares the exact size of his own foot. He stood upon those tiles while a jeweled arch solidified around him, standing free, sheltering him. The jewels formed the pattern of the comnet nodes known to every Interface. The white-hot lava oozed down to the far end of his mind, forming a pond. The pain ebbed.

He knew now what was within the kyralizth—a ceremonial pond room designed to represent the soul-mind bond. It was a truth echoed in every pond room, the truth of the door.

"Master Interface, is *Epitasis* on orbital station?"

Zref answered before he realized he'd opened. Then Zref shook his head ruefully, feeling almost normal again. "I'd have been afraid to open, if I'd thought about it!"

"You're all right?" asked Khelin in wonderment.

Never for a moment had Zref thought Khelin doubted what he was doing.

It was a bright, sunny morning when they arrived at the Sorges River site.

Over the millennia, the Sorges River had carved a huge canyon across the interior of the continent. Above, on the plateau, there was nothing but a waterless desert, while the narrow strip at the floor of the canyon was fertile. But the climate was too hot for the natives, so they'd gladly sold Lantern the site—before Madlain and Nunin Lakely, the parents of Dennis Lakely, had discovered the Crystal Crown.

Arshel babbled brightly on the way down, pointing out the

changes made by Lantern since the early days. But Zref had caught her the night before, curled on the bottom of their pond. She'd admitted her fears, but wouldn't let him go alone. He'd been too exhausted to argue, but now it haunted him. What was he doing to his bhirhir, bringing her here?

The Crystal Crown was under the river bottom, and at first, the river had been held at bay by a cylindrical forcefield so the mud could be cleared to expose the Crown. They'd used a two-car tramway to get down to the Crown then.

Now, the course of the huge Sorges River had been diverted into a flume encircling the Crown, leaving the sparkling white stone circle in a hole cut into dry mud.

From their angle of approach, Zref only glimpsed the brilliant white tops of the standing stones, but he knew instantly he was in trouble. It held the same sort of vivid life Stonehenge had, though far sharper even now. How could he enter *that* to be Interface for these students?

Zref tore his mind away, concentrating on Arshel's lecture. The original, workers' tramway was still in place, but a gaudily painted, larger tramway had been rigged at the upriver end of the excavation for the Lantern Tour groups.

Further upriver, beyond the site of a First Lifewave village the Lakelys had also uncovered, stood a fifty-story hotel complex, built in a hyperbolic curve so that virtually every room had a spectacular view of the excavations. A small touchdown pad had been built behind the hotel to accommodate orbital shuttles bringing tourists.

As their shuttle circled over a compact group of huts, Arshel pointed them out. *"That's* what we lived in then. I used to go down to swim in the river every morning."

"I'll bet that hotel has pond-rooms!" said Khelin.

"What?" teased Ley. "You don't want to rough it?"

They were scheduled to stay at the Sorges site for two days—one at the Crown, and the other at the village. The shuttle spilled them into a tunnel leading directly into the air-conditioned hotel lobby. Zref couldn't help noticing the massive vacancies, and wondered, with a sudden chill of suspicion, why they'd been delayed in orbit.

After settling in their rooms—and the hotel's pond-rooms were as magnificent as those aboard ship—they had to report directly to the front lobby to ride out to the Crown.

That ride was in automated ten-passenger carriers. Zref and his group, among the first to arrive, filled one. Arshel hung back at the groundcar's door. "Zref, I don't know if I can make myself go out there."

Ley looked back as Zref answered, "You don't have to. Or if you go, you don't have to read."

Behind Ley, Iraem voiced the question on Zref's mind since he'd seen the Crown. "Zref, how are you going to make yourself go into that thing? It's no toy like Stonehenge!"

Ley said, "It isn't just the Crown. There's something else. Awful."

Shui pulled Iraem into the shuttle, saying, "Ley, let them in. We're conspicuous holding up traffic here."

Ley clambered in, and Zref waited behind Arshel until she said, "Talents are to be mastered—and used." And she heaved herself up the steps into the cool dimness.

The smoky dome of the car was polarized against the hot glare of the sun. Soothing music played. The seats were luxurious—large enough even for Arai, easily adjusting down to Arshel's size. As Zref was seated, the car moved, the music giving way to a lecture on the site, which they ignored.

Khelin had heard Ley's remark, and now scrutinized Ley's eyes, saying, "Ley seems to be our sensitive. He's responding now as he did when Mautri aklal was violated. I don't think *I* want to go out there."

"This car will take us there now, whether we want to go or not," said Waysjoff, perched precariously on one of the seats, anchored by one hand-foot.

"We're not trapped," said Zref. "I can take us back to the hotel, or anyplace else there's a road."

"I hadn't thought of that!" said Waysjoff with relief.

"But we can't do that," protested Neini. "Zref is required to work this site just like all the others."

Zref fought the temptation to suggest he have the bus take them to the village while he went alone to the Crown. That would break up their aklal. To keep his mind off the seductive temptation, Zref checked his files. He was running several simultaneous scans, sifting for news of interest to them or the Cruise. Now he found an unexpected one.

He rose on his knees and turned so they could all hear him. "Bad news." He caught Khelin's eye and indicated Ley. When the kren was prepared, Zref said, one hand on Arshel's shoulder to reassure her, "The ship carrying the new serums against this plague has disappeared en route to Camiat, and is presumed lost to pirates. The situations on Camiat and Sirwin are worse. Could this be a move of the Enemy?"

Ley growled, "If it is—for that, I'd kill!"

"I think we all would," answered Khelin in his mildest blue priest's tone. "But until now, the pirates have been Her enemies. An alliance?"

"Maybe," said Zref. "But that would mean She believes we're really close to beating Her. Which means whatever's out there at the Crystal Crown must be faced and conquered."

Ley looked up at Zref, "For the children."

Khelin squeezed Ley's hand and flashed his fangs at Arshel. "Whoever's behind this plague, has made a grave error." There was a general murmur of agreement as renewed personal strength overcame their reluctance. Even Jocelyn who had been glassy-eyed, became animated with new life.

They were almost at the dock of the tramway where brilliant green, gold and pink gondola cars waited in a row when Jocelyn said, staring wildly about, "The Enemy believes the Object is here, and has come to get it."

"That's some kind of next move!" breathed Neini.

"I don't believe it," said Waysjoff.

"It's not too farfetched," allowed Arai. "The Crystal Crown was built by Zref to house the Globe of Ossminid, created by Arshel to symbolize the Galactic Habitation. This Crown's the only one to survive *so* alive. What better place to hide a Maze-heart than in a Crown where Persuaders won't go—even in future incarnation?"

Khelin was unresponsive when everyone looked to him. Arshel said professionally, "The Object isn't here. I've been all over here, and up and downstream, too. I'd have found anything from the City. The Enemy must know that."

Zref said, "I think we should convene our aklal, leaving the green sphere and the white cube out of it because Mautri and Glenwarnan are too debilitated to help. Let's use only our own image, the Maze as seen from above, colored as Arshel suggested." He called the image down from *Epitasis* and put it on the demonstration screen at the front of the car.

As the car pulled into a stall at the gondola dock, the incomparable warmth of the group enfolded Zref, solidly with him. The image on the screen blazed up to a searing intensity and seemed to come off the screen into the very air. Zref cleared the screen and led them outside.

The gondola dock was becoming crowded now. As soon as they had vacated their groundcar, it moved off and another discharged passengers, and then they came in a steady stream.

Laughing, chattering, the students piled into tramway gondolas and were swung out over the ditch that had once held the Sorges River. The overhead lines sang with power. The cars swayed in the wind. The sun beat down mercilessly. A bright, cheerful day—and yet somehow sinister.

Zref went to the railing to get a good view of the Crown. It gleamed white in the torturous noon sun. The lintel that had been pulled down by the villagers and set up as a monolith in the center of the village was back in place, completing the Crown. There was a model of the Sphere of Ossminid on top of the lintel now, a solid gold sphere in which were embedded other solid gold spheres representing the artificial suns which had been set in a huge globe of stars.

The white crystal uprights were connected to each other by many lintels, forming a building made of doors to the room without walls. It was as if this edifice had been built from a set of superconducting tuning forks, then one had been plucked, the eternal sympathetic echoing of one to the other preserved forever.

The molten lava at the pond end of Zref's mind stirred. There was a memory here. But Zref clutched his aklal about him like a protective cloak and deferred exploring memory, saying instead, "We're expected to take one of these gondolas down to the Crown. Could we walk down instead?" He craned his neck over the high railing to inspect the bank beneath them.

Arai, who could see it all quite well, said, "It's dry, crumbling mud. I'd try it only if my life depended on it."

Arshel said, "We could use the other tram, the original one." Then turned grim as she surveyed the old gondolas: peeling, faded orange paint, rusty-seeming mechanisms.

Zref checked the maintenance records and said, "They're in good condition—used by grounds-keepers. Let's go."

Off the planked trail, the going was rough. But they had dressed for the outing in good trail boots and tough clothing. They reached the platform of the old cars, and Arshel showed them the controls. "You used to be able to swim out to the forcewall," she said wistfully.

"I'm glad we don't have to do *that!*" said Waysjoff.

Zref had never seen a wet Jernal. He suspected they didn't swim at all.

Inside the gondola, the seats were worn, stuffing spilling out. Soon they were swinging out over a vast emptiness, vulnerable if anyone meant them harm.

Zref wondered if their effort to do the unexpected was of any avail. He still felt like going it alone, telling himself it was unnecessary to endanger his friends.

When they got out of the gondola, they were on a high platform that had once been even with the river surface when it was held back by the forcewall. They trailed down the narrow stair past the river bottom to the level of the Crown.

It was awesome. On this side, no planked trails led across the dried mud bottom. There was no sign of civilization at all—just the Crown looming above them.

It was a vortex of real power. "Do you feel it?"

"If it still had a mate," said Khelin, "this Crown could be used to span the galaxy. I wish Sudeen could have lived to know he was right about the Crowns."

Khelin rarely mentioned his brother, but before Zref could comment, Ley whispered, "Somehow, I think he knows."

The heat in the pit was oppressive. Zref suggested, "Let's go look it over," and led the way. The real entryway was on the other side where the tourists were. He was only going to touch one of the outside stones, then he'd walk all the way around to the entry. But he couldn't go in. No.

"No," said Jocelyn in a thready voice. "She's here!"

Ley wrapped his arm about her shoulders. "I know." But he urged her after Zref. The rest followed, only Waysjoff walking easily on the clods and ridges of mud.

But once, it had not been mud. Visions began shooting through Zref's mind. Standing on this very spot, watching these very crystals arrowing down through atmosphere, glowing white-hot with reentry friction, surrounded by a toroid of minute flying craft, impacting like missiles, their pointed ends burying deep into the ground, right on target, an incredible sense of pride swelling within his feathered form.

His hands were on one of the columns now. It was smooth, warm from the sun, throbbing under his touch as it had that bright day when it had buried its nose in the ground, quivering like an arrow.

He drew back, shaken deeply, the surging waves of hot lava in his mind lapping at his feet.

"Zref?" Arshel dragged him aside until they were standing between the uprights, but turned to face the others.

"I'm fine," he said.

"He looks pale," declared Neini.

"You remembered," accused Ley.

"A little," confessed Zref. "I—can't. Remembering hurts." The Maze image shimmered in the air around them.

Arshel clung to his elbow, half supporting him. "You can do it," she said, pulling him to circle deosil around the Crown. "You're not going to break the Guarantees. It won't harm the comnet if one Interface remembers his own past."

That floor was in his mind for a reason; he had no way of knowing if it could be dissolved without penalty. But stopping the Enemy would be worth any penalty—except destroying the comnet. They walked in silence, gazing raptly between the uprights as they passed. They were more than halfway to the entrance when they cleared the edge of one of the large uprights, and Zref saw beyond the inner circle of stones, the swarm of students pouring into the Crown. Their irreverent chatter drifted on the still air. Many of them were probably looking for him to make recordings for them.

Arshel pulled him a few steps beyond to where two uprights were so close one could barely stand between them. She put one hand on each of the stones. "Try again, Zref."

Her venom sack pulsed as determination won over her fear and she stepped aside, pushing Zref between the stones. The others huddled around Zref, as if against a vast darkness.

At that moment, feeling the solidity of the aklal around him, closing Interface, trying to accept the surging lava pond boiling at one end of his mind, while he stood secure under the arch of the door to the room without walls, Zref glimpsed a flash of scarlet at the center of the Crown.

It was a daub of color flittering between two uprights. *Probably some student*, he thought, nudging his mind back to the life he and his aklal had breathed into this Crown. *We built it on a different principle. That's why it's lasted.*

The knowledge just appeared, rousing intense curiosity, and the comnet answered with all the data on the Crystal Crown. He dumped that file, and summoned the Crown memories.

Again the flash of brilliant scarlet—like a wild bird within the straining force lattice within the Crown. He could *see* that lattice as he could the strands of the comnet.

It was the same pattern as used in all other Crowns, of course, to make them resonate. But the strands were elastic, larger than normal, formed like cable not string, the largest running along the ground and into the bases of the uprights. The cables glowed to his altering vision, blue-white cores surrounded by pastel rainbows. They thrummed with vibration that set standing sine waves along their lengths; vertical along the higher ones, horizontal waves along the ground level ones. The Crown was still perfectly tuned.

Where the cables entered the crystals, they bent into an unimaginable dimension—beckoning alluringly.

Zref remembered anchoring each cable to specific molecules held in the lattice within each crystal. He'd assembled the aklal to grow each of these crystals in huge vats under the pressure of many joined minds, working to create for eternity. He'd assembled the aklal to guide each of the crystals from orbit into its proper position. He remembered standing right where he was standing now, guiding the central crystal into its place to complete the lattice.

And he remembered how, during that ticklish operation, he had fought to keep his mind from wandering—because suddenly he *knew* how to build the Maze, to create an aklal of Persuaders. In a fit of intuitive insight that made ordinary consciousness seem moronic, he comprehended the thirty-two principles of reality. He would go down in history as the greatest of the Philosophical Engineers.

With all of this boiling in his mind, Zref caught again that illusive flicker of scarlet. The familiar, yet changed and matured, aklal behind him tensed. On the largest of the ground cables, walking a good handsbreadth above the baked mud, a magnificent Almurali female approached.

A film of scarlet chiffon draped from the jeweled tiara sparkling between her upright ears and fell like a regal train to her feet. A twist of the scarlet circled her body, revealing most of her silken, smoke-gray fur. With felinoid grace she walked the cable as if it were substantial.

She was slightly built, but radiated giant confidence. She was nothing like the hard, efficient Captain of *Epitasis*. She was sumptuous, seductive—and deadly.

And Zref knew her. The Enemy. Ossminid, Emperor of Crowns and Mazemaster. Before that, the Persuader candidate he'd been most proud of.

She had worn feathers then, when he was Mazemaster for the second time, under the Forty-second Emperor of Crowns. Her feathers had been as scarlet as the material she decorated herself with now—to remind him?

Standing with one hand on each of the two upright crystals, his feet embedded in the cable she walked upon, Zref remembered in rapid sequence, their lives under nine Emperors of Crowns. He'd built the Maze under the Fortieth Emperor, admitted her in his next incarnation as Mazemaster under the Forty-second Emperor—and discovered the Selector, the Mazeheart Object, didn't always disperse the soul of one who'd misuse its power. She'd gone on a rampage of abuse—Persuading to gain power over others, using her crude, half-learned aklal techniques to disperse rebellious souls. And since then, Zref had stood responsible for the disaster.

At least, I stopped her before she learned to construct a Selector of her own!

But then, under the Forty-forth Emperor, when Khelin was Mazemaster, Zref in training under him, she'd returned, become a Crown Operator, rising rapidly in the Crown Council. Arshel, also among the Crown operators, was unaware of her colleague's identity. She spent that life obstructing Zref viciously so by the time Zref had the power to oppose his renegade student, nothing could be done. Zref died in old age leaving his student Forty-fifth Emperor of Crowns.

In her next incarnation, she became the Forty-ninth Emperor, naming herself Ossminid, Emperor of Crowns and Mazemaster, the first Emperor to retain a personal name. By then, nothing could stop the maniacal amassing of power, or the consequent downfall of the Empire.

The beginning of the end was when Ossminid, having walked the Maze, reentered the Emperor's Crown and sent his Persuader's powerful thoughts to a rebelling planet to stop a disastrous war. Fear of his domination spread the rebellion. Planets were devastated, Crowns destroyed.

Seeing his chance, Zref led Khelin and many of his Persuaders—Ley among them—in a stealthy move to recapture the Maze from Ossminid. They occupied the Maze and outbuildings, under siege from the Emperor's troops, refusing to abuse their powers and Persuade the troops away from their lawful duty to obey the Emperor.

Ossminid, determined to retake the Maze, went into the Emperor's Crown and aimed wave after wave of Persuader power at the Persuaders—urging them to suicide.

Ordinarily, a Persuader could not Persuade a Persuader, but Ossminid's method worked. Persuaders flung themselves into the weapons fire of the Empire troops. Seeing defeat imminent, Zref gave his life to dislodge the Mazeheart, setting it to self-destruct if it were ever used again, and giving it into Khelin's hands. His student and oft-times teacher was more powerful now than he, but still ignorant of the Selector's construction. He would guard that secret, and Khelin would guard the location of the only functional Selector ever made.

He had sent Khelin and Ley away with the Selector, by a secret passage he'd built under the Maze during construction.

Zref remembered dying, the walls of the Maze he'd built crumbling about him, impotent before Ossminid, his other student who was now more powerful than the Master. His final emotion had been dismay that the Selector hadn't dispersed Ossminid's soul, so he'd never be reborn. Once, just once, the Selector had malfunctioned. Zref didn't know why. Until he did, it must not be used again. He'd clung to that determination for millennia, and been tempted away from it only in this lifetime—by the lure of the Lantern aklal, the power of the Meguerian titles.

By sheer force of will, Zref banished the memory and focused on the soft-furred Almurali female before him. Only the scarlet draperies reminded him of that sharp young Persuader candidate, so eager and promising. But the manner of controlled ferocity wielding deep power was pure Ossminid.

His heart quailed, responding to blurred memories of defeats at those hands. He had to master this gut-wrenching fear or it would defeat him.

Shaking, he pulled his hands away from the white stones. They seemed to stick like magnets to metal. His shoulders screamed with pain. His elbows had forgotten how to bend. Every hairsbreadth of movement cost him dearly, but he freed himself and stepped back from in between the uprights.

With an effort, as if moving through cold molasses, he put one arm around Arshel, and the other around Khelin, just touching Ley on that side. They were transfixed by the apparition before them, as Zref was. Behind Zref stood Waysjoff, close enough that Zref could feel the warmth of its fluff against his legs. Neini and Jocelyn were behind Khelin, Shui and Iraem close behind Arshel, and Arai stood behind Waysjoff, peering over Zref's head. They hardly breathed, and Zref was sure they were all seeing the braided lines of force, and the Almurali gliding toward them.

She stopped. The heat shimmer rising from the crystals invaded the space between them, billowing like smoke until they stood in a limbo surrounded by walls of smeared color, floored by rainbow cables.

She raised one scarlet draped hand, beckoning Zref forward. He felt his feet slide toward her of their own volition. Gritting his teeth, he forced them back, hissing, "Our image. The Maze!" And his aklal solidified about him.

Her body, rippling like a flame, brightened as she gestured, gathering her aklal. Pulsing waves of yearning battered at Zref, calling him into the Crown scintillating about her. "You can't escape this time, Mazemaster. Come, tell me what you've done with it! I won't be put off again!"

Inwardly, Zref quailed, but held his ground. "You'll never get what you want from me." Even here, beyond reality, he was still bound by the Guarantees of truthfulness.

"You don't remember yet? Well, there're remedies for that!"

She strolled toward him, her hands motioning as if she were reeling him in on a line. He felt that tug in the middle of this body, as if his guts were spilling out a hole. She announced to his aklal, "I shall gather his innards and throttle him until I have what I came for—the location of the Mazeheart!"

Zref, in a peculiar heightening of awareness, felt Khelin tense, resisting the temptation to save Zref. Zref, helpless, felt his aklal disintegrating about him as each of them wavered. In that instant of weakness, Jocelyn suddenly dashed forward to the inner edge of the Crown circle and blurted, "He doesn't know, but Khelin does!"

Freed by the Almurali's astonishment, Zref lunged to snatch Jocelyn back from the brink of the Enemy's control. But meanwhile, the attack had focused on Khelin, who went down on his knees, consumed by a private agony, his venom sack pulsing irregularly. Shoving Jocelyn into Arai's arms, Zref threw himself before Khelin while Ley embraced his bhirhir protectively.

The Enemy's eyes burned into Khelin with all the implacable strength of Lantern's millions, focused through the presence of the onboard aklal—dozens of students and faculty who were now flickering phantoms glowing within the walls of distortion about them, feeding their energy into the Almurali.

Zref was prepared to throw himself into the Crown to save Khelin, and the secret, but he hadn't even the strength to move. In anguished desperation, he wrenched at the fabric of their reality, banishing the braided rainbows and blurred walls, substituting the pastel Maze as seen from above, themselves floating in midair over it.

The Almurali gasped, the first time Zref had scored. Encouraged, he found his voice, and proclaimed his aklal, "At ten, we are One!"

They took that up, making it a chant, weaving it as a wall between themselves and the Enemy. But before it could solidify, Khelin emitted a hissing scream that should never have issued from a kren throat. He reared back, Ley clinging to him doggedly. As a look of orgasmic satisfaction suffused the Enemy's Almurali countenance, Khelin, venom sack distended to painful thinness, struck Ley, pumping venom into his bhirhir with savage grunts of agony.

Then, laughing, the Enemy turned and vanished. Zref, staring after her, realized she'd gotten the location from Khelin and would race them there. Again, without thinking, Zref gathered the fabric of reality and transported them back to the Crystal Crown's own reality.

The braided rainbow cables were gone, the heat shimmer rose according to mundane laws of physics, and the crystals stood starkly bare of magic. The Almurali strode across the circle, breasting a wave of moving people converging on Zref's position. It was the students and faculty of the Cruise, led by Cruise Director Plath. Plath was a big man, superbly muscled, easily Zref's physical superior.

The approaching people moved woodenly, as if animated by another's will. Some of them dropped out, leaving the advancing wall full of holes. The ones who faltered had been won over by *Phailan Atrocities*. Zref reached out to them, willing them to stop their fellows—wake them from the clutch of an unnatural control, and leave.

Some of them indeed began shaking their compatriots, but the enspelled ones worked free with a negligent strength and closed ranks. What would they do if they got within reach?

Behind Zref, Ley sprawled limply next to Khelin who crouched, sides heaving, consumed by anguish.

Arai suggested in his deep, calm voice, "Now we summon Mautri and Glenwarnan, for we battle all of Lantern."

Zref said, "Yes, we've no choice. Visualize with me, green sphere on top of a white cube. See glinting sunlight, the sea depths of the sphere glowing. Feel reality singing like a choir of all who have ever climbed the kyralizth or discovered the cube." Zref kept on, evoking the experiences he'd had with Jylyd and at Glenwarnan.

He felt the heavy summer heat abate in a breeze of a hundred presences. The blazing power of Presence joined them, but it was much weaker than when they'd brought Jocelyn back. The plague had taken too heavy a toll.

But the Almurali swung around in shock and dismay. The mob she was focusing on Zref shattered into bewildered individuals. She gathered her red chiffon and lengthened her stride toward the exit from the Crown.

Distantly, they could her the Almurali exhorting the students and faculty as she passed, "They're wanted on Camiat! That's why they inveigled themselves onto this Cruise." She accused Shui and Iraem, as well as Khelin and Ley, of starting the plague on Camiat and conspiring to spread it so they could make a fortune in venom-futures, because the cure was venom-based. "Get them!"

The mob milled around, beginning to reform. Ley was beginning to stir as Jocelyn fought free of Arai and went to him, her glassy-eyed stare gone now. Zref approached Khelin with all caution, whispering, "It wasn't your fault. It's all right, now. Ley's not hurt. Come on, Khelin, get up. We've got to run for our lives!"

CHAPTER FOURTEEN
City of a Million Legends

Khelin finally focused on the converging mob, absorbed the situation, and rose, shaking Zref off. He helped Ley up, draping one of Ley's arms around his shoulders, grudgingly accepting Jocelyn's help on Ley's other side. Together, they began a stumbling run around the outside of the Crown.

Zref dragged Arshel after them, toward the entryway and public tram cars docked there awaiting the students.

As if their movement was a trigger, the half-formed mob within the circle coalesced amid shouts of, "Stop them!"

They had farther to run, but the mob had to squeeze through arches single file, or detour around uprights.

Arai and Waysjoff had drawn into the lead, the top of the Jernal's fluff coming barely hip-high on the Theaten, but its six legs blurring with speed. They could have run much faster, but wouldn't leave the group. Neini was slowly losing ground, falling behind Khelin, Ley and Jocelyn to where Shui and Iraem deliberately brought up the rear.

Zref had to slow, or let go of Arshel's hand. He chose to slow, pacing Khelin, Ley and Jocelyn. Iraem called, "We're not all going to make it. We'll have to fight them."

"No!" said Zref. "They don't deserve to be hurt!"

Zref's side ached already, and he wished he'd spent more time in Jocelyn's dance classes. Arshel's grip was weakening so he had to hold her and pull her along.

Clearly, they weren't quite going to make it. Almurali laughter floated over the growl of a mob's bloodlust, and Zref caught a glimpse of scarlet between the stones. She was still down here with them!

Zref could not use his newly remembered powers as a weapon. Instead, he reached for the comnet and took over the programming of the tramway cars. He sent all but one back up to the dock. Then he took over the groundcars and sent all but one of them away from the dock—to wait at the village.

When Arai first saw the tram car move, he looked back in panic at the mob filtering across the circle of stones. But then he glanced at Zref, saw his smile and returned it with a fierce grin. He raised one arm in a Theaten victory gesture, and forged ahead aiming to secure the tram for them.

Zref couldn't follow Waysjoff's mental processes so easily, but it also doubled its pace and kept up with Arai.

Ley was running now, but still supported by Khelin and Jocelyn. Zref and Arshel were just ahead of them, while in the rear, still losing ground, came Neini with Shui and Iraem. That was the order in which they approached the planked tramway deck from one direction while the leaders of the mob came at them from the right side.

Arai made it to the tram door, and Zref signaled it opened for him, glad it didn't take any breath to send a comnet command. Then Plath swept out of the mob, his eyes wild, ferocity distorting his features as he bore down on Waysjoff. The human swept it off its feet, lifting the wispy Jernal over his head, clearly intending to slam it into the hard planking—surely a killing blow. Its spindly legs flailed in all directions and a thin shriek filled the air.

Zref would have shouted at Arai, but he had no breath. Arshel was an increasing weight on his sweat-slicked hand, and his right clutched the pain in his side.

Arai turned at the Jernal's cry, and his ruddy features twisted. He threw himself at the Cruise Director, seized the pink puff of a Jernal and ripped it from Plath's grip leaving two tufts of pink fluff in Plath's hands.

Waysjoff's scream pierced upward into the supersonic, a silent white-hot agony that seared into Zref's head, leaving him dazed. He wasn't sure if the pain was just the unheard sound, or if he was actually feeling Waysjoff's agony.

Arai wound both arms around the Jernal, trying to stop its flailing legs with their sharp claws. Bent double, hugging the Jernal to him, he dived for the tram's door.

Zref threw himself on Plath, knocking the large man down, scrabbling for advantage until he could land a punch to his jaw. Before Plath lost consciousness, a slender, long-legged Sirwini with gleaming sharp horns, pulled Zref off Plath.

Arshel leaped onto the Sirwini's back, her lean legs wound about his waist, grabbing him by the horns and pulling his head back as her venom sack pulsed.

With a roar of outrage, the Sirwini pushed Zref away. Zref stumbled and fell backward, hitting his head on the baked mud, the world darkening around the edges. But he saw the Sirwini jackknife forward, throwing Arshel over his head to land in a graceless heap. Zref got his knees under him, but before he could rise the Sirwini charged, head down, ready to use those horns to disembowel Zref.

Khelin skidded in front of Zref, fangs down, venom sack distended and throbbing. His stance alone—seldom seen among civilized kren—would have stopped any sane attacker. But the Sirwini was driven by a madness.

He charged. As the Sirwini came within reach, and Khelin sidestepped to avoid the horns, Zref lunged forward and up, ramming his fist into the Sirwini's soft midsection. The Sirwini sprawled—horns unblooded—in an unconscious heap over Khelin who shoved the limp body aside.

Plath, only stunned, was regaining his feet. The roar of the approaching mob heralded their emergence from the edge of the circle. Zref, almost retching with every breath, grated, "Into the tram!"

Jocelyn was struggling with Ley's weight. Khelin staggered back to help her. "Hurry!" she cried.

Zref collected Arshel and followed them into the tram. They eased Ley onto the floor between two seats where he promptly passed out.

Arai was huddled over Waysjoff on the rear seat of the tram. Shui arrived carrying Neini, staggering to his knees before he could make it to a seat. Iraem came through the door backward, yelling, "Get this thing moving!" Zref slammed the door and ordered the tram up to the dock. They were all heaving air through hot, dry throats. He upped the percentage of oxygen— carefully, because they couldn't afford to get drunk, and for the first few car lengths of the trip, they all gulped air noisily.

Zref dragged himself onto a seat and peered down at the mob which now seethed around the platform. The Almurali stood near the edge of the circle, grinning up at him.

Horrified, Zref saw the mob, robbed of its prey, turn upon

itself. It started near the center of the platform. Someone went down. Immediately, they were on the downed one—some defending, some attacking.

Shuddering, Zref turned to his own. Khelin was kneeling over Ley, moaning softly.

Iraem knelt on a seat, leaning over Khelin at a distance safe from his strike. "Peel back his eyelids, let me see."

Khelin did so, and leaned back to let the paramedic see. Iraem asked, "How's his pulse?" And when Khelin answered, Iraem said, "He's throwing it off. He'll be all right."

Zref hurt everywhere, but he managed to fold himself into a seat. Neini had joined Arai and Waysjoff. But the whimpering screams were still coming—some of them registering in the supersonic. Not only had its fluff been ripped out—probably leaving naked patches—but Arai must have actually felt its whole body when he picked it up. Nevertheless, they had no time now for personal hysterics.

The tram was almost halfway to the dock. Zref advanced to stand over the three writers, saying gruffly, "All right, Waysjoff—that's enough! You've lived other lives than as a Jernal!"

The keening hesitated. Zref went on, "Ley's out. We may have to carry him. You can go on your own feet."

Arai leaned away from the rumpled and wilted ball of fluff, picking at its frothy pinkness in a vain effort to make it feel decently clad in public. Its legs were completely hidden.

"I'm sorry," came the reedy Jernal voice.

"It couldn't help it!" defended Neini.

Zref took off the jacket of his Interface's uniform, thrusting his medallion into his shirt pocket, then offered the jacket to the Jernal. "Here, wrap up in this."

As he was turning away, without waiting to see if his gift was accepted, the tram car ground to a swaying halt—dangling midway between anchorages.

A murmur of fear rose from them all, but Zref cast it aside and opened. Something had triggered the safety brake.

The probability of this happening was so vanishing small that Zref knew immediately that Almurali/Ossminid had done it. His new memories told him such manipulation of small probabilities was a trivial magic to her.

But he was not going to fight her power—not yet. So far,

she did not know what—if anything—he remembered. He felt his way into the circuited programming and planted a new override, releasing the safety brake.

The car started to move again, hissing and grinding, but moving. He explained what had happened. "Khelin, before we get to the ship, you've got to tell me where the Object is, or she will get there first!" There was no time to let the kren come to terms with his betrayal. Quickly, Zref related what he'd remembered of the Almurali, while instructing the workers' tram to return to its dock—hopefully stranding the Enemy in the pit.

As they arrived at the dock, he opened the door and they began climbing out before they'd stopped moving. He helped Khelin with Ley, who roused enough to shamble between them. Weary beyond measure, they piled into the ground car. Zref noted that Waysjoff had the black jacket wound all the way around itself. As they drew away from the dock, Zref instructed the system to shut down until morning.

"That should do it," he announced with satisfaction. "She might get them out of there within the hour, but she'll have to deal with the ambulance squad." The operator on the Infirmary comtap was frantically punching queries into his board while Zref's orders scrambling the first-aid teams to the pit spewed out. Then he moved to the seat in front of Khelin, who had Ley slumped against him. The pain of what he'd done was written in the way Khelin held his bhirhir.

Softly, wishing he had time to be sympathetic, Zref said, "Khelin, I remember. All of it. Even the part you described. I remember the end, and why I sent you and Ley away with the Selector. It was simply so that I couldn't—no matter what— let her know where it was. I didn't think, even if she made me tell her how, that she could make one for herself. Now—maybe she could."

"How did we get out of the Maze?" asked Khelin.

Zref told him.

"You do remember it all! And you're still alive!"

The feeling that the Guarantees would clamp down and kill him if he summoned memory was gone, and memory was there. At that point, he realized that the entire sequence of events from the moment they'd sighted the fragment of red material to the second when he'd opened to send the tram cars away was not recorded in his private file. But he remembered it. He remembered Sudeen and Tess—vividly, with all the accompanying emotional overtones. By some other contortion of mnemonics, he could also call up any memory in his private file—and they were as ashen as ever.

"Apparently, I can be either person or Interface at will now," marveled Zref. *Free of the Guarantees?*

"And she doesn't know that!" exclaimed Neini.

"We're going to win!" said Arai with a hearty smile.

Khelin's eyes locked on Zref's, facing his disgrace and failure unflinchingly. "This's what she got out of me. After we left you, I sent Ley on ahead to place the marker declaring the Selector had been removed. Then I hid it right there in the tunnel, under its own place. I'd have known if it had been disturbed. It's still there."

"So we go to the Maze!" said Iraem.

"Right in the midst of Lantern exploration!" added Shui.

"Diabolically clever!" saluted Neini. "We'd never have dared suggest that in a novel!"

"I should hope not," said Arai. "Even if I'd known, I'd never have suggested it. But how can we get there?"

"It's not far," noted Arshel thoughtfully.

"All the way across the Globe of Stars!"

"Six days travel," said Zref. "In *Epitasis*."

"We can't wait for the students and everyone to get aboard. They'll be tied up in infirmary here for days!"

"I wasn't planning to wait," said Zref. Already the ground car was circling the hotel, through glorious lush formal gardens hiding aquatic residences.

"Steal the ship?" challenged Khelin.

"Commandeer," corrected Zref. "We'll return it, with all the accounting right. Those people back there are going to be held in the infirmary and by the Pallacin arm of LEAHPs, answering to charges of assault and such. The ship will be back in time to take them on the rest of the Cruise."

"This has got to be against the Guarantees," said Shui.

"I'm not sure why I can do this—except I know it's got to be done to save the comnet and our civilization. Look, Interfaces run ships all over the galaxy—whether they're personally inside them or not. I haven't been ordered not to instruct *Epitasis* . . ."

They all looked at one another, comprehension dawning. Arshel said it. "She wanted to make sure you couldn't take *Epitasis* to run from her. That's why she had you locked out to begin with!"

"She knew Zref could regain the wholeness to maneuver around the ironclad walls of the Guarantees! After all, she made the Wild Interface—and Zref was made using a derivative technique. So she would know."

"You make me sound like a criminal," said Zref, dodging the words *Wild Interface*.

"No," replied Khelin. "You're human again."

"Maybe," allowed Zref.

Shui said, "Come to think of it, I recall being told we had to protect you physically because an Interface couldn't be physically aggressive—even if the situation called for it."

"True . . ." said Zref. He hadn't been asked a question, yet he'd responded without effort. *Alive again!* But did this mean the Guarantees had no force? If that were so, then he'd have to be very careful.

The groundcar glided to a halt at a dock beside a gleaming silver orbital shuttle with *Epitasis* markings. "Come on," said Zref, getting to his feet.

As he went, he instructed the shuttle to prepare for an orbital jump, and began alerting *Epitasis* itself. He didn't know how the Almurali might affect the probabilities against them. Their only chance lay in moving faster than she could think. And that was a slim chance.

Zref clamped his Interface medallion onto the edge of his shirt pocket, and led the way into the shuttle, speaking briskly to the pilot and assistant pilot. "I'll handle the takeoff. We're in something of a hurry."

The assistant, a belligerent Sirwini, began to argue, but the Ciitheen pilot only grumbled at the kren passengers and said, "Your ship, Master Interface!"

It wasn't that easy aboard *Epitasis*. Zref had the departure clearance sent through from Astrogation, and cut orders for the Escorters not to follow, for they were very likely controlled by the Enemy. As their shuttle docked, *Epitasis* slipped away from station and turned out-system, leaving all the other shuttles on the ground.

But, by the time they had unstrapped and reached the shuttle bay doors, the Captain was waiting.

Her ears were tight down to her skull, and her voice was low and dangerous as she said, "You have no authorization for this. Return my ship to me at once!"

"Captain," said Zref. "Let's discuss this in private."

"There is nothing to discuss. Get out of the *Epitasis* systems! Now!"

Zref felt the reflexive move within himself to obey, but was able to override it. He shook his head, repeating, "We are going to discuss it."

She drew herself to her full height, only her flashing eyes betraying her inner rage. She was formidable indeed, but Zref wished their Enemy were merely this formidable.

After holding him with her gaze for a very long time, she said, "In my quarters." She wheeled, and strode away.

Zref pulled Arshel along and sent the others to their quarters, then followed the Captain in a separate lift.

"What are you going to tell her?"

"I don't know," answered Zref.

Arshel wrapped her arms around herself, shuddering.

"What's the matter?"

"Another Almurali. I might end up hating them, and that's irrational."

Not to mention dangerous for a kren. "Ossminid isn't Almurali. That's just his/her body this lifetime. She probably doesn't have any Almurali cultural traits, and doesn't even identify with them. Most of them I've met have been decent, like this Captain."

When she admitted them to her quarters, she was pacing restlessly. Sizing up her mood, Zref said impulsively—barely noting this was his first truly impulsive utterance as an Interface—"You don't like feeling helpless. It's a unique experience for you."

She whirled, astonished. Her ears came up pointing at Zref. Arshel tensed, but Zref put a hand on her elbow. "I'm sorry," he added, meeting the Captain's eyes. "Very truly, I am sorry. I would have discussed it with you first—but there just wasn't time."

"Wasn't time?"

"The fate of the Hundred Planets might depend on the outcome of this mission. The accounting will be handled by the Guild. Star-Treader and Lantern will be paid, and your crew will get overtime. Don't worry about fulfilling your contract. The faculty and students on the Cruise were detained on Pallacin by an unfortunate mishap. Your ship will be back in orbit by the time they are ready to leave. Is there anything else I can say to reassure you?"

She was silent, staring in open astonishment at Zref. "Reassure me? Master Interface, I firmly intend to lodge a full protest—and I expect Star-Treader will as well."

Zref bowed formally, his whole body protesting the exercise. "Your privilege, of course, Captain."

With that, he escorted Arshel to the door.

The suite, which they'd left only a few hours before, seemed like a sweet home. As they entered the sitting room, Arshel turned to him and asked, "Are we away free, really?"

"Passing Pallacin's outer Orbital Checkpoint." As he was scanning, he noticed, "And, they finished the antenna repair!" Simultaneously, the antenna spat out a signal. "And the Captain is lodging her protest without delay."

"Then we're in trouble," said Khelin. He was sponging Ley's forehead and plying him with an herb tea which Ley was resisting because of its vile taste. Zref sympathized.

Zref explained what he'd done. "The trouble is going to come from Ossminid—and from the Guild itself." He told them what their Almurali Ossminid had done to force the tram to stop. "I'm not sure I entirely understand it yet, but I know she did it. She might do the same to *Epitasis*."

Zref turned as the big Theaten came in followed by Neini. Apologetically, Neini said, "Waysjoff wanted to be alone for a while." She handed Zref his jacket. "It said to thank you. I don't think it will show itself in public willingly for weeks."

"I don't always understand Jernal," said Arai folding himself onto a leaning rack. "I think it would rather have been dashed to death than rescued. But how could I let such a brilliant writer die so uselessly?"

"I think you did the right thing," answered Zref. "It will know that when it gets over the embarrassment."

"I could have a talk with it later," said Khelin, "about public embarrassments."

"It wasn't your fault, Khelin," said Ley roughly. His color was returning to normal, but he remained supine on the lounge. "It was my clumsy stupidity. I'm so sorry!"

Khelin sighed, "It wasn't your fault. She broke me."

Zref said, "I'd have broken. Any of us would. She's stronger than any of us alone." He looked at Arshel, "But not collectively. With Arshel, we're stronger than her whole aklal, because we're at peace with our opposition."

"Opposition?" asked Ley, struggling to sit up. "It seems to me, Jocelyn classifies—"

Jocelyn had come out of Khelin's and Ley's room onto the mezzanine just in time to hear this. Her face was blotched, eyes red, and she twisted a tissue between her hands. Her voice sounded as if she had a cold. "I came to apologize, though I don't know what could possibly make it up to you."

Zref whispered to Khelin, "What did Ley say to her?"

"That's private," answered Khelin. Plainly, he wasn't any happier with Jocelyn than Ley was.

Alone, Zref went up to Jocelyn. She stared down at the twisted tissue, fighting more tears. "You remember betraying Khelin?" She nodded, and Zref asked, "Do you remember now starting the rumor that the pirates were really after me?"

She looked up at him astonished. "I didn't—!"

"Maybe not, but it seems logical. Jocelyn, I knew—we all knew—you were open to our enemy, and dangerous. But our aklal can't convene without you." He told her what he'd told Khelin. "Don't be embarrassed you succumbed to her. She knows our weaknesses because she's known us all a long time."

"She might have killed—or dispersed—Khelin!"

She was about to cry again. Zref put his arm about her steering her down the stairs. "Yes. And you once told me you understood bhirhirn. Now's your test. Ley's waiting."

At the bottom, she left Zref, and calmly approached Khelin and Ley. She locked gazes with Ley, who was standing now, one hand on Khelin's shoulder. Then unable to bear his silent recrimination, she crumpled at his feet, sobbing, "I can't promise not to do it again! I wish I were dead!"

For a moment, Zref thought Ley would turn his back and coldly walk away. Lifetimes ago, he probably had. This time his heart melted, and he raised her up, tears in his eyes, and kissed her passionately.

While still holding Ley's hand, she threw herself at Khelin, apologizing hysterically, trying to kiss him, too, and compromising by planting one near his invisible ear. The kren flinched, then laughed and embraced her in return. "With two bhirhirn, how could I ever take the white?"

Arshel joined in hugging Jocelyn, saying, "Three."

"Four," corrected Zref, joining the group hug. That sense of exile, felt so keenly in Jylyd's chamber, was gone.

Neini wormed her way in to Jocelyn, kissing her.

Arai leaned over and stroked Jocelyn's head. Shui and Iraem joined the outside, laughing self-consciously. The close-packed knot of people enjoyed the outpouring of emotion. At last Ley said, "Zref, you've got to order us in some food! I'm starved!"

Khelin would soon be in the grip of intractable post-strike hunger cramps if he didn't get fed soon, and Arshel's sack was quite full. "Sensible idea," he agreed.

"With great deference, Master Interface, Venerable Sir."

It was the middle of the ship's night. Zref and Arshel were in the suite sitting room. Unable to sleep, they'd pulled lounges up to the big comlink screen and were studying the inscription stating the Object had been hidden.

One of the kren stewards, padding on silent feet, had come in. Zref said, "Yes, Swirn?"

"The suite stewards, all of us, wanted you to know—whatever it is you're doing, we're on your side." He scanned the ceiling as if he could spot the bugging devices. "We don't consider that disloyal to our employer, for we were hired to be loyal to the inhabitants of this suite. But, well—we would be anyway. Venerable."

Zref was taken aback, so Arshel answered smoothly, "We are most grateful, Swirn. But we wouldn't ask anything against your employer. Just continue to service this suite in the same excellent manner you have been, and think kindly of us even when others don't."

"Those who would not think kindly of you are only fools to be ignored," replied Swirn in his most formal accent.

Zref smiled, lips carefully covering his teeth. "I thank you, Swirn. I would ask an unusual service."

"Anything, Venerable."

Zref flinched inwardly at the accolade. "Could you perhaps

begin the hot drink service early this morning? And refill the fruit bowl?"

The kren brightened as if Zref had conferred honors upon him. "Certainly. We took on ripe zwingus at Pallacin—sweet and juicy. Would that please the Venerables?"

"Perfect!" said Arshel delightedly.

They returned to staring at the screen and in short order, delightful aromas drifted their way from the bar. Swirn moved so quietly, they didn't notice as he brought them drinks and a bowl of the succulent purple fruits, wrapped in artfully folded absorbent paper to catch the drippings.

Before long, Khelin joined them, barefoot, wrapping a robe bearing the ship's monogram around himself. "Early for breakfast. But it smells great."

They related Swirn's message, and Khelin joined them, nibbling zwingus and pondering the inscription.

"Zref, how many people are reading *Atrocities*?"

Zref opened and answered. "About 57 percent of what a Lantern would pull at this stage. Not bad."

Arshel nodded, "And they get to keep all the profits! What will Waysjoff have left to worry about?"

Khelin laughed. "It'll find something."

"Such as," said Zref, "our enemy isn't going to quit." He explained how he and Arshel were trying to read the missing text in order to corroborate Zref's memory about the Object. "I don't intend to use it to make it self-destruct. There has to be another way!"

"If I could get my hands on the actual plaque," said Arshel, "I might be able to learn more."

"Khelin," asked Zref, suddenly remembering, "where's Ley? *He* wrote that thing. If he remembers, maybe he can translate it!"

Khelin answered, "He's asleep. He needs it."

"I don't know if we dare take time to sleep," said Zref.

"Perhaps if you had," said Khelin, "you might have thought of looking up our enemy's identity via comnet."

Stunned, Zref shut his gritty eyes.

"Do you still need question form input?" asked Khelin.

Silently, Zref nodded. Apparently, he did.

Khelin obliged, adding, "I'll go see if I can wake Ley."

By the time Khelin returned, followed by Ley, who was dragging his heels and squinting against the light, absently scratching his chest as he descended the stair behind Khelin, Zref knew a great deal about their enemy.

They all took refills on their drinks, and appreciated the zwingus, while Zref told them, "Her name is Thsee Rith, an Almurali aristocrat, majority stockholder in Lantern Enterprises. She bought in when Lantern was just a failing tourist outfit and created Lantern Novels and Lantern Digs. She sits on a number of Lantern's governing boards, but her strength is felt only through the proxies she votes—by instruction, so she claims. But she owns most of the stock."

"So it's all of Lantern, we have to fight," said Khelin.

Zref flashed some diagrams on their screen. "It'd take me days to trace her holdings. She's like a spider at the center of a web. See? Many of those strands disappear into limbo at the edges. She has underworld connections—and uses them. She was behind Balachandran, though maybe we'll never know if she put him up to calling himself the modern Ossminid. She obviously wants Imperial power again."

Zref put the inscription on the screen beside the translation. "Ley, do you remember carving this plaque?"

"I don't remember very well, just a flash here and there—studying under Khelin. Tutoring Jocelyn. Being jealous of Khelin when he had Jocelyn—even though I was of a different species! I was such a juvenile idiot—"

Khelin clamped a steadying hand on his shoulder, saying, "We were all juvenile idiots! Young souls are, you know."

"I was cowardly, too. I could have done a better job on that plaque. But I knew I was going to die. Stupid. I was scared to die. I couldn't remember dying before, so the idea frightened me. Now I remember almost nothing but my deaths!"

"But do you remember what you wrote?" asked Zref. "You learned the language, when you were working for my parents. Can you remember, and translate the missing parts?"

Ley squirmed in his chair, and Khelin looked as if he was sorry to have wakened his bhirhir to face this. Just then, Shui and Iraem came in, sniffing the pervasive aroma of assorted hot drinks. By the time the two kren were brought up to date and had confessed their only clear memory, other than memories of people who weren't here, was helping Zref build the Selector, Ley was able to tackle the hard one.

"I left Khelin with the Object—the Selector—and I knew I'd never see him alive again. At the end of the tunnel, I found a building tool discarded since the tunnel was finished, and I cut a panel from its wall. I used some sort of levitator to haul it outside, as far as I could from the mouth of the tunnel. Crashing explosions shook the ground. Debris was raining down. People ran screaming all about me. I squatted in the midst of it, concentrated, and carved the inscription with the building tool." He got up to finger the screen where words were missing.

"I remember each of these distractions. Here, a child with a burn-blackened arm ran by screaming. There, a large stone hit beside me and knocked me over. And here, at the end— two space ships trying to take off rammed each other and exploded, raining more fire on Thiarac—the City."

The name rang true. "Yes," Zref agreed. "Thiarac. But what did you write, here?" He didn't have to ask why Ley's distraction had caused the words to crumble with age. He understood now how a trained worker could make a product virtually eternal, or time-degradable. "I don't blame you for being distracted. Even I would have been."

Ley flashed Zref a thankful smile, and went on, verbally underlining the missing or incorrect words. "The *secret* of how the *Selector was constructed* dies with us. Know only that we dared not *drop it* into a *black hole*. All our *theoretical knowledge* would not let us predict what would happen." He glanced sheepishly at Zref and shrugged. "I was trying to write something frightening enough to keep people from looking for it." He continued. "If the *Selector* is found *and used by the untrained, many will die, and it will* destroy itself." Again the sheepish glance at Zref. "Close as I could come to a traditional curse." He tapped the signature, THE LAST PERSUADER. "Juvenile melodrama."

CHAPTER FIFTEEN
Thiarac

Later that day, *Epitasis* systems reported unidentified ships pacing them in and out of hyperlight, and the Captain demanded Zref's presence in her office. She paused in her storming rage only long enough for the purser's assistant to show Zref in and close the door behind him.

"Now do you see what comes of sheering away our Escort! We're not armed. We've survived the last two attacks by sheer luck. Now what are you going to do?"

Zref said, "Our destination is held by HP security, and I've alerted them we'll be coming in with pirates in our wake. Already, they've got ships breaking orbit to meet us."

She paused in her pacing, an icy stillness filled with all the menace her ancestry could muster, but even so she couldn't emulate Thsee Rith's implacable menace. "They had better be in time, or I shall hold the Guild responsible—*if* your Guild can buy out Star-Treader and Lantern!"

Zref met her gaze and took his leave with all elaborate courtesies, wishing he felt as confident as he appeared to her. He knew how the Guild would react if they knew the Guarantees no longer held him. If they could catch him, they'd disconnect his interface, leaving him a vegetable.

But before he faced the Guild, he had to outrace the pirates. After they'd calculated their destination, the pirates would still have to pry the exact location of the Selector out of Thsee Rith. That would take time if they were her enemies. If they were her allies, she still wouldn't trust them with the location. They had some time.

On his way back to the suite, through empty halls where crewmen were lackadaisically tending low-priority chores, Zref received a private file drop. *"Do you have an explanation for commandeering* Epitasis? *Rodeen."*

Zref had thought over many versions of the truth to tell the

Guild, for he must behave as if he were still bound by the
Guarantees, and he'd prepared a text detailing the story for
her. *"Rodeen, this is for File # 9777. I have the location of
the Mazeheart Object, and I'm using* Epitasis *to race the creator
of the Wild Interfaces to it. I'm awaiting instructions on its
disposal after I secure it. Zref."*

Rodeen did not ask for verification of Zref's sending. She
didn't have to. There could be no mistake. She replied, *"I'll
try to straighten this all out for you. Rodeen."*

The entire group had assembled by the time Zref finished
telling of his visit to the Captain, while putting his exchange
with Rodeen on their big comtap screen.

"You didn't tell me, you planned to turn the Selector over
to the Guild," said Arshel indignantly.

"With its Selective properties eradicated," said Zref, "it's
just a relic, as good as destroyed. All the Guild's scientists
couldn't figure out how to recreate it."

"The Guarantees," said Khelin, "require him to obey Guild
Officers like Rodeen."

"Of course, because they're also bound by the Guarantees
to uphold the integrity of the comnet. If Rodeen knew what I
know, she'd order the destruction, or at least disarming, of the
Selector. But I doubt she'd believe me without extensive verification. In any event, after this is over, they'll call me in for
a thorough lab study, because I've taken more initiative than
I should have been able to take."

A short time ago, Arshel would've objected to going to
Guild Headquarters on Hengrave when Zref had promised to
see her through Mautri. Now, he saw she'd meant her promise
to release him from his obligation. "I think I like you better
now," said Arshel. "Not so many blank looks when I forget
to form a question—or weird answers when I ask instead of
stating. Interfaces can be hard on the nerves."

Shortly after this, *Epitasis* began to experience a rash of
minor malfunctions. Zref immediately convened his aklal and
encased the ship in a protective green globe.

They suffered one more major disruption of power when a
conduit slagged down. But it was quickly fixed, and the ship
plunged on. For a while, Zref feared sabotage by crewmen of
Thsee's aklal, but it seemed she'd called all of them to her at

the Crown. The skeleton crew was reliable.

When Zref was certain they'd fended off Thsee Rith's influence, and she knew it, he dared to drop a note to Youta who was still under quarantine on Camiat. *"Do you have any news of Mautri or MorZdersh'n for me? Zref."*

Youta replied the epidemic had developed a second phase which often left nerve damage. A ship had brought a limited supply of serum, allocated to high-risk patients in hope it would forestall the secondary infection. Mautri had refused treatment; MorZdersh'n had accepted only for children.

Firestrip, as most major cities on Camiat, was shrouded in a deep silence. A few Ciitheen, the species most resistant to the plague, were operating essential services. Youta sent Zref the official death roll; those closest to Zref had escaped. *"But I expect they're as ill as the rest of us, or struggling to care for the fallen. Youta."*

Zref sent back, *"I understand. But please deliver the following messages to Skanqwin, or if you can't reach him, to Jylyd. We are all well, and proceeding rapidly. We may call upon you for assistance unexpectedly, if we must. Zref."*

Zref also queried Sirwin where the situation was similar, and sent the same message to Glenwarnan.

Over supper on the fourth day out of Pallacin, Zref told them this news. With the ship so empty, they ate together in their suite, food brought from the officers' mess. "I really don't think we should count on them at all," said Shui. He had been worrying about Jylyd. Iraem wasn't much help, for he, too, was worried about his ex-bhirhir and family.

"They gave us some support on Pallacin," argued Khelin. "Or we never would have gotten out of that."

"They gave us their last strength," said Iraem. "We've got to settle this ourselves, even if it costs all our lives."

"That's awfully grim," objected Neini.

"Realistic," corrected Waysjoff. It was huddled in a hemispherical chair suspended from the ceiling, the bald spot in its fluff carefully hidden.

They'd shared the fragments of memory they'd recovered, sifting out ones pertaining to other people not here now. "I think," said Zref, "each of us has to evaluate independently— or as bhirhirn—the price of a life."

Jocelyn said, "Thsee Rith means to kill me. I don't mean to let her."

"That's a good attitude," said Ley. "I'm with you."

"Of course," said Arai, "we'll fight for our lives. But destroying the Selector is more important than surviving its destruction. We built it. It's our responsibility."

"Jernal don't make good heroes," said Waysjoff.

"None of us do," said Zref. But Arshel had already put responsibility above life in striking her bhirhir. She was the only one of them who'd passed that test of heroism—in this life. "We must do our best. If we fail we'll only have all this to do over again. That is—if Thsee Rith doesn't disperse our souls to the winds of chaos."

Every spare moment, they studied Thiarac. They pored over the maps of the City showing the shuttle pad near the cluster of dwellings, almost a village, at the edge of the once teeming metropolis. And they planned strategy.

Zref spent much time in the astrogation nodes trying to track the ships that were dipping in and out of range of their scopes. Most were pirates, not registered with local Astrogation. But far to the stern, and gaining, came a yacht which could only belong to Thsee Rith.

One day out of Thiarac, two pirate ships exchanged fire, one of them was destroyed, and the winner pulled ahead of the rest, closer to *Epitasis*. Zref relayed this to the HP ships approaching and watched the yacht veer away from that aggressive pirate. No friend of Thsee's then. And her enemies had had a falling out among themselves.

Half a day later, their HP Escort closed with the pirates. Zref projected the encounter onto the suite screen for his group, as he and Arshel watched it from the bridge.

"The Guild does things right for the ships it hires," admitted the Captain. The Guild had squared everything with Lantern and Star-Treader, knowing as they did, *Epitasis*'s real mission, thus which HP officials to bargain with behind the scenes. Thsee Rith had let Zref have *Epitasis*, he surmised, because she was utterly confident in her yacht's ability to overtake them. His musings were interrupted when the Captain said, "That's a much more formidable Escort than Lantern sent us at Pallacin. They're winning."

This, after three hours of maneuvers, they saw only as slowly shifting colored dots in a three-dimensional tank. The pirate that had destroyed another pirate had also destroyed two HP Escorters and still survived. Two other pirates maneuvered skillfully in concert with the shark pirate. The Captain sent terse tactical suggestions to the HP ships, which were often taken by the fighter captains.

"You could have been an Escort Captain, yourself," said Zref. "You think fast enough for it."

"It has always been an interest of mine," allowed the Captain, drawing herself erect. "However, I'm satisfied to run a passenger liner." But something in her manner made Zref suspect this wasn't wholly true.

Zref watched the battle probing back at the yacht which was closing on them, but still far astern. It made all legal recognition and astrogation signals. Its systems were as sophisticated as *Epitasis*, with independent decision capability. But it was blocked to Interface control.

He abandoned that avenue, waded into the shallows of the lava in his mind, and reached out with his other senses. He still perceived it, but now it shimmered insubstantially.

As the survivor pirate and its three cohorts broke and ran from the HP ships, Zref said, "If you'll excuse us, Captain, we'd like to see how the others are taking this."

She acknowledged, giving orders for the approach orbit into the system of the synthetic yellow star with its single planet, an engineering feat far beyond the HP. *Epitasis* injected into a synchronous orbit over the City of a Million Legends lost amid a horde of other ships, large and small. With Thsee Rith's yacht closing fast, Zref hustled his group into the shuttle. The comnet had been extended to cover the planet since he'd first been here, and there was even a small ancillary comnode below. Zref had no trouble insinuating his command for a hopper to meet them at the shuttle pad.

The shuttle's screen showed them the City from space, laid out like a target. The effect was enhanced by a maze of boundary fences set up by cataloguers charting every rock, every artifact, every grain of sand before anything could be moved. Some areas were run by Lantern, but the dominating hand here was HP, which was lavishly cooperative with the Guild. There

was no other Interface on planet, but the HP obviously hoped
to get one sooner by welcoming Zref.

"Master Interface," the Explorer Corps Groundmaster, a
Sirwini male of middle years and stature, greeted. His horns
were dull with age, but still sharp. His complexion showed
long exposure to the dry desert now lapping at Thiarac. But
this day was only pleasantly warm.

"My mission is urgent," said Zref, projecting dignified haste.
"Later, I'll be glad to explain as best I can. But for now, will
you order everyone out of areas H-7, K-7, H-6, and H-8? There
may be some danger."

The Sirwini threw his head back in respectful assent. "Our
pleasure to cooperate with the Guild."

Even at the hopper's best speed, it took long minutes to
reach the area where Zref and Arshel had found Balachandran
dead. The beige, dust, white and pink stone that had once
composed the City was crumbling, holding a pattern only when
seen from space or by the experienced eye.

Yet they were seeing it through newly wakened memories.
Zref remembered high building terraces and sweeping avenues,
dotted with lush vegetation of parks and gardens, throngs of
brightly colored beings, feathered and scaled, or even haired;
mingled cooking odors; music of a thousand languages. His
breath caught in his throat over a futile pang of homesickness
evoking the emotion he'd felt when he'd "seen" Thiarac in
Jylyd's green globe, an overwhelming sense of a long, painful
exile finally ending. And, oh, he ached to bring this new family
of warmth and belonging home with him for a lifetime.

"Why is that hopper following us?" asked Waysjoff.

"It's not—" started Zref checking its route program. Dozens
of similar hoppers were rising from the area of the Maze,
evacuating on the Groundmaster's order. But this one, slipping
through the patterned confusion, was indeed pacing them. "It's
part of a Lantern crew," said Zref.

"Thsee Rith controlled?" asked Khelin. "From so far?"

"We dare not underestimate her," warned Arai.

"Nor harm innocent bystanders," added Iraem.

Zref said, "Let me see if I can ground them." He wrestled
the suspect hopper free of traffic control by pulling rank on the
machine, then sent the hopper off into the choked tumble of

streets—far enough that the occupants couldn't get to them in less than a day on foot.

Arshel eyed the trajectory saying, "You're going to have a hard time explaining that to Rodeen. Interfaces aren't supposed to strand people."

"They'll be all right," said Zref, knowing she was right, and knowing why the Guarantees were so very strict. It would be easy to fear the kind of power he had. *Surely they'll disconnect me.*

Their hopper set them down just outside the area where the two landers had plowed arrow-shaped scars in the rubble. Balachandran's lander was still there, deactivated and rusting away. The one Zref and Arshel had ridden down in was gone. An archeologist's demarcating field outlined Balachandran's body prone before the replica of the stone slab with Ley's final inscription on it.

They picked their way carefully over the undisturbed debris. Knee-high forcefield fences laced the area into a grid pattern, and they had to help each other over them. Arshel said, "No. This place is still as bereft of a past as a newly made shoe. The Object's not here, Khelin."

But Khelin was looking up the broad avenue that led to the Maze entrance. "We've got to find the tunnel."

Ley glanced about. "Nothing looks right. This thing might have been dragged—any distance, by anybody."

"Zref, where did the tunnel exit?" asked Khelin.

Ley was right, nothing looked familiar. But Zref summoned the image of the ruins from above, and the memory of how the City had once been laid out. Superimposing them as he cast about him for a landmark, he finally settled on an area strewn with rubble. "It was like an exit from the basement of a building—the wall must have collapsed on it."

"We should have brought tools," said Arai.

"The hopper's fully equipped," suggested Neini.

Arshel and Neini climbed back in to search, returning with a force-lever and a pounder capable of reducing a boulder the size of a man to dust in half a minute. Arshel said, "We can't use this!" brandishing the pounder.

Arai took the force-lever from Neini and puzzled out the controls with long, graceful fingers. "I think I can move that chunk there. Maybe we can hand-clear the rest."

He inserted the shaft of blue energy under the largest fragment and extended the fulcrum field. With his height for leverage, he leaned his weight on it. It wasn't enough, so he ran the lever's field out behind his hands, grunting, "Zref, lean on this with me. If only we had a levitator!"

Zref stretched up awkwardly, grasped the handle and put his entire weight on it. The chunk of wall tipped, then slid away exposing a slanted hatchway covered with rubble.

The others fell to, clearing the doors, but when they tried them, they were—of course—jammed.

"No," said Khelin thinking. "Not jammed with age. Arshel, can't you feel it now? *That* is not dead."

She knelt, felt the eroded surface, a drab-colored door in a pile of pink rubble. "Yes, but nothing's there—" She halted, astonished at her words. "That's nonsense. But I swear, there's no reason to go down there. It's empty . . ."

Khelin grinned as Zref lifted Arshel away. "Zref, I remember now! I set up a kind of standing wave of Persuasion— surrounding the Selector with unutterable boredom."

Zref clapped his hands. "Always knew you were clever!" He knelt on the door, dusting off a gleaming panel, reevoking the ambience of this place as the heart of a galaxy. It didn't hurt now to remember building the Maze—and its escape route. He was aware of the droning of the yacht's systems as it contacted local orbital control, and of the efforts of the downed hopper's crew to take off again. One of them had climbed a mound of rock and spotted their hopper. Thsee Rith would know, might already know.

But he remembered the tunnel's lock. "Waysjoff," said Zref. "You have good, hard claws. Come here." He traced a figure in the dust, saying, "Draw this right there. Draw it while visualizing the Maze from above." It was no accident they'd chosen that figure for their aklal focus.

"I don't know if I—"

"Of course you can," encouraged Neini.

Waysjoff rotated as if to glance at her. Hairpins held bits of its fluff together over the holes left by Plath.

"Try," she pleaded.

It rotated again, applying itself to the task. Four times it tried, then hid its legs. "I can't concentrate!"

Zref was struggling with unruly thoughts, too. He said, "Arai, will you help him as if you were writing a book?"

Arai turned stricken eyes on Zref, glanced at the sky, and shuddered. Neini said, "You've got to face it."

The Theaten nodded, and bent over the Jernal with Neini, forming their triune aklal. Waysjoff traced the pattern—very accurately—on the sensor panel. Arai described the Maze for it. Four more tries, and the door slid aside presenting them with a black pit.

Iraem said, "Too much to ask the lights to work!" He dashed back to the hopper, returning with an arm load of hand torches while Zref ventured waist deep into the hole.

"It's cold down here," Zref said, "but not unbearable."

The clear sky and warm sun for which they had forgotten to be grateful were left behind as Shui pulled the doors shut on top of them. "Is there some way to reset that lock?"

"I think it resets automatically," said Zref. "Try it."

Arai put his back to it, but no matter how he heaved and grunted, the doors wouldn't budge. "How do we get out!"

Arshel shivered. "I don't like it down here! Kren aren't underground creatures."

"Neither are Jernal," said Waysjoff.

"It's nothing like Firestrip's heated underways," agreed Khelin. "I hope we can get out. Last time, I didn't."

"The lock should work from the underside as well as it did above," said Zref. "Just find the sensitive panel, and trace the figure." He had erased the figure he'd drawn in the dirt—erased it physically and mentally, so perhaps Thsee Rith couldn't read it.

Jocelyn said, "We get out only if Waysjoff lets us out."

"Don't say it," warned Neini as Waysjoff began to speak. "You'll do it. When the time comes."

Zref could visualize Arai holding the poor Jernal over his head while it used a claw to trace the pattern. Zref hadn't realized his feathered form had been so tall.

They started down the narrow, stone tunnel. Waysjoff's light was slung from its underside, all six legs picking its way along the rock-strewn floor. But it wasn't complaining.

They crossed obliquely under the city streets. Sections of

the tunnel were relatively clear of debris, and they made good time, but the yacht was orbiting when they came to a wide chamber with bright, glittering walls.

"This looks familiar!" exclaimed Jocelyn.

"It's alive here," whispered Arshel. "But—I don't—I've never been here before."

"You haven't. This's where we built the Selector," said Zref. He didn't know how he knew that, but he'd fallen into the habit of speaking, then listening to what he'd said. "And this is the only place we can destroy or disable it."

"Destroy!" said Arshel.

Khelin didn't give Zref time to argue. "Has the Guild instructed you concerning the Selector?" he asked.

"No, they're debating." He looked around fighting off a dizzy sense of déjà vu. "But we haven't found it yet."

The cavern was roofed with a groined dome over a floor that was a square with two isosceles triangles grafted onto opposite sides. One of the triangles was tall, its depths shrouded in shadows. The other was short, and held at its blunted apex a glistening model of the galaxy made from precious gems to color the suns. Around it, giant rubies clustered like succulent fruits on a twining vine. A white sun-opal formed the eye of a mythological creature and seemed to glow intelligently. Opposite, bizarre gems reflected light making a rainbow haze in the center of the chamber.

Zref knew there was a pattern and a precise reason for each and every gem's choice and its placement. But his memories were gestalts rather than details. He couldn't reconstruct this science, though it was founded on elements of the Mautri and Glenwarnan teachings.

Khelin put one hand to the wall, running his fingers along it as he followed the wall, searching. Waysjoff folded its legs and settled to the floor. Neini sat down near it, her forehead on her knees. Zref could feel the dead weight of boredom, pricking him with anxious impatience to get out of there. Shui and Iraem posted themselves on either side of the tunnel entry. Zref examined the dome, and dusted a section of floor. Its intricate mosaic pattern seemed to speak to him. And where was the other entry?

Suddenly, Khelin gasped. Ley dashed across the chamber

to where the kren had entered the tall triangle. "What's—
uuuhhh!" And then in a reverential whisper. "It's *you!*"

Zref joined them, with everyone else. "It's your skeleton,"
affirmed Arshel. She shuddered clinging to Zref.

Khelin, after the initial shock, grabbed at Ley as if he were
his only hope of sanity. Zref could well imagine what it was
like to come upon your dead self while in your living body.
And the memories of that death weren't pleasant.

He urged the two bhirhirn aside and squatted to examine
the find. "Let me record this just as is." The remains were
scarcely more than a dust smeared horny carapace and a wisp
of what might be hair. When he'd finished, Khelin had recovered his composure.

"The means the Selector has to be—" Khelin turned, dragging Ley with him straight across the chamber and into the
shallow triangle. "—here!" He squatted at the apex, running
his hand over the jeweled pattern. "Zref?"

Zref hunkered down, shining his torch on the area. "One
of these jewels?" *No, that can't be right.*

Khelin sat down, running both hands over his head where
his ears would have been had he been human. "I don't know!"

Zref fingered the jewel encrusted wall. Many of the brightest
gems were unknown in the HP. Manufactured by First Lifewave
technology? Selector could be a jewel—but—his fingers engaged a chink at the edge of the block forming a section of
wall. "Look!" He traced the block. "Help me!"

They scrabbled at it, then Arai said, "Zref, if it's a secret
compartment, you built it. Tell us the opening code!"

The yacht was making orbit, sending a shuttle down.

"Khelin—you must know."

"I—I can't remember."

"Think back to when we built the thing. It took a long time.
When it was only partly finished—we kept it here, where it
couldn't harm anything. Khelin—when you hid it—I wasn't
even aware of this hole. You must have remembered it as you
were preparing to flee. Think—remember!"

They both ran hands over sections of wall around the corner,
until Khelin rose and spun about, and charged back to where
his body lay. "Of course." He pointed. "Under. Me."

Ley caught him away from the gruesome task, grunting,

"Not you." He gestured to Shui and Iraem. "See if we can move it without breaking it."

"Don't watch," said Zref. But the kren was transfixed.

The carapace broke into several pieces, and the tufts of hair disintegrated. But they got the thing moved aside with a lot less damage than expected. The floor mosaic here looked the same as it did everywhere else.

Coughing, Khelin knelt and scraped dust aside. "A sensitive panel. I don't know the combination—"

Zref did. "I used my own name—as it was when we built this. Fahamin. Kinrea cursive script. I can still do it!" He knelt and traced the figure over the sensitive area of the floor. It felt right—but his hand should be a claw, and there was a mental image trigger. What? Ah! The Crystal Crown!

"Waysjoff—your hand again, please," said Zref. He traced the complex figure several times, but even with Neini and Arai helping, the Jernal just couldn't copy it.

"Waysjoff," said Zref, standing to ease his cramped legs. "Remember we talked about heroics? Do you think—do you think you could allow me to—guide your touch?"

It whimpered, and Zref wished he could snatch back his words. But he pressed, "Thsee's entering atmosphere."

With the oddest sound Zref had ever heard from a Jernal, it agreed, hunching down to hide its legs, allowing only the one claw-hand to protrude from its pink fluff. "If there were any other way—" said Zref.

"Just hurry," urged Waysjoff, trembling.

Non-Jernal had been prosecuted for assault for less. But Zref took the living tool, visualizing the Crown, and on the third try, the corner of the shallow apex across from them slid out like a drawer.

They all rushed back the length of the chamber, Zref sliding to his knees in front of the drawer. Arshel hung back, averting her gaze, radiating fear. Zref said, over his shoulder, "Don't worry, it's deactivated now."

Reverentially, he shined his light within. At first sight, the Selector was an unprepossessing globe of white crystal, with colorless windows showing a complex inner structure. But in moments, it flared with invisible energy.

Zref knew the Selector was made of the same time-fixed substance as the Crystal Crown. The Globe of Stars had suggested its structure: nine spheres plus an elliptical spheroid, linked by two triangles.

Zref reeled, his untrained brain unable to encompass it. Tucking his torch under his arm, he lifted the Selector out of its dusty drawer. He rose letting them get a good look at it, walked to the center of the chamber, and said, "Arshel, because you've never been a Persuader, there's no guarantee you'd survive looking into the Selector." And if she did, she'd become what she feared most. "While we work, go out into the tunnel and turn your back on us. Don't look!"

Absently hunting for something his arms and legs knew was there, he directed the others to form a circle. Then he reached out to place the Selector on its pedestal—and found the floor rising to meet his hands.

He stared. A small round section of floor rose on a slender column and took the Selector out of his grasp, elevating it to nose height. *No doubt. We were taller!*

"Arshel!" he commanded, noticing her lingering despite his order. "In the tunnel. Warn us when Thsee Rith comes."

She scuffed into the tunnel, with two torches, but Zref scarcely noticed. His mind was probing the Selector, looking for cracks or discolorations of dangerous deterioration. Yet he could simultaneously read his private file drop.

"Have you found the Object yet? Rodeen."

"Yes, though it doesn't look very imposing. Zref."

"Package it carefully. Epitasis is standing by to bring you two directly here. Thsee Rith has claimed it for Lantern. Move fast, she's in orbit though I've had her landing privileges denied. Rodeen."

"She's on the surface here, gathering her allies among the workers. She'll soon know where we are. Zref."

"Your friends will be richly rewarded if they can help. Rest assured the Object will disappear into Guild vaults not even to be studied by Guild researchers. The Guild is unanimous on this now. Bring it to us, Zref. Rodeen."

"Don't be surprised if you don't hear from me for a while. Zref." The dominant part of him didn't intend to follow more than the letter of that instruction.

When he relayed the Guild decision, Arshel called, "What are you going to do?"

As always, Arshel tapped his inspiration. "Shatter the interior, so it looks like a crystal that's undergone severe thermal shock. That'll disarm it so nobody could rearm it. Even *we* can't destroy it without making a new Persuader!"

Arai called, "Arshel, join us as you always have. We can't do this without you."

"Yes," agreed Zref. Arshel was the key. They had to have an aklal one member more than that which had constructed the Selector, and that extra member had to be an antagonist they'd embraced in harmony. It'd taken all these millennia to do it. "Arshel, visualize our Maze—as you colored it for us. All of you—think now—we're in a chamber under the Mazeheart. Remember how it once was—alive, glowing. Remember how you walked it. Remember what you discovered—of yourself. Of the One. Be there with me now. Be here, with me then— about to activate the Selector and establish the Persuader Corps by becoming the first Persuaders."

Awareness narrowed to his richly feathered, athletic body. He looked down on the Selector on its pedestal, circled it inspecting from all angles. When he'd gone halfway, he looked back where he'd been standing and saw a short pale stranger of some odd species. He shrugged, knowing the entity was friendly, a sleeper's projection.

He turned the Selector until it was oriented exactly, and he was satisfied. He rustled his feathers impressively, and proudly called in his aklal. The multiple awareness settled about him. He was everywhere in the chamber, looking in every direction. He was even in the exit tunnel which was only half finished now. No, that one was a projection, too.

With a snap of his attention, he called the aklal to the work, giving them the key image, the interior structure of the Selector—with each sphere spinning, and orbiting the center, while the ellipsoid spun first on its long axis, then on its short axis, moving to the heartbeat of the observer. Within each sphere, the pyramidal form inscribed within it rotated its colored sides this way and that, reflecting the energy states of the observer.

In this case, "the observer" was not one being, but an aklal. It made no difference in principle, for their minds beat as one, and all the mobile sections of the Selector whirled smoothly in their appropriate patterns.

With dismay, he heard the thoughts and echoed them willingly within his mind, adding his own power to it.

DISINTEGRATE! DISSIMILATE! DISSIPATE! DIS-LODGE! DISJECT! DISPEL!

The concept was one, the expression many, and the thought voices formed a perfect chord. The silence rose to a crescendo that suspended in midair over the Selector which glowed invisibly, whirling faster and faster, hotter and brighter, and in the end the Selector screamed—

No! That's Arshel! The contact fell away from his hands, and Zref whirled in his tracks, stumbling toward the tunnel—because his legs were too short. But he recovered and raced to her while the others were still clutching at their eyes to break the contact with the Selector.

Hand over her eyes, Arshel was pointing up the tunnel. Now Zref felt an immense impact, a thud that shook the world.

"It's a pounder!" yelled Arshel.

Local traffic control indicated Thsee Rith's shuttle had grounded at the port and she'd taken a hopper—picked up the workers Zref had stranded—and was now at the tunnel.

The intensity in the chamber behind them had faded. The Selector was quiescent, armed and able to self-destruct.

Zref squirmed out of his jacket, saying to Arshel, "Here, take the prybar. Guard the tunnel until I call you. And don't look this way until I say it's all right!"

He raced back to the chamber, pushing through those crowded around the doorway. As he flung his jacket over the Selector and scooped it up, he said, "That door isn't going to hold forever. We've drained a lot of the power that was sustaining this place. Here—take this now!"

He handed the Selector, wrapped in the black Interface's jacket, to Khelin. He didn't take time to snatch his medallion from the pocket. Then he grabbed Ley and Jocelyn, putting them on either side of Khelin and shoved them into a position halfway between the pedestal and the open drawer.

He dropped to hands and knees, scrabbling in the dust. "Waysjoff! Quickly! Visualize the Maze. Write my name."

This time, despite the ominous pounding, Waysjoff did it on the first try. A circle of floor detached itself and raised Jocelyn, Ley and Khelin toward the ceiling—which opened, then closed behind them.

"Come on Arshel!" called Zref. "You can look now."

Meanwhile, he sent Neini, Arai and Iraem up.

Arshel ran to Zref. "We didn't succeed, did we?"

"Almost," said Zref, urging Waysjoff onto the returning lift, and motioning Shui on after him. "I don't dare believe this thing will work one more time! But it has to! Go on, Waysjoff, activate it!"

The pounding had stopped after a mighty crash.

The Jernal reached a hand-leg over the side and drew the figure. Shuddering and wobbling, the platform rose.

"Come on!" called Zref, pulling Arshel toward the tunnel. "This is the only way out now."

CHAPTER SIXTEEN

Bhirhirn

The tunnel was dark.

Arshel panting beside him, Zref could still feel Waysjoff's shock when the Jernal realized that Zref and Arshel weren't going to crowd onto the plate, too.

But it was a small lift plate, old beyond all reason. It shouldn't have functioned at all, let alone carry the four of them. With no way to activate the control, the tunnel remained their only escape. He drew Arshel forward, knowing Thsee Rith and others were already rushing toward them.

The tunnel was just wide enough for two to walk abreast. Zref doused his light as they approached a bend. Immediately they could see the lights of the approaching party.

Restraining Arshel, he peeked around the corner. The section of tunnel ahead was empty. He tugged her forward.

They dashed the length of the increasing light of the approaching party. Zref stationed Arshel behind the right angle bend, and leaped out into the new branch of the tunnel.

Blinding brilliance.

He shut his eyes, then dared to squint. "Thsee Rith! Ossminid! You are not Emperor here! You trespass!"

Oddly enough, the party stopped. A murmur, and from its rear, a figure worked its way toward Zref—forcing the others aside. But they didn't all hug the same wall. They alternated, so if Zref wanted to run that gauntlet, he'd have to zigzag and would surely be caught.

The Almurali female emerged from the group of six dusty, sweaty humans who'd been peacefully working their site before Zref came. She gestured her men to aim their lights down.

She was wearing a forest-green cape—the Imperial color. A gown of pure white draped her torso and fell to the floor behind her, stopping above the ankles in front. Her feet were booted. Zref noted the cant of her ears: forward now, willing to listen. "So. You've come to welcome me."

The lack of sarcasm in her tone underscored her contempt for him. Zref demanded, "State your business here."

She strolled into the space between her men and Zref. "You never were as good as you thought you were—as teacher, as Mazemaster . . . or lover. You just never could seem to understand the value of power. Almost four hundred million years and you still don't know when you're beaten."

She sounded as if she were amazed at a precocious child. Zref glanced behind him, worried Arshel might be goaded.

"Your little kren can't help you. I'm immune to her."

At his astonishment, she laughed—the Almurali hiss of pure pleasure. "Now, do you understand, Fahamin? You're outclassed. Join me and together we'll found a new Empire of Stars. Alone, I could make it as great as its predecessor. Together, you and I could make it even greater!"

Those years, when the Empire was growing, every life had felt sweetly successful. Zref found a knotted tension within him, the knot that'd resisted disarming the Selector, and knew it to be a hunger to recreate the goodness he'd known then. A vibrancy in the air made it so real to him, he moaned, feeling as if he held a hatchet and were about to chop off his own foot. With her, he could be whole—

Throwing off Thsee's enticing grip, he lunged a step forward and snarled, "No!" The breeze from the smashed door was chill on his sweat-coated face.

Arshel stepped out beside Zref. "You aren't worth defying!" she spat. "The glories you say you created never existed. The memories that made this the City of a Million Legends were based on the works of forty-eight emperors—but not the forty-ninth! We'll help you remember it correctly!"

Arshel snatched at the remaining wisps of the aklal and wove them anew. In her hands, the aklal was barely self-aware. Zref sensed Khelin's presence, and then concentrated on backing Arshel. Perhaps they could win Thsee Rith over.

He drew himself up into his Fahamin persona, and then recalled being Thsee's teacher, preparing her to walk the Maze. He recalled his doubts of her readiness, overcome by her earnest enthusiasm, and burning will to serve. She reminded him of Khelin, the indefatigable investigator of the Odd Occurrence.

But he'd never been able to discern what she was dedicated to, only that the dedication had the purity needed to walk the Maze safely. He let her go, only half instructed in the secrets of the universe known to him.

"Half instructed!" she scoffed aloud, breaking their fragile concentration. "Your Maze completed my instruction! Now, I've come for the device. Don't tell me it's not here. I felt you activate it. You're not going to set yourself up again as Mazemaster independent of the rightful government—like your precious Guild!" Her silky tones roughened as she spoke, her haughtiness growing. They'd reached her.

Arshel, unable to be silent when her bhirhir was pressured, answered, "We've destroyed the Mazeheart."

"You lie!" But panic underlay her words. She reached behind her and threw one of her men at Zref. "Kill him!"

The man was virtually a zombie—eyes glazed, movements dull. He was a puppet under her control—and that control was frightening to see. As the first man stumbled into Zref, the others moved as if joined by an invisible string.

Zref retreated, afraid Arshel might be triggered into a strike if it came to hand-to-hand. Mentally, he stretched for the bonds holding these men in thrall. He'd been part of the Lantern aklal himself, held spellbound by tales of the greatness of the Empire, the peace and security, the ease of taking up a life of mighty deeds. Those books had been written by Meguerian, but even these men had read them. Probably, they'd also read *Phailan Atrocities*, and that was the avenue Zref found into the man's consciousness.

From those threads, he wove a transparent wall between himself and the six men. "How did you do that?" asked Arshel, mystified.

But there was no time to lecture on Philosophical Engineering. Thsee gestured, and created an archway in his wall. Her men charged for it, and Zref created a solid computer-locked door and slammed it. She materialized a programmable sounder, attached it to the door and picked the lock. Zref built a stone wall just inside the door which stopped the door from opening, but also cut off their view.

It was all illusion, palpable to the six hapless tools she was using, but meaningless to Thsee and Zref. While she pondered,

Zref scooped Arshel behind him, wrapping her arms about his waist. "Stick with me, no matter what happens."

He knew they'd probably die here, but he had to give Khelin enough time to get the Selector offplanet. She'd be roundly defeated, and would know it, while he hadn't struck a blow or harmed anyone. Perhaps she could learn from observation what she couldn't seem to learn from instruction. Trust. The simplest of all lessons, and the hardest.

What Zref did not reckon on, though, was loyalty.

Summoning memories of incarnations both before and after his lives at Glenwarnan, he flung a cloak of invisibility around himself and Arshel, confining their auras within it, and stepping back into shadow, dissolving his wall.

He swallowed a burble of delighted laughter when the bewildered men swept the area with their hands, and shined their torches around the next corner.

"Gone!" exclaimed Thsee. "We'd have heard them running—teleportation! I never would have believed—"

Zref hadn't thought of that. Rummaging amid fragmentary memories, he couldn't find any way to do it. He could only do things when the situation suggested them—if he didn't think about it. *Much like an amnesiac who's lost personal identity because of trauma.*

As the men searched the next tunnel, Zref edged toward the entry, trying to muffle his breathing and his step. Understanding, Arshel moved silently with him.

Beyond the lights, it was easier to seem invisible. The six men were making enough noise, and Thsee was shouting at them, so Zref picked up his step and they made about half the distance to the door before Thsee divined their trick. "That way!" she exclaimed, pushing her men back toward them.

The men pounded back around the corner, their torches probing ahead. The powerful, collimated beams shone directly on Zref and Arshel just as three more people came down the tunnel from the entrance. *We're trapped!*

"Zref!" called Khelin.

The kren was carrying the Selector still wrapped in Zref's jacket. Behind him, Ley and Jocelyn slid to a halt.

Behind Zref, Thsee Rith pushed through the six men who were now brandishing pounders and prybars with their fields turned on, and roaring at the top of their lungs as if taken by a killing rage. Thsee had her green cloak caught up over one arm, and a torch in the other. "Get them!" she cried. Ears laid back, she led the charge.

Khelin's venom sack pulsed, his fangs flicking down into strike position. Then he recovered, and closed with Zref and Arshel, thrusting the Selector into Zref's hands. *"Now* call the aklal!" he commanded, as if impatient with the prior feeble attempt. "Come on Ley!"

Khelin squeezed by Zref and Arshel, heading for the on-coming force. Ley slid by, cast an exasperated look into Zref's eyes and yanked the jacket away exposing the Selector, saying, "Wake up! Don't let her hypnotize you. Call us!"

Several things happened simultaneously. Arshel whipped around, shutting her eyes to avoid sight of the Selector. Khelin downed the lead man with one punch. Ley snatched the man's prybar to fence with the two behind while Khelin pushed on. Thsee caught sight of the Mazeheart as Zref, confounded at finding it in his hands when he'd been so sure it was being spirited offplanet, fought feelings of betrayal.

A mental contact coalesced between Zref and Thsee in which she magnified Zref's feelings. *See? You can't trust them!* For three breaths, Zref was taken by that insidious self-righteous pride. *How dare Khelin!* Then her grip wavered, and Zref felt her start with new fear, and then glory in it as if fear were the epitome of pleasure. She was blinded to all true pleasure and beauty by the purity of her dedication to power.

He squirmed in her grasp, rejecting the lure she offered, seeing her reflected within himself yet determined that part of him would whither from starvation rather than gain the upper hand. His choice was made. There was enough beauty in the universe to provide satisfactions; no need to seek satisfaction in recreating what had been.

Now Thsee tried to pull away, but Zref held as she inadvertently let him gaze through the eyes of her aklal. The three remaining pirate vessels now fighting the HP ships in orbit had been trailing her to the Object to steal it from her. She was contemptuous of them, but perversely joyful, for their obliteration would sweeten her triumph.

Disgusted, Zref gained command of the nexus of the Mazeheart and drew his aklal around it, shutting Thsee out.

Suddenly, he stood with his feet on the floor of the dark tunnel, and his head at orbital height over the City. His body stretched between, insubstantial as a chiffon scarf.

Below—or within him—Waysjoff, Arai, Neini, Shui and Iraem scrambled to find a way out of the Maze. Though they remembered the pattern, many paths were blocked by debris.

Above, the remaining HP ships deployed to engage the pirates. On the bridge of *Epitasis*, the Captain fumed helplessly. As Zref's awareness touched her, she started and looked about, "Master Interface?" Just as Khelin had been downing the lead man, one pirate ship opened fire on an Escorter, and the Escorter became an incandescent ball expanding into a rain of fragments some falling to the surface. The Almurali Captain swore luridly, and watched impotently as pirates fired on unarmed small civilian craft to clear the scene for their maneuvers.

The other two pirates swooped down into atmosphere, dangerously low, letting out a swarm of fighters and landers and then riding out of sight, orbiting the planet, struggling to gain altitude again before the atmosphere tore them apart. Three on one, the remaining HP ships dispatched the lone pirate and maneuvered to meet the other two.

Meanwhile, Khelin and Ley had fought past Thsee, and Jocelyn had thrust past Arshel to follow them. She came up face to face with Thsee—and Zref didn't like the way her aura pulsed as she recognized the one who'd used her cruelly.

Zref caught at Jocelyn, weaving her deeply into the aklal, soothing the fury that had almost possessed her. Now the entire aklal faced the Almurali form of Ossminid.

Beyond them, the physical fight continued, leaving Zref and Arshel alone, guarding the only exit from the tunnel.

Above, tiny fighters were engaging the HP ships, blazing energy bolts visible against the daytime sky. Landers were circling toward the City—bearing hordes of fighting men prepared to kill for the Mazeheart and its power.

One ship came down on the near edge of the Maze, disgorging armored men who spread out in a search pattern trying to find their way out of the Maze and to the open hole in the ground they'd spotted from the air. From atop one crumbled wall, Shui leaped down on one of the pirates, wrested his weapon from him, and rolled, firing into the thick of the squad. Four of the ten fell before one of them drilled the kren through the chest.

Iraem, seeing this, screamed and leaped on Shui's assailant, sinking his fangs through the elastic seal between helmet and armor, and into flesh. The pirate dropped in his tracks, but another got Iraem while he was locked in the throes of his strike.

Zref struggled to hold both Shui and Iraem in the aklal.

Arai appeared atop a mound of rubble as the pirates regrouped and headed for the tunnel entry. He pulled Neini up beside him, and Waysjoff popped up in a Jernal's peculiar leap. Seeing Shui and Iraem amid the bodies, divining the pirates' objective, he gathered Waysjoff and Neini away from Zref's greater hold. *I will do this, Zref. Keep Thsee from getting the Selector.*

The sub-aklal split off, blurring to Zref's perceptions, and suddenly, the entire squad of pirates was teleported back into their ship.

Zref knew he had to end this quickly, no matter what. Back in the tunnel, he was dismayed to see the six men struggling to their feet despite their wounds. Arshel yearned to destroy the Selector. Fear of its uncontrollable power no longer ruled her. And she knew one sure way to make it self-destruct. It took all her courage, but as Zref struggled to reform the aklal, she looked into the Selector. If it made a new Persuader, it would self-destruct.

Zref, caught off guard, could not stop it. The Selector flared. Zref was aware that the chamber beyond flared also, as if an image of the Mazeheart remained on its pedestal.

As light and not-light gathered about the Selector, the attention of the six men was drawn to it.

Six deep-throated cries of agony ripped the air. Zref felt heat in the Selector as it rejected the unprepared six. He was almost torn from his own anchorage to reality as the whirling forms caught at each of those souls, ripped their fabric to shreds and flung the tattered bits to the far corners of the unreal.

His head spun. He tumbled to the floor of the tunnel, the Selector clutched to his belly, his whole body attempting to shield it from the view of Arshel and the men. Too late.

Already the bodies of the men were subliming away, a rot of the very molecules. The tunnel became cold, dry-piercing bone-numbing cold. But the Selector was hot—glowing hot.

Zref was numb with the tragedy happening inside him— that had happened already—spellbound by the vision above of a deep space pirate ship, hurtling to ground, trailing billows of black and green smoke, falling helplessly toward the Maze itself—to this very spot.

Still stunned by the dying—the ultimate, true-dying of six innocent men—one corner of Zref's mind knew he should use the aklal to deflect the plummeting, and already dead pirate ship. But Thsee caught him in his benumbed, shocked weakness—to her Dispersals were nothing new—caught him and held him one precious instant.

She summoned Lantern. She seemed to grow beyond her mortal body, with strength no woman, even an Almurali, could wield. She thrust Jocelyn aside as if she were a wraith, and her hands reached toward Zref, reached to pluck the Selector like a ripe fruit, utterly confident. But Arshel rolled Zref over, and snatched it from his arms, gazing deep within it.

Arshel screamed—her whole body in torment, her hands burning, and her piercing scream ululating from every throat of the aklal.

Thsee saw it, too—now that Zref wasn't shielding it with his body. And Khelin and Ley, stumbling back along the tunnel, tripping over clothing and kicking torches and tools out of their way, came to the Selector as to a homefire.

Thsee backed as if from pain too excruciating to bear, her body blocking Khelin, Ley and Jocelyn.

Arshel, body rigid, held the pulsing hot globe aloft, her mouth open, her fangs down but her venom sack quiescent.

Zref felt the energies change, the Selector pulsing now with the life peculiar to Arshel Holtethor Lakely MorZdersh'n.

Harmony came in pulsing waves, each sweeter than the last, wiping away the pain and anguish echoing from the destruction of the six.

Transfixed by the sight of the Selector, Zref became caught up in the very essence of Arshel. He went with it—gave himself to it because it was for him, as Arshel always was, the link between himself and his true self. The Selector wove the two of them together into a symphony.

Thsee Rith backed, whimpering, and tripped, falling at the feet of Khelin and Ley.

When the sweetness was beyond bearing, and Zref had surrendered to imminent death, the globe of the Selector throbbed brighter and then brighter until the light made the solid walls transparent.

And then, in one instant, the Selector shattered to dust and was gone from between Arshel's uplifted hands.

The image seared into Zref's brain, a white-hot brand that sank deeper and deeper into his being. He clutched at the pillars of the door to the room without walls and watched the magma surge over his feet, dissolving his safe place away. The Interface opened.

The comnet lay before him, a bright, ethereal webwork of latent energies. Delicate beyond imagining, powerful beyond belief, here was a new philosophical engineering in its embryonic stage. The energy from the Selector lanced out into the comnet, incompatible, deadly.

Zref knew he couldn't surrender to death—for if he did, the power shafting down into his being and out into the comnet, would destroy this civilization as it had the first. He had one shattering vision of the entire Interface Guild turned into one massive Persuader. Then with nothing but his will, he drew himself back from the brink, wrestled with all the skills of an Interface to lower his blood pressure and close. Barely, just barely, he managed it. But as always, the crack was left open to his private file.

The energies, cut off from the nearly infinite comnet, splashed into his private file. Pressure collected as he struggled to squeeze off that access. He almost made it, but in the end circuits blew, and he felt a searing overload, and then the crack—open since the day of his final operation—closed. *Disconnected.* The last thing he knew before the world shattered was that he'd contained it to his own file. That was the only damage. He surrendered his life triumphantly as he felt the aklal rapport drop apart followed by a black emptiness.

His awareness terminated. But he knew when the pirates sallied forth again from their ship and picked off the three writers as they swayed in shock. He heard Arshel cry out, saw her venom sack pulse.

The pirate ship struck.

The ground shifted hard. Arshel fell on top of Zref. The walls shuddered. Powder rained down from the ceiling. The shattering blow was a physical wave smashing the body and the senses. Ground subsided. The ceiling crashed down between Zref and Thsee Rith, Jocelyn, Khelin and Ley.

"Run!" screamed Zref over the thunder.

Walls crumbled. More debris rained down, filling the tunnel between Arshel and Zref—and Jocelyn, Khelin, Ley and Thsee.

Zref grabbed Arshel up and stumbled toward the entryway, ceiling falling in behind him, rock shards pummeling his back, tripping him. Choking and coughing on the dust, he fell on Arshel, dragged himself up and without pausing to see if she still lived, picked her up and pushed on.

After a worse nightmare than ever he'd dreamed, Zref saw light rays dancing in the dust. The entry had been enlarged by the crash, not buried. He gave thanks to God the Creator of foolish mortals, and weeping shamelessly, staggered out into the light of day.

The air wasn't any better. Fumes from the burning ship tainted the hot breeze. It had left a crater where the Maze had been, shock-wave-piled debris burying the pirates, Shui, Iraem and the three writers. The emptiness ached, paralyzing him inwardly, and he shut off the aklal awareness.

In his arms, he held the only reason to go on living.

Arshel stirred, and he went a few steps farther to put her down on relatively smooth ground. She choked on the fumes, coughed, spat, then voided venom. He held her until the spasms subsided.

At last, she looked up at him. "They're not all dead?"

He could only nod. "Buried alive. Or burned. Look." He made her look at the still-smoking crater. "They were all dead before it hit. Khelin, Ley and Jocelyn—"

Stunned, horrified, she said numbly, "Thsee called it in! It couldn't have happened by accident! She'd rather die than let you have the Selector!"

"She did die, and so did the Selector. It's all over, Arshel. Over. Done."

She absorbed that. "We're the only survivors..."

The reality clutched at him, emotions he hadn't felt since before his surgery to become an Interface. Grieving for Tess,

Sudeen and his parents had paralyzed him for a year. Only Khelin had been able to pull him out of it. With Khelin and Ley, there had been that whisper of warmth, the end of exile. He'd felt it full blown when they'd all hugged each other, accepting Jocelyn back. And now it was gone, wiped away by a cold blackness.

He hugged Arshel, feeling such a tiny echo of that warmth, that it was more pain than pleasure. But he still had her. She was all he had. And he was now a threat to this entire civilization—a true Wild Interface, without even a private file and all its limiting, failsafe programs. If any of his private file circuitry survived, it held—he didn't want to think what it held. The Guild would know him dead, because his file was closed. *Can't take time to cry now. Later. Grieve later. Their souls weren't dispersed. We'll all meet again, in happier times now we're not bound by the Selector.* Even Tess, Sudeen, his parents—they weren't gone. He'd grieved hard because he hadn't known that.

He massaged his throbbing head, and abruptly, curiosity about the battle raging above the sky brought him the entire resource of the local comnode. It was a weird sensation, without the echo of his private file recording everything, monitoring, enforcing the Guarantees. Yet he had no trouble reading the scope recorders to ascertain that dozens of the little lander crafts had been destroyed, along with many of the fighters. The sky was full of the little ships though. And the big ships still fought beyond sight. "The pirates don't know the Selector is gone."

He spotted a lander headed for the area where they now stood, and another disgorging its task force beyond the Maze. Nearby, was the hopper Thsee Rith had come in.

"Come on!" he said, and led the way to the hopper.

Tumbling inside, he ran a quick check, and as Arshel climbed in, he took off, overriding all the safeties.

Keeping low, he put the hopper down on the shuttlepad outside the village. Nobody was on the streets now. Even the shuttle-launch control shack was empty.

But Zref anticipated no trouble, until Arshel balked at the yacht's shuttle. "Zref, this was *hers!*"

"I know! Her yacht's the fastest thing within ten days of here!"

He pulled her in and strapped her into the copilot's seat.
He took control through the comnet, launching them through
a window between the fighting ships.

As acceleration hit, she was saying, "But what's the hurry?
You can file your report via comnet, and we can get to Hengrave
in our own good time!"

"We're not going to Hengrave," he gasped as g-force pushed
the air out of his lungs.

They fought it silently all the way up, Zref making course
corrections until they mated with the yacht, which he had
primed and ready to receive them.

It was a one-man ship, but could accommodate half a dozen.
It was almost fully stocked. It would take the two of them
twice across the HP and back.

They were still in the shuttle when Zref pulled the yacht
out of orbit—not waiting for official clearance.

"Zref, *what* are you doing?" demanded Arshel.

On the way to the control room, Zref said, "We're not going
to Hengrave—or Camiat, either. We're leaving. Leaving the
HP—for good." He strapped into the pilot's seat, aware of the
residue of Thsee Rith's presence but ignoring it. He was haunted
by whispers of his aklal, too. It often took a long time after a
body was dead for the death processes to complete, especially
in death by violence.

"Arshel, do you remember Final Duty?"

She pulled out of her distracted shock, comprehension
dawning. "We can help them!"

They joined one last time through their aklal symbol. Shui,
Iraem, Waysjoff, Arai and Neini were there, drifting, per-
plexed. They greeted Zref and Arshel with joy. "Guide us
back!"

"You've nothing to go back to," said Zref, replaying his
memory of the ruination of their bodies and all that came after.
"You must go on now," he added, the hardest thing he'd ever
said in his life. "That way!" Hugging them all within himself,
he turned them toward the light and propelled them onward.

They understood at last. Clinging to each other, they turned
back to Zref, who was weeping openly, and Arshel, who was
raising venom, straining to go with them. "Don't grieve," said

Arai. "It was worth it. We'd all dedicated our lives to this—and we won free of the debt."

Shui hugged Arshel, saying, "We invoked. We knew the price. There'll be other chances, Arshel. You've earned the rest of this life with Zref—many times over. Live!"

As the five drifted toward the light, Zref heard Waysjoff say contentedly, "I've nothing to complain about."

And then Zref was sucked back down into his body. He hadn't had a chance to search for Khelin, Ley and Jocelyn. But since they weren't with the others, Zref could only assume they'd found their own way. *Leave it to Khelin to keep oriented!* His cheeks were slick with tears.

He could barely see his scopes, which showed exactly what Astrogation was telling him—one pirate left, one HP Escorter left. *Epitasis* still in orbit. Smaller ships scattered everywhere amid fragments of their fellows.

As the yacht began to move, Zref threw his trajectory onto *Epitasis*'s scopes, asking them to move to allow the yacht out, adding, "Captain, I'd appreciate your cooperation. Zref." He knew he shouldn't have signed it, leaving the HP a means of tracing him, but he couldn't bring himself to invade her ship and move it without her assent again.

Meanwhile, Zref followed an exchange between Astrogation and the Escorter. The occupant of the yacht had landed illegally—over Guild protest. Now the yacht was breaking orbit without permission. The HP Escorter was ordered to stop the yacht or destroy it before it rammed *Epitasis*.

Zref flipped the radio on so Arshel could hear that, and piled on all the g's the yacht's in-system drives had. But it was clear even before the on-board computer displayed. The Escorter was going to catch them.

As the Escorter turned its attention from the pirate, the pirate turned and bore down on *Epitasis*, tumbling to bring a gunport into play. Zref grabbed the whole local comnode to calculate, and knew the pirate's plan—to take out Thsee's yacht with the inferno of *Epitasis*'s explosion.

Suddenly, *Epitasis* lifeboats scattered in every direction, and simultaneously it spun about on its short axis, and broke orbit with a pulse of its hyperlight engines.

Zref understood. The Captain had left only herself aboard, and was going to use her ship as a weapon.

And it worked. *Epitasis* and the pirate went out in a stellar magnitude blaze of glory that blanked all the astrogation sensors in range for a good two minutes.

The shock of yet another death of someone he admired beat in upon him, but he couldn't absorb it all now. Later—later for a tribute to the brave Almurali Captain.

Right now he saw that the radiation sphere from the blowup engulfed the yacht, sending instruments crazy, and he had an idea. He convinced Astrogation's trackers that the yacht, too, had been blown up, leaving false tracks on their scopes, wiping out the remainder of the yacht's visible orbit before it went hyperlight.

Finally, he glanced aside at his bhirhir. "Arshel, are you with me? Can you leave everything you've ever known?"

"Become an outlaw?"

"I am already, several times over." He explained what had happened to his private file and the Selector's energies. "I don't understand what's happened, Arshel, but I know it's best if the HP believes we died down there in the wreckage with everyone else. What's left of our lives—we can live out peacefully on some little out-fringe planet like Laleen."

"Zref—Zref—am I a Persuader now? I survived . . ."

He hadn't thought of that. He swore, a most un-Interface practice. "There's no way to tell for sure. You don't seem different to me—but I looked into the Selector, too. A Persuader can't Persuade another Persuader."

She kneaded her hands, worrying the problem. After a long silence, she said, "Zref, I am, I know it. But I don't want to be. I wish I could have gone with them!"

"No! Arshel—oh, no. Arai said it. We've earned the right to a little peace together. I want that—somewhere we can do no harm. Where they've never heard of Lantern Novels— where settlement is just beginning and they're not nosey about who settles. Laleen would be perfect."

Thoughtfully, she stared at the scope that showed the planet dropping away astern. She pulled her eyes to focus on him, putting one hand over his where it rested on the arm of the chair. "Promise me one thing. If we are active Persuaders, we'll never use that power on anyone. If ever anyone seems likely to discover what we are, to try to use us, we'll die first."

That was exactly what was in his heart, and he was about to promise when he remembered. "When we first met, you bound me with such promises. Are you still so insecure? Do you really need my promise? If you do, you'll have it."

She considered. "You're right. We couldn't resolve this mess until I released you from your promise and began to help you. It remains to be seen if we're still bound by your vow— I certainly hope not! I don't want any more promises."

He put his other hand over Arshel's. "My bhirhir."